COCOON

COCOON

Book I of the Cocoon Trilogy

DAVID SAPERSTEIN

TALOS PRESS

Talos Press books may be purchased in bulk at special discounts for sales
promotion, corporate gifts, fund-raising, or educational purposes. Special
editions can also be created to specifications. For details, contact the
Special Sales Department, Sky Pony Press, 307 West 36th Street, 11th
Floor, New York, NY 10018 or info@skyhorsepublishing.com.

Talos Press is an imprint of Skyhorse Publishing, Inc.®, a Delaware
corporation.

Visit our website at www.skyhorsepublishing.com.

10 9 8 7 6 5 4 3 2 1

Library of Congress Cataloging-in-Publication Data is available on file.
ISBN: 978-1-940456-05-8

Printed in the United States of America

To

My dear wife Ellen-Mae, my son Ivan and my daughter Ilena
for their love and patience

and

My dear brother Bert, who always encouraged and believed.

Other books by David Saperstein

Metamorphosis: The Cocoon Story Continues—Book II of The Cocoon Trilogy

Butterfly: Tomorrow's Children—Book III of The Cocoon Trilogy

Fatal Reunion

Red Devil

Dark Again (With George Samerjan)

A Christmas Visitor

A Christmas Passage (With James J. Rush)

A Christmas Gift

Table of Contents

SO NATURE DEALS WITH US, AND TAKES AWAY
OUR PLAYTHINGS ONE BY ONE, AND BY THE HAND
LEADS US TO REST SO GENTLY, THAT WE GO
SCARCE KNOWING IF WE WISH TO GO OR STAY,
BEING TOO FULL OF SLEEP TO UNDERSTAND
HOW FAR THE UNKNOWN TRANSCENDS THE
WHAT WE KNOW.

—Henry Wadsworth Longfellow

COCOON

CHAPTER ONE
A STRANGE CHARTER

The large cruiser moved slowly down the canal past the sleeping residents of Coral Gables. Schools of leaping mullet made the only sound other than the chug of the powerful twin inboard diesels of the *Manta III*. The houses along the canal were sparkling shades of pastel pink, blue, and green, and the lawns were perfectly manicured. The docks were immaculate with at least two boats moored alongside each one. It was very quiet and very early.

The *Manta III* turned into the main channel and left the tranquil, misty scene behind. The engines responded as Jack Fischer urged them up to six knots. He stood on the flying bridge, spun the wheel hard to the right, and then positioned the *Manta III* to the left of the channel markers. It was a mile run to the sea wall and then out into the open ocean.

Jack sipped his coffee and breathed in deeply. This was the best time of day for him. The rim of a red sun rose in front of him, and there was peace and quiet. All was well this morning, and if his clients below were a little strange and secretive, well, that wasn't any of his business. The short bald guy was obviously in charge, even though he never spoke.

A pelican flew across the path of the boat in search of breakfast, which reminded Jack of the buttered roll he had not eaten. He found it and took a healthy bite. Yes, it was going to be a good week. These folks were paying top dollar to charter the *Manta III*.

Jack glanced back toward the stern and eyed their equipment. He counted ten scuba tanks. There was an assortment of flippers, weights, masks, and markers. The large suction pump and hose were off to the left—a vacuum cleaner of sorts. The other cases were unopened so he could only speculate as to what they held.

This was not the first diving expedition that had chartered his boat. There were a few treasure hunters, although it was rare that they didn't have their own boats. Actually, these people had never said they were after treasure. In fact, they hadn't really told him the purpose of the trip.

He studied the map and the overlay they had supplied. It marked an area that he had fished many times. It was just to the southeast edge of the reef. In season, that was a good spot for trolling for barracuda. He took another bite of his roll and a sip of the coffee.

A noise below made him turn to see one of the three divers moving a crate to the center of the deck. Jack watched as the man opened the crate and lifted out what appeared to be a small transmitter. There were two coils of silver wire that he placed on the deck. He then turned and began to climb up to the flying bridge.

Jack checked the channel markers, judging that they were now about five minutes from the open sea. The young man, was his name Hal or Hank, came onto the bridge and smiled.

"How's it going, Captain?"

"Fine … we'll be out in a few minutes and I can open this tub up. Then we can make some time. It's going to be a great day."

The young man looked at the rising sun and smiled. "Can I use the outriggers? I want to string an antenna like this." He outlined the shape of a triangle with his fingers, indicating that he would use the tips of the outriggers as the base and the vortex would be attached to the stern. Jack could find no reason to say no, and he was curious to know why they needed a transmitter.

"What kind of radio is that?" he asked.

"Oh, well, it's not really a radio … just sort of a direction finder for working under the sea. Actually, it's a new piece of equipment that we designed and were going to test out today." The young man seemed uneasy, but Jack dismissed that as part of asking permission.

"Sure. Go ahead. You're Hal?" Jack asked.

"No. I'm Harry. Hal is the guy with the blond hair." He disappeared from view as he quickly went down the ladder to the deck. Jack heard the squeak of the pulley attached to the outrigger. His thoughts then quickly turned to the sound of a motor ahead of him.

The sleek bow of a Hatteras emerged from the canal that led to the site of the new condominium dock. That was some development— brand new and built in record time. It was the talk of the Gables. And what a name. Antares. It took the local newspaper two weeks to track down the owners and another week to report that Antares was an obscure star in the constellation of Scorpios. Why they called the place Antares was a mystery.

The Hatteras was out into the channel now and in front of him by about fifty yards. As the bow swung around he could read the name— *Terra Time*. He observed that her outriggers were spread and that thin silver wires were attached to the tips and joined on the bow. There was a blond young man attaching the lead to a double of the transmitter on his own deck. As they passed the sea wall, the sleek Hatteras throttled up. Her heading was due east into the rising sun. Jack revved up his twin Volvo engines and turned toward the southeast and the reef. Behind him other charters were emerging from the main channel and he had to pay attention to the traffic. He reminded himself to ask about that antenna setup later. Now he had to get down to the lower bridge and get on the radio to check the weather. His customers had also asked him to check to see if there would be many boats in their area today. Jack took a quick look around and then set the auto pilot down to the lower controls. He gathered up his coffee and roll, leaving the chart and overlay in place. One of these days he would run a radio mike connection and speaker up to the flying bridge on a permanent basis, but for now he would have to go below.

Harry had finished attaching the antenna setup and was opening another crate as Jack negotiated the last rung of the ladder and dropped to the main deck. The crate contained a gas cylinder and what appeared to be a shiny metallic cloth. Jack sensed that this was going to be a different kind of treasure hunt. As he turned to enter the main cabin, the bald man emerged from below decks and nodded hello.

He was short, perhaps five feet, two inches, but extremely well built. He appeared to be in his early forties. He had stripped off his clothes and was wearing only a pale green bikini bathing suit. Jack nodded back and went into the cabin as the man passed him and knelt next to Harry.

There was something strange about that guy, Jack thought. He seemed to glow, yet he wasn't sweating. As a matter of fact, he was as dry as a bone. Then it hit Jack—the man had no hair! Not just on his head, but on any part of his body. Jack glanced back to confirm his thought. Yes, no hair. Probably a result of a severe case of scarlet fever. Or chemo? Too bad. The radio crackled as he turned the "On" switch and moved the squelch knob. He punched in channel 27.55 and keyed the mike. "This is KAAL-9911 … *Manta Three*—Phil, you out yet? Over."

A voice came back immediately. "Hey, Jack, how are you this morning? Yeah, we're out about five miles … gonna take a shot at some sails over in the Stream. Picked up two yesterday … What are you up to? Over."

Jack keyed again. "I got a party for the week here … gonna do some diving over by the south reef. Anyone say they were heading that way? Over."

"No … no way. That's been real dead over there for the past two weeks. Not even a stray cuda. Strange, because it was really hot, and then … nothing. Let me know if you see anything over there … I'll give you a call around noon … over."

"Roger, Phil—what the hell!" Jack was startled as a huge shadow nearly blocked his view. He saw a flash of silver and then realized that Harry and baldy had launched an enormous silver balloon. "Sorry, Phil, I gotta go have a talk with these folks about rules and regulations … I'll look for your call around noon. Over and out."

He placed the mike on its hook and pulled the throttle back to slow. The engines responded immediately and their forward motion slowed. The swells caught the bow and the boat began to roll. Jack sensed something, turned around and found the bald man standing directly behind him. For a moment he was startled and then realized that he was looking into the coldest eyes he had ever seen. It was as though he was looking at them for the first time. They were ice blue (hadn't they been brown before?), and the man did not blink.

"What did you guys do with that balloon? I don't think we're allowed to let things like that go without the proper permission."

The man's expression didn't change. "We are," he said. "How long before we reach the reef?"

"About an hour, if the sea stays this way. Hold on a minute. What do you mean *we* are? And are there any more surprises in store?"

"… really sorry, Captain. I should have told you … it's my fault." A voice emerged from behind. It was the man who had originally made the charter arrangements. His name was Bright. Amos Bright. When he came aboard in the dark this morning he had been wearing jeans and sneakers and a sweatshirt. Now he was wearing a metallic diving suit. It was copper-colored and had wires hanging from the shoulders and knees. Mr. Bright continued his apology. "That's a high-altitude marker to test some new equipment … that stuff out on the deck. We're going to bounce an underwater signal off it and make some calculations. There won't be any more surprises. I'm truly sorry." He had stepped between Baldy and Jack. Harry, who had followed Amos into the cabin, placed his hand on Baldy's shoulder. The shiny little man and Harry left and walked to the stern of the boat.

The moment of silence was now interrupted by a toot from the horn of an approaching charter boat. Jack realized that he had better get underway. The traffic was getting heavy and he was an obstruction. "Okay … okay … I was just startled. Sorry. I didn't mean to yell."

"No harm done," Bright answered. Jack was about to ask him about the Hatteras and the antenna, but Amos was moving away to join the two men at the stern. *None of my business; besides, the money is good*, he thought. He pushed the throttle. Once again the diesels responded and soon they were making twenty-five knots. The skyline of Miami Beach was visible off the stem, while the near shore was dominated by the new Antares complex.

Nearly a half hour had passed since Jack had gone back up to the flying bridge. He estimated they would be at the reef site in another fifteen minutes. It had been a while since he had seen another boat. The charter party seemed to sense that they were nearing their destination because they had all assembled. The only one missing was the bald man.

5

DAVID SAPERSTEIN

There were a total of six men below on deck. Mr. Bright, Harry, Hal the blond, two other men dressed in the copper suits, and another short, hairless man who could have been Baldy's brother. The only difference was that this man was jet-black. It was as though he had been sprayed with hi-gloss enamel paint. He stood apart from the others and was looking up at the sky. Jack's eyes followed his line of sight and saw the large silver balloon hovering over the boat. He couldn't tell how far above it was because he hadn't really had a chance to see how big it was close up. He guessed it was about five hundred yards slightly off to port. For a moment Jack thought he saw two balloons. He rubbed his eyes and looked again, but there was only one.

The pings from his depth finder's sonar bouncing off the ocean floor came quicker, indicating they were nearing the reef. He eased the throttle back and checked the overlay on his chart. Jack figured that he was about a half mile west of the site and slightly to the north. He turned the wheel and peered out for the Coast Guard marker, reef buoy number forty-three Green. It lay off the starboard, about one hundred fifty yards. He swung the wheel so that they would pass to the south of the buoy. That would bring them straight to the site.

As Jack reached for the ice chest on the flying bridge, the white bald man came on deck. He was carrying a black rod. Attached to the rod were two wires. One wire ran to a silver disk that was stuck to the center of his bald head. The other wire was held in his hand and had a disk at the end of it.

Jack reached into the Styrofoam chest and grabbed a cold beer. He opened the can and looked up. The second wire was now attached to the black man's head. Both knelt at the bow and placed a hand on the antenna wire that ran from the outriggers. The black rod was being lowered into the water by Mr. Bright. As the rod sank into the greenish water above the outer reef, Mr. Bright stepped back below the bridge. All the others followed except Hal, who knelt and moved some switches on the equipment.

A faint humming sound reached Jack's ears just as the antenna wire began to glow. The morning sun was up now, yet the light from the wire was brighter than sunlight. It looked like a triangular welding machine in operation. Suddenly, a bright red glow appeared beneath the water off to starboard. Jack estimated that was the position of the black rod. The glow broke the surface and a red beam of light flashed directly up to the silver balloon hovering above the boat. The humming increased. Jack didn't realize that Harry had come up onto the bridge, but he felt his presence and turned to him. "What the hell is going on here?"

Harry put his finger up to his lips to silence Jack and whispered, "Just watch … we'll explain shortly."

There was yelling from below as Mr. Bright and the two other copper-clothed men were pointing off to the starboard beyond the red beam. Entering the water was a blue beam. Jack glanced up to see the source of the blue beam was a second balloon. So he had seen two balloons! Mr. Bright shouted up to him, "Captain … over there! That's the place we want to anchor. Right at that spot. Quickly. Please." Mr. Bright turned and signaled to Hal, who immediately turned off the transmitter device. One of the copper men reeled in the black rod and the bald twins let go of the antenna. The beams stopped, but Jack had already marked the spot by triangulating it with the buoy and reef edge.

Jack looked at Harry. "So, what the hell is this all about?" Harry, who was obviously excited, assured Jack that Mr. Bright would explain it a lot better than he could. The important thing was to get to the spot quickly. He then scampered down the ladder to the deck below.

Jack eased the *Manta III* toward starboard and the spot indicated. He took a sip of beer. It had a metallic taste. He set it down next to the compass. His eyes went quickly to the compass because it was spinning wildly and undulating so that the needle was hitting the glass covering the face of the instrument. It made a rapid, clicking sound. The closer he got to their destination, the faster the needle spun, and when they were directly over the spot, the glass cover popped off the compass, spilling his beer. He moved back as this happened, which was fortunate because the needle flew out of the compass, missing him by inches and whizzing off into the air. *What the hell is going on here?* he thought. Then, angered to his boiling point, he stopped the engines and rushed down the ladder to the deck below. But there was no deck, only a bright flash, and then a blue black void as his body seemed to melt.

CHAPTER TWO
CARGO FROM THE STONES

If death had an odor, then that was the first sensation Jack was aware of as he awoke. The second sensation was that his body was attached to a huge vibrator. As he opened his eyes, the pleasant face of Mr. Bright came into focus. Harry was there, too, removing a sticky white substance from Jack's neck. They were in the below deck cabin.

Mr. Bright spoke first. "Captain, please … I want you to collect yourself and try not to be angry. Relax if you can and please just listen to me. I am going to tell you a story that you most likely will not believe, but in time, you most assuredly will. Let me begin by saying that we need you, and that we hope you will come to understand our requirements and help us. We thought that what we had to do here, we could do ourselves, without … shall we say … uh, outside help? But we now know that this is impossible. Please listen, and try to understand."

Jack settled back on the bunk, calmed by Mr. Bright's reasonable and soothing voice. Harry set the white goo aside and smiled reassuringly. The deathly odor now seemed pleasant and his body stopped vibrating. He became aware of activity on the deck above as he turned his attention to Mr. Bright. "What happened to me? Did I fall? And what are you guys doing up there?" Then he remembered the compass needle and chill went up his spine. "What are you going to do to me … to my boat?"

Mr. Bright spoke calmly and softly. "Jack. May I call you Jack? Do you know exactly where you are? I mean, do you know what this place, the reef, is called?"

"The Stones. I fish out here all the time."

"And do you know why it's called The Stones?"

"Sure. Because of those stone slabs imbedded in the reef. People say they are from a lost city or continent or something."

Bright smiled. "Fine. Now let me tell you what this place really is … what those slabs really are … and who we are … and," he sighed, "… why we are here."

Bright spoke for almost an hour. Jack interrupted three times—once to ask Harry to get him a beer because fear had made his mouth go bone dry, once to play spy, and once to ask the black bald man to take his face off again.

Actually, the story was simple. Believing it was difficult. He could understand the words, but not the concept. He was just not prepared. Now he was up on deck, and, by his oath, part of the team. Three of the charter party were on deck with him: Harry, Mr. Bright, and Hal. The shiny black, whose name was Bill, was in a small yellow rubber raft about ten yards off the stern. The white bald man and the two others in copper suits were working underwater on the reef. Amos Bright had removed his copper suit and was dressed.

The balloons were still overhead, but now Jack knew only one was a balloon, and the other was a spacecraft. What was it they had told him? Oh yeah—not really a spacecraft. A guide ship. Their mother ship was a spacecraft from Antares and was moored on the far side of the Moon. This balloon shaped vehicle was expendable and would self-destruct after it finished the mission.

Suddenly there was excitement on deck. Bill was shouting in a shrill voice, "It's coming! It's coming!"

Off to the left of the raft, the surface filled with bubbles and two copper-suited divers popped up. They were followed by a canister … no … more like a large white roll-on deodorant container. It was covered with a white gooey substance. Its presence filled the air with the same odor that Jack had experienced earlier when he woke up below deck.

The copper divers guided the canister toward the *Manta III*. It took ten minutes and a great effort to lift it aboard. Five minutes after it was on deck a second canister popped up. Within two hours there were six more, and the *Manta III* resembled a World War II P.T. boat with torpedo tubes secured on bow and stern. It was only after the seventh canister was on board that the hairless white man came to the surface. Jack had forgotten about him, but at this point, after hearing the story and seeing the containers pop up, it did not surprise Jack that the man was able to stay underwater for such a long period of time. It didn't even seem strange that he wore no breathing apparatus.

Mr. Bright had a few words with baldy white and then turned to Jack. "This is the final member of our unit, Jack. I'd like to introduce you." He gestured toward the shiny white figure that came toward Jack. The eyes were no longer icy and menacing. They were brown and friendly. "This is James … uh … Jim, yes, Jim is better."

Jack extended his hand, and Jim did likewise. A vibration surged through Jack like an electric shock shot and he pulled back. "Sorry," said Jim. "I have to control that better."

Jack nodded and smiled as the sensation passed. "Good idea." Mr. Bright suggested that it was getting late and that they should head back to the dock. That would be the dock at the Antares condominium complex.

As the rest of the group packed their crate and removed their suits, Jack climbed to the flying bridge. Hal was on the bow to make sure the anchor chain was clear of the canisters. He waved an okay to the bridge. Jack started the engines and glanced at the compass. It was repaired and working perfectly. He turned the bow toward Miami and reached for another beer. He also decided to stay up on the flying bridge by himself. There was a lot to think about and only one hour to make a decision that might affect the world … his world, and his race. The human race. The ones these people called "dwellers." Jack definitely belonged to the "dwellers."

CHAPTER THREE
ANTARES QUAD THREE

Jack mulled over Bright's revelations as he headed toward the Florida coast. Atlantis was a misnomer. Actually, the island had been named Antares Quad Three by those who built it. It had been a thriving Antarean colony for almost five hundred Earth years—a large island, stretching from the islands known as the Azores westward to the islands of the Bahamas. Its northern shore extended close to Greenland, and to the southernmost point of the island was a mere two hundred miles from what is now Brazil.

Antares Quad Three was a trading post, and in its final days a military base and the site of the signing of the Quad Three Peace Agreement that settled all space wars in this quadrant of our galaxy. That happened seventy Earth years before the colony was destroyed. Antares Quad Three had been wiped off the face of the Earth five thousand Earth years ago when a section of the planet Saturn, having torn away from its orbit, passed close to Earth. The inhabitants of Antares had ample warning about the impending disaster and were able to evacuate their colony. At that time they chose to leave a portion of their army behind.

Jack's mind raced. Bright's story was overwhelming, but he realized that he had to understand. He forced himself to organize his thoughts and go over the story from the beginning, just as Mr. Amos Bright, Antarean Commander and force leader, had related to him. He began with The Stones. "Yes," Jack had said. "I know this place … we call it The Stones because of the slabs that are beneath in the reef." Then Bright had said, "I want you to picture a large island filling most of what you now call the Atlantic Ocean. There was an island here once.

You actually suspect that, and you call it Atlantis. Well, the name was Antares Quad Three. It was our colony … here, on this planet, in this place. We were thousands there because we were settling this quadrant, the third quadrant, of this galaxy that our planets share. You call it the Milky Way. "In the beginning we avoided contact with the 'dwellers' here because they were quite primitive, and we did not want to interfere. Besides, we had our hands full with some rather aggressive and advanced beings on a planet near the red star you call Rigel. We had a minor space war on our hands. It lasted sixty-one Earth years and ended with Rigelians joining in a pact of peace that is in effect to this day.

"After the treaty, this colony became a thriving center of interplanetary trade and government. I wish it were here today so that you could see it. Beings from all over our galaxy gathered … different languages … customs … evolutions. So much was happening everywhere you looked. Once we had a governmental meeting here that lasted three years, and several important ambassadors were in residence. At one time we maintained forty-seven different atmospheres for the conference."

At that point, Bright had a faraway look in his eyes. "I speak of those times because I was here often."

"But you said five thousand years and more. How is that possible?" Jack had asked. "We have a long life. There is death in our system, but it is at our choosing." That concept startled Jack.

"After the disaster, interest in this planet waned as we opened exploration beyond our galaxy. Ships had been developed that enabled us to enter the black holes in space and explore other galaxies. The first was in Andromeda. Ah … those were times. We were like children with a new toy."

"But you left an army behind, right?" Jack asked.

"True. Our leaders saw fit to leave a modest army behind in case the Rigelians had second thoughts about the peace treaty. That is why we are here now."

Jack had interrupted again and asked about the army. He had served in the army in Vietnam years ago as an artillery spotter. He was not yet sure of the actual mission these space travelers were on and felt that perhaps he was in an enemy camp. He wanted to know about their strength. He sensed Bright knew why he was asking about the army, but believed the Antarean told him the truth.

"An army is an army," Bright had said. "Ours numbered nine hundred forty-one, and they were some of the best combat soldiers we have. They fought in units of ten, with each unit possessing a unit leader, and nine specialties. There were ninety such units. Every ten units had a group leader." Bright had been a group leader at one time and still carried that title along with force leader. "Then there were thirty transport beings, again in units of ten with a unit leader. They had a group leader. Their responsibility was transportation and logistics for the fighting units. Finally, there was what you would call a commander. The hairless ones who are with us … the light and the dark ones … they are commanders. They are special beings and we must honor them with great respect."

Bill had just smiled and then reached under his chin and peeled off his shiny black face. Behind it was another face. There were eyes that were slits and they wrapped around both sides of the head. Through the slits Jack could see a glow, but no more. There was no nose … no mouth … no ears … no hair. Then Jack heard words inside his brain. The words were not coming through his ears … but were just present in his brain. The voice was Bill's voice, and it told him that he was telepathing to Jack. He said he could read Jack's mind and control his body if he so chose. He could do this to all beings that were carbon-based. He then put his face back on and left the room. At that point Jack didn't need any more convincing.

Bright continued the story of Antares Quad Three. "About five thousand years ago they became aware of a celestial accident that was going to affect their colony. A comet had passed close to the planet Saturn and had torn off a rather large chunk of matter. It had also affected the orbit of the planet and caused debris to be scattered out into space. Thus, the rings of Saturn. The large piece of the planet broke out of the planet's orbit and was pulled along by the comet for one hundred years. Then it broke free and by pure luck, bad luck, headed for Earth. The inhabitants of the colony had sixty-three years' warning, so it was not a disaster as far as life was concerned. In fact, the decision was made to alter the orbit of the earth as much as possible so that there would not be a direct collision, but rather a glancing blow, at the worst. In order to accomplish this, a thruster was set on a predetermined spot on the Earth and ignited. Of course, the dwellers in the area were evacuated. They were unable to understand what was happening. The effect worked and, with some minor disturbances to life here, the planet was saved but calculations showed that the chunk of matter would pass directly over our colony and destroy it. So we evacuated. The army left behind was put into a form of life that you would call suspended animation and sealed deep in the rock of the island. Our city was destroyed. Eventually, that piece of Saturn became the planet you call Venus.

"We have passed this way many times since that destruction. Some of you might have even seen us. You have advanced from those primitives we first encountered. Perhaps you are ready to learn more about our Universe. We shall see. Right now we have a need for our army in a place far from here. So, to put it simply, we have returned to get our soldiers. They are sealed in containers, like cocoons, buried under The Stones, waiting to be hatched. We have to get them out, and we need your help. We mean you no harm. When we have our soldiers we will go. But first the cocoons must be retrieved, opened, and the soldiers reprogrammed at our base in Miami. Will you help?"

Those words, will you help? rang in his ears. Why in the name of whatever did these advanced space travelers need him, charter captain Jack Fischer, and his boat to raise nine hundred forty-one cocoons from under the sea floor? Why not just buy a boat? Or build one and get the army out? And why was he believing all this fantastic mumbo-jumbo, anyway?

He had answered, "Yes, what do you want me to do?"

Bright had said, "Just do what we ask, and stay with us until we are finished."

"How long?" Jack had asked.

"Three months. It will take three months to raise all and process them," answered Bright. "We will pay you well and we will make you a very important man on this planet."

Jack sat on the flying bridge and steered toward the sun, although this time it was setting behind Miami to the west. He was still confused and unsure about what deal he had made with Bright. And those commanders who could get into his mind frightened him. They could probably will him dead or, at the very least, fry his brain. But he had to admit that he was also dying to have a look inside one of those cocoons, and the idea of living five thousand years hadn't been lost on him either. Nor had the promise of money and importance.

The *Manta III* passed the hotels and condos along the beach, silhouetted by the setting sun. He steered toward the channel outside Coral Gables. Off to the port side he saw the Hatteras wending its way home, too. He had forgotten about that boat. What was it called? *Terra Time?* Then he remembered that he had asked Phil to call at noon. The radio had been off, and Phil should have the Coast Guard alerted. But there had been no Coast Guard. Strange. Jack wished he had run a mike up onto the flying bridge. Once again he reflected back on Bright's story. He spoke of their base here now. That was something he had to see.

CHAPTER FOUR
CONDO HUNTERS

Bernard Lewis was once known as Bernie Lefkowitz. His wife, Rose, was always Rose, except at their wedding, when the rabbi had called her Rifka. Their red Buick was a gift from their son, Craig, which made it a business expense because Bernie was still listed as the Florida representative of Bernal Woolens, and that meant that it wasn't really a gift at all. Bernie understood that maneuver. Rose thought it was a marvelous thing for her son to do.

When Bernie was active with the company in New York, few people ever asked him twice about the Al in Bernal Woolens. The first time one asked, he answered, "I don't talk about Al anymore." His tone of voice made it clear—don't ask again. And no one did.

Bernie and Rose were driving, in their new red Buick, to look at the Antares condominium complex. They were in the market for larger quarters. Bernie wanted to move because in the past eight months more than fifteen people had passed away at their present condominium complex, Sunset Village, because all the patios faced west. The more he lived there, the more Bernie felt that it should have been called End of the Trail. Rose had explained, "Sweetheart, old people die, and Miami is full of old people."

Bernie answered in a tone that was similar to his answer about Al: "I don't want to talk about old." So they were looking.

After turning into the driveway of Antares, the Buick moved along a dirt road edged with palm trees that were still unplanted. They noted that the roots were wrapped in burlap balls and the trees were dying. Bernie puffed on his cigar and tapped his diamond pinky ring on the red steering wheel and pointed to the trees. "Well, so far, at least here only trees are dying…."

"I don't want to talk about it," she said.

He grunted and swerved to hit a pothole. "Got it." He grinned.

But Rose was not responsive this morning. Looking for a new place meant leaving her bridge ladies. That was unthinkable, but deep down she knew it was going to happen. Kismet, she thought, and she began to hum "Stranger in Paradise" as the car pulled up to the unfinished entrance of Antares Building A.

Tony Stranger sat behind his desk and stared in disbelief at the couple seated across from him. They were on the verge of killing each other. He had learned a half hour ago that to interfere with these people was to risk his life. At the moment they were discussing the wedding of a niece—his brother's daughter who had been married six years ago. She was reminding him that they served chicken and no hors d'oeuvres and that they were "cheap, no good, I-don't-know-what," and that she would never have them as house guests after the way they treated their son Harold with such a cheap "I-don't-know-what" gift for his wedding five years ago after they had given such a generous gift to that cheap "I-don't-know-what" daughter and the bum she married, so they didn't need a larger apartment because they didn't need an extra guest room. And that was the final word.

"So, Arthur, what will it be?" she asked, pointing to the floor plan laid out on the desk. "This apartment, with one guest room for fifty thousand? Or the one with two guest rooms for fifty-seven that I won't live in?"

Arthur Perlman blew his nose and studied the plans. He smiled at Tony and then leaned closer to the floor plans. He then turned his face toward his wife so that Tony could not see him mouth the words, *Bess, I'm going to kill you.* He sat up and said to Tony, "Does the condo with one guest room have a patio on the corner?"

Tony checked his available list and found a corner apartment on the fifth floor of Building A. "Yes, Mr. Perlman, we have one left."

"They always have just one left," Bess grunted. He looked at his wife. "Okay, love of my life, you have it. You'll be able to pay it off with the life insurance, because in this place I'll be dead in two months."

Arthur Perlman was saying those words as Bernie and Rose walked into the salesroom. Bernie stopped dead in his tracks. Rose smiled and said, "See, people are dying all over Miami. You can't get away from it by moving, unless you want to move to Alaska, and even in Alaska people die. But from the cold."

Bernie walked over to the wall and studied a floor plan. "I'll be a few minutes, folks," Tony said smiling. "There are brochures and more floor plans on that table and some coffee, if you'd like."

Tony turned back to the Perlmans and handed them an application form, credit form, and insurance form. "You folks can fill these out and bring them back, or mail them in. It takes about two weeks to process them. We'll need a deposit with the forms. It's all spelled out there in plain English." He chuckled a little and added, "That's the law these days. It has to be in plain English so you can understand. I'm sure you'll be very happy here. There's still a little construction going on, but Building A is ready for occupancy immediately, and as I told you, it's almost full. You were fortunate to come in when you did." His voice, louder than it had been, was not lost on Bernie, who was pouring coffee into a plastic cup. He didn't notice that the coffee machine had not yet filled the glass coffeepot he now held in his hand, and that hot coffee was spilling down onto the hot plate and the brochures.

Rose shouted, "Bernie! Put back the coffee! You're making a mess." He muttered something about stupid machines and placed the carafe back on the hot plate with such force that the puddle of coffee that had collected there splashed onto his oyster-colored slacks and white cane shoes.

Amused by the scene, Tony made no move to help. He had his orders—discourage everyone he could from buying an apartment. He was one of the worst salesmen in Miami, so he was perfect for the job. But in spite of his efforts, he had accepted twenty-seven couples who wouldn't be dissuaded; people would live in the middle of a battlefield if they thought that they were getting something exclusive, or a bargain. He had made the mistake of trying to discourage them up front. They took that to mean they weren't wanted, or that the builder had made a mistake and underpriced the apartments, or something was going to raise the value of the apartments soon and the owner wanted to hold on to them.

CHAPTER FIVE
DOCKING

Terra Time was already at the dock as Jack eased *Manta III* toward the Antares complex. He could make out three people on the deck in the late-afternoon light. The sun was setting behind the two buildings that made up the complex. The dock was in shadow.

Harry had come up to the flying bridge as they entered the channel, but had not spoken a word. Jack sensed he was there to keep an eye on him. Harry motioned for Jack to dock the boat in the right hand slip. Jack eased back on the throttle and then shifted into neutral. The boat edged toward the slip and just before entering he reversed the engines and came to a stop.

Hal and Mr. Bright jumped onto the dock and secured the bow and stern lines. Jack noted that they had remembered to put the bumpers over the side. It appeared that this slip was perfect for his boat. They must have scouted him for some time, and were sure he would agree to take on the job they had offered.

The commanders were directing the two other men, whom he had not met yet, to begin unloading the cocoons onto the dock. Two more men from the *Terra Time* had come over to help. Hal and Harry were heading up the path from the docks that led to Building B. Hal stopped within sight of the dock and Harry continued on ahead to the door of the building. Jack was able to see the activity from his vantage point on the flying bridge. The men continued to load the cocoons onto a flatbed that was pulled by a small tractor. Jack counted ten cocoons. He did not hear Mr. Bright call him at first because he was distracted by the activity. The second time he not only heard his name, but he felt it, as though someone had poked him in the ribs.

These guys can play rough, Jack thought. He waved okay, took the ignition key, and put it in his pocket. He quickly checked around as he descended to the main deck. Things were reasonably shipshape and buttoned down. There was no food to clean up because these people had not eaten, and there was no mess because they had not been fishing.

Mr. Bright was waiting for him on the dock and extended a hand. "Welcome to Antares, our home away from home. It will be your home for the next few months, too, I trust?"

Jack just smiled, shook Mr. Bright's hand. "If you say so, boss."

"Good," said Mr. Bright. "Now, let me show you our lab and equipment and what is actually inside these cocoons." They headed toward Building B. Behind them the tractor started up, on its way to deliver the cocoons to Building B.

CHAPTER SIX
BEN AND THE POOL

It took two weeks to get the swimming pool filled. Ben Green had taken it upon himself to accomplish the feat. He met daily with the manager and the maintenance chief. With this morning's meetings done, Ben made his way toward the pool. It was time for the daily gin game to begin, and his three cronies were waiting as usual. Bernie Lewis and Art Perlman were setting up the chairs. Joe Finley was shuffling the two decks. The score pads were neatly placed on the table next to Ben's chair.

A meeting of the totally bored, Ben thought as he approached his buddies. Retired life was aimless and boring. Without each other's friendship they would have been committed to the funny farm long ago. Four healthy, educated, and bright men with almost two hundred years of combined business experience, put out to pasture.

Ben mused back on this morning's meeting with the manager and maintenance chief. He had handled them well, just like the old days at the ad agency when he was account supervisor in charge of their biggest account. He could really throw the bullshit at a meeting and terrorize those creepy creative people. Just do your homework, cover all the bases, and then sit back and wait for them to put their foot in their mouth. Then attack … attack … attack until they were so confused that they would agree with anything just to get back to the safety of their cubicles. Ben was physically a big man. He was gaining too much weight in this sedentary life, felt it in the hot Florida sun. He stood over six feet, three inches and weighed two hundred thirty pounds. His height had been helpful in business, especially when he would storm into the art department and throw layouts onto the art V.P.'s desk. The head art director was a diminutive man, just five-foot-five, and even when he stood up to argue with Ben he had to look up. It was a child-parent scene, carefully orchestrated by Ben with a devastating effect on the little man. Those days were gone now and there had been little fun of that sort until Ben met the manager and maintenance chief. It was like the old days again. Ben planned each step of his campaign against them.

The first time he had tried to speak to the manager, the condo office secretary had been curt. She told him he would have to make an appointment because Mr. Shields was a very busy man. Ben had then asked for an appointment, but the girl told him that Mr. Shields' appointment book was in his office and that was locked. Ben would have to call or come by later. She suggested he call first. Ben did that, but of course Mr. Shields was out. The game went on for over a week. At first Ben was annoyed. Then he realized that this conformation gave him the same rush that he used to have at the agency before a contentious meeting. With that realization joy filled his life. He was reborn—fulfilled with a sense of worth that he had not felt for years.

The next day he stopped into Mr. Shields' office and, of course, the manager was out. The secretary's dismissive manner had not changed. Ben approached her desk slowly. He added a slight shuffle to his walk and forced his hands to shake a little. He tried to look as old as he could. It worked, because the snotty secretary began to speak slowly to him and explain things as though he were a child. He listened as she told him that the pool was not quite finished yet. They were waiting for delivery of a special paint to seal the lining. The paint had been ordered from the manufacturer, in Ohio, but it would be several weeks until the order could be filled. Her final words were, "Do you understand that, Mr. Green?"

Ben had tried to look as confused and beaten as possible. He smiled and started to turn away from her desk. Then he stopped and turned back to his original position. The girl had gone back to her typing, but stopped typing when Ben came back to her desk. She was about to speak when Ben, in a clear deep voice, spoke to her. (It was the same voice he had used once to tell the executive vice president of the agency that he was about to take the three biggest clients to another agency if the stupid son-of-a-bitch creative director was not fired.) "There is just one other thing, young lady. You tell Mr. Shields for me that if his ass is not in this office at two-thirty this afternoon to discuss the swimming pool, I will personally find him and kick the living shit out of him. Good morning, dear." He turned and left.

Mr. Shields had greeted Ben at the door at precisely two-thirty. He was shorter than Ben by several inches. Although he had the title of manager, it was obvious to Ben that this man was not calling the shots. He was a front for someone else. Shields had given Ben the same story about the special paint, and Ben had answered, "Bullshit." When Shields tried to explain, Ben asked if he had been out to the pool. Shields said yes. Ben asked him to try to remember what kind of lining the pool had. Shields couldn't, so Ben reminded him that it was plastic and it was a stupid ploy to tell him they were going to paint a plastic pool.

"That's what they tell me, Mr. Green," the manager said.

"Who tells you?" asked Ben.

"Well, the maintenance chief. Perhaps you would like to hear it from his lips?"

Ben smiled and said politely, "Yes, by all means, let's meet the expert."

Shields buzzed the secretary and asked her to get Wally Parker on the two-way radio. Ben heard the girl calling, "Wally? Come in, Wally." That went on for about a minute. She then came into Shields' office and told her boss that Wally must be off the grounds because she couldn't raise him.

Ben muttered "She couldn't raise anything" to himself just loud enough for everyone to hear. Shields suggested that they would contact Ben and arrange a meeting with Wally Parker as soon as possible.

As he left the office, Ben told Mr. Shields that he expected to hear from him within twenty-four hours. He did not say good-bye this time.

It took three days before the meeting took place. Friday Ben had been told that Wally Parker had to go up to Fort Lauderdale because they thought that a wholesaler up there might have some of the special paint. Saturday Wally was in for only half a day and he had several emergency repairs to supervise as a result of the storm Friday night.

Sunday was Wally's day off.

Monday found Ben greeting the secretary as she opened the office at nine A.M. She was very polite to him now and told him that Mr. Shields would not be in until after lunch. Ben told her, "Fine. I'll be back at two, and have Wally the Wonderful paint wizard here, too."

He left, but instead of going to his apartment, he went over to Joe Finley's condo. Joe's second bedroom overlooked the entrance to the office. Finley made some coffee. His wife Alma was at the Green's condo for the "girls" morning coffee klatch with Mary Green, Rose Lewis, and Bess Perlman. Ben and Joe kept a vigil and they were rewarded by the appearance of Shields slinking along the edge of the building toward his office. He stopped at the door and waved toward the parking lot. A blue Chevy door opened and a very fat man in overalls slid out of the driver's side and made a beeline toward the office. "Wally the Wonderful, we have you now," Ben muttered, and he motioned for Joe to get to the phone.

Joe dialed the manager's office and identified himself to the secretary as Mr. Bonser, of the Florida Attorney General's office. He asked to speak to Mr. Shields on official business. The girl put him on hold and then Mr. Shields got on the line. Finley nodded to Ben, and Ben left the apartment on the run.

"Mr. Shields, this is Mr. Bonser, of the Attorney General's office. I'm calling about a complaint we received from a Mr. Green, who says that services … let me see, I'll read the complaint to you … that services herein described and duly paid for have been withheld without cause justified *en corporatum per legalum.*… What that means is that this Mr. Green is charging you with … let's see … ah, yes … not fulfilling a contract to provide a swimming pool according to contract. Now, Mr. Shields, I know what a pain some of these old people can be, but they are citizens of this state and they vote. We have to follow up on these things. What seems to be the problem?"

Just as Shields was about to answer, he heard a ruckus outside his office and then Ben burst through the door into the room. Shields asked Mr. Bonser if he could call him back, and Bonser agreed. The manager hung up just as Ben reached across the gray metal desk and grabbed him by the lapels of his blue blazer with the Antares logo on it.

Wally Parker started to get up, but Ben glanced over at him and suggested that Wally remain in his chair. He turned back to Shields and let him down into his chair. "Good Morning, Mr. Shields. Good morning, Mr. Parker. I'm really glad you could both make our meeting this morning. Tell me, Mr. Parker, were you able to locate that paint in Fort Lauderdale on Friday?"

Parker looked at Shields with an expression that told Ben he knew nothing about the trip to Fort Lauderdale.

Ben pulled out a piece of paper from his pocket. It was the score sheet from yesterday's gin game. He studied it for a moment, then put it away. "Now, Mr. Parker, I would appreciate it if you would explain this special paint to me. I had a pool in Connecticut, where I come from, and the lining was quite similar to the pool *we, the condo owners,* have here. I don't recall ever having to paint it, because it was a special substance that sealed the pool. But I'm an old man and tend to forget things from time to time. Perhaps we did paint it." Ben slid into his old-man act again, realizing that Wally had just met him and that Shields hadn't told Wally too much about the situation.

Before Shields could say anything, Wally proceeded to patronize Ben, explaining slowly that this lining required painting. He said, "You know, Mr. Green, here at Antares we pride ourselves on having a facility that is not just beautiful, but durable, too. We expect our tenants to be with us a long time and we want things to be right for them. We want things to last. This special paint will add years to the life of the pool, and that means years of enjoyment for you and Mrs. Green. I'm sure you understand." He smiled at Ben, secure in the feeling that he had set this old buzzard straight.

Ben smiled back and put up his hand just as Shields began to speak. "No, Mr. Shields, allow me to speak first." His voice was still that of an old man.

"Wally, may I call you Wally?" Wally nodded and smiled again. "Wally, you are a fat, stupid asshole." Ben's voice was that of Ben the adman again. "I will tell you three things. One, I am not a tenant here; I own the goddamned place. Two, that is a freaking plastic pool liner out there, and any kind of paint would peel in one day. Three, we will meet here at ten tomorrow morning and you will have a schedule for me of when the pool will be filled. This meeting is over."

CHAPTER SEVEN
A PLANET OUTSIDE IN

Amos Bright was amused when he telepathed Jack Fischer from the dock. The first time he had summoned him by inner voice only with no response. Then he sent an electric impulse to the charter captain's brain. It startled Jack and made him shudder. Amos made a mental note to cut his telepathing to the Earth dwellers several milli-volts. But Jack got his message and caught up to Amos at the end of the Antares dock. They walked silently toward the Building B complex. The sun had nearly set. The lighting along the path was mercury vapor lamps, glowing with an eerie greenish light. The only sound was from the small tractor behind them as it made its way along the service path to the back of Building B's delivery entrance. Jack glanced back to the tractor and noticed that the cocoons, now dimly lit, had a faint glow of their own that came from within. He had not seen that in the daylight. Amos, who read Jack's thoughts, knew the reason for the glow. It was the power system installed in each cocoon to maintain life-force elec-trics. The glow was caused by the fuel cell, a small piece of the mother planet core. Literally a piece of home to keep the occupant alive and warm.

Home for Amos Bright was Antares, a near Earth sized ice planet whose sun was growing cold. It orbited in the constellation the Earth dwellers called Scorpios. By all reason it should have been abandoned millennia ago, but the Antareans were an old race that had adapted as their world cooled and its surface froze. It appeared desolate. Ice covered the entire planet and the poles had more than fifty miles of ice through which one had to travel before reaching the surface of the planet. It was another eighty miles below the surface that water could exist without freezing. That point was the beginning of the planet's temperate zone where, it was, in fact, very much like Earth, except Earth zones were on the surface in a lateral dimension and temperature was dependent on the distance from the sun and the altitude of the surface terrain. Most planetary life depended upon energy from without—usually a nearby star. On Antares it was a matter of depth. Heat was determined by the vertical plane. The closer one got to the core of the planet, the warmer it was. So Antarean heat and energy came from within. It was this fact that formed the basis of Antarean thought and philosophy. Examination of the inner self had rapidly brought the Antareans to develop their energy and life centers, the things the Earth dwellers called brains. Telepathic communication was discovered early. But as they developed these inner powers, a well-developed Antarean brain could move mountains and navigate spacecraft. It could also melt ice and refreeze it in milliseconds. Amos let his mind wander with thoughts of home and he grew slightly taller. Jack Fischer thought Amos had just straightened up, or stretched. They had reached the outside back door to the B complex. It opened without Amos touching the knob.

It was cool inside. They walked down an unfinished corridor. Jack thought it was a bit strange that the building was air-conditioned at this stage of construction. Then he noticed that the air-conditioning duct work was not complete, and he realized that it was cooler on his left, the side closer to Amos Bright. As he moved a bit closer to the alien, it became even cooler. Amos was putting out his own air conditioning.

They turned a corner and stopped at a stairwell. Again the door opened, seemingly by itself. They walked up the stairs to the second-floor landing. When they entered the corridor, Jack saw that it, too, was unfinished. He also noticed that the coolness emanating from Amos had stopped and that they were now in an air-conditioned area. They came to a blue door painted and Amos stopped. "We will go in here for a while. The others have preparations to make before we open the first cocoon. Are you hungry?"

Jack answered, "Yes, and I'm also a bit cold."

"Of course," Amos said. "You will get used to that soon, I promise.

This room will be comfortable for you." He opened the door with his hand this time and motioned for Jack to enter. Amos Bright followed him into the room.

CHAPTER EIGHT
AFTER THE EMPTY NEST

"Four bam. Two crack. Soap." Then silence. Rose Lewis and Bess Perlman looked across the table at each other. It was Mary Green's turn and she was staring down at her mahjongg rack and card, deep in thought.

Alma Finley spoke first. "Come on, Mary, you've been playing for two months now. You should know the card by now." Mary looked up with a hurt expression. "I'm trying to play a hand I never played before, and I think I just went dead."

Bess leaned over and looked at Mary's rack. She thought for a moment and then suggested that Mary call the soap and play an exposed hand.

Mary looked at the mahjongg card in front of her and then smiled as she realized that she could do what Bess suggested. "Thanks, Bess. I guess you have to be Jewish to be really good at this game."

Alma laughed. She was the best player of the foursome, and she was a Presbyterian. Bess and Rose had made her an honorary Jew the day she cleaned them all out after only three lessons in mahjongg. Actually, she was a terrific card player and she approached this game the same way. She could count tiles the way she counted cards and therefore knew the odds at any given time. She played the percentages. Before Joe had been forced to retire they made a few trips to Las Vegas. She always won at the blackjack table because of her counting ability. Joe admired her for it, but he always believed that the next time it wouldn't work. He never allowed her to gamble with more than a few hundred dollars. Even so, she had managed to stash away over ten thousand dollars from her winnings in a bank account that Joe didn't know about.

Mary called the soap tile and the game progressed.

"West," Bess said.

"Take for mahjongg," Alma called, and she exposed her winning wind hand.

Rose looked at her with disbelief and said, "Somewhere in your WASP past a Jew must have snuck in. Either that, or you cheat."

Alma laughed again. "Actually, from what I understand about my sea captain paternal great grandfather, it was probably an Asian."

That started the laughter again and Bess Perlman made a mental note to have a talk with Mary regarding exactly what a Jew was, and was not. Now was not the time or place.

They dumped the tiles into the center of the table and began turning and mixing them for the next game.

"Joe told me that the pool was going to be filled soon," Alma said.

"Ben told my Arthur today," Bess said. She was a woman of few words.

Rose looked at Mary and asked, "So, is it today?"

Mary answered, "Yes. Ben told me that he was having a meeting with the manager this morning and that the pool was going to be filled today. It's a crusade with him, but when he says something will be done, usually it's done."

That was the way with Ben Green. He was a man of action, not reaction. He was a leader, and until Mary had realized that she was a person unto herself, she had been a follower of Ben Green. At times he could be an overbearing pain in the ass. But it wasn't Ben's fault. It fact, he had pointed that out to her on a day she would never forget. They had been married twenty-two years and their three children were out of the house. The youngest was nineteen—a marine biology major at Cornell. Their middle child had been drafted, sent to Vietnam and was now a permanent resident at Arlington National Cemetery. Whenever Mary saw a golf bag being shipped on the plane to Florida, it reminded her of Jimmy, because she had seen pictures of body bags being shipped back from Vietnam and, although they had received his body in a casket, she knew that at one time it had been in a bag like that. Her third and oldest child, Patricia, was married, living in Chicago, and soon to make Mary and Ben grandparents. She was in her sixth month. Her husband was Michael Keane, an up-and-coming product manager for General Foods.

On a particular day in May 1965, Mary had followed her usual routine. Ben had been up and out of the house by seven A.M. It was eleven A.M. and she was still in bed. She heard the key in the front door and then Ben's voice calling to her. "I'm up here," she said. He came into the room and looked at her. Then he shook his head and went to the large walk-in closet and took out his mid-sized suitcase.

"Where are you going?" she asked. "It's Friday."

"I have to go to Los Angeles this afternoon. I'll be gone for a week. We have to rush through a pool of commercials on that new cereal account." While he spoke, he continued to pack.

Suddenly she felt very depressed and alone. Then she got an idea. "How about my coming with you?" she asked.

He had stopped packing and stared at her. He knew then that what he was about to do was cruel but necessary. He truly loved his wife, but in his mind she had become a vegetable. Her life had always been the children and the house and taking care of him. Now that was over. The kids were gone—one of them, tragically in war. Mary had become a slug … a sloth … she was going to seed. Ben knew women older than Mary who worked at the agency. They were vital and exciting. Mary was a disaster, and if this way of life continued for her, he knew that it was just a matter of time before they would drift irreconcilably apart. He decided that now was the time to speak directly to the problem. He loved her, but he was a coward when it came to fighting with her. Years of living a relatively easy life around children and other homemakers had dulled Mary's fighting spirit. She was a pushover in a logical argument and her perception of the world was twenty years old.

Ben sat down on the side of the bed. "My dearest Mary," he began, "I want you to listen carefully to what I'm going to say. I love you very much. I think you are a good woman. I think you are a beautiful woman. I think you are an intelligent woman. A wonderful woman. But I also think you are becoming a pain in the ass and a bore. You can't come with me because I have a long hard week of work in front of me. It's my work, which is a part of my life. It is what I do, and I do it well. It really has nothing to do with you other than that it provides money for our standard of living. I happen to love what I do. It is stimulating and exciting. But that's for me. I think that you should take a good hard look at yourself in the mirror, and a good look at this house, and then sit down and find out who you are and what you want to do and be in this world now that our children are grown. You can do anything you want. I'll be back next Friday or Saturday and we should talk about it then. Now, please don't say anything. Just let me finish packing and get the hell out of here."

He got up, quickly finished packing, and left without saying another word. He slammed the door and she had heard the tires of his MG squeal as he drove out onto their quiet Westport Lane.

Ten minutes later, with tears drying on her cheeks, she screamed, "Screw you, Ben Green!" Then she poured herself a glass of bourbon.

The next four days were spent in and out of a hazy drunken stupor. She wandered through the house spending time in each room. She had drawers, folded their contents neatly, and then refilled them. She threw out a stack of *Good Housekeeping, Redbook,* and *McCall's* magazines that dated back fifteen years. She stripped naked and stood in front of a full-length mirror in their bedroom and examined her body. She saw the beginning of flab and the flattened breasts. She studied the slight bulge of varicose veins on her legs. She gently touched the wrinkles around her eyes and mouth. She let strings of four-letter words fly out of her mouth on a regular basis. Some of them surprised her because she hadn't remembered knowing them. In the beginning they had been directed toward Ben, but as time passed they poured out in a general, undirected way.

The morning of the fifth day she woke up with a start. She had slept for only three hours. It was seven in the morning. She was naked. There was a sound coming from the kitchen and she realized that Betty, her cleaning lady, was in the house. It must be Tuesday. Mary Green got out of bed and walked slowly to the bathroom. She hadn't bathed since Ben left. She smelled her breath. It was foul. She smelled her body. The odor was unpleasant.

Then she recalled the punch line of a joke that her son Jimmy had told about a hermit who had a long beard. He fell asleep one day in his cabin. Some kids crept in and rubbed Limburger cheese into his beard. When he awoke he sniffed the rotten odor. He went outside his cabin and sniffed again. It was a clear, bright day in the mountains. Still he smelled the cheese. Finally, he muttered to himself, "The whole world stinks."

Mary said it out loud. "The whole world stinks." Then she thought: *No, it's only me and my body. I can brush my teeth, and wash my body, and perfume myself. Then what?* Mary desperately wanted the answer to that question, and she knew she had three days to find it.

Betty was washing the kitchen counter when Mary came into the room. "Miss Green," Betty said. "What's been goin' on here? This house is one fine mess." Betty had been working for the Greens for seven years and took a proprietary interest in the comings and the goings of the family. She had been the only person who had been with Mary when news of Jimmy came to the front door in the person of an Army Captain and a Chaplin. She had cried like a baby with Mary. She had hovered over the family and cared for them all. She was a Catholic, just as they were. She was black and they were white and that made a difference, but only outside of the house. She truly loved these people and felt their love for her in return. Now, as she looked at Mary Green, she realized that a very troubled woman had entered the room.

Mary stopped near the kitchen table and sat down. "Is there any coffee, dear?" she asked. Betty poured her a cup and brought it to the table.

"You want some breakfast? You're up kind of early." Mary didn't answer. She just looked down into the cup. Betty saw a tear drop into the coffee. Mary's hands started to shake. She sobbed. Betty sat next to her and put her arm around Mary who leaned her head onto the big black woman's shoulder and cried.

Betty held her. "Okay, honey. I'm here. Let it out. Let it all out."

It was ten minutes before Mary could talk. She sipped her coffee and told Betty what had happened. At first it came slowly and with difficulty. Betty listened patiently. She liked Ben Green. He was a fair man, a bit pushy at times, but nevertheless fair. She knew the truth of what he had told his wife. It was the method that she didn't approve of, but what was done was done. Her concern now was for Mary.

"What have I done wrong?" Mary asked. "You're married. Does your husband think you're a vegetable or a slug? What does he want?"

Betty was slow to answer. She wasn't sure this problem was in her domain, but she did love this woman. "Well, Miss Green," she said, "I don't know exactly what is on Mr. Green's mind, but I can understand how he might be feelin'. You know folks get on, we all do, and the years seem to go by, and suddenly we get to be forty and then fifty and the kids leave and being a mother and father isn't there anymore like it was. Mr. Green, like he says, he has his work. It keeps him feeling … well, sort of alive. Maybe makes him feel younger than his years. Gives him a reason to get up in the morning and be tired at night. Me and George, we have that, too, both of us. We have a nice small house and a good car and we travel a bit and go out a lot. But we each have a life of our own too. I have my friends and he has his. Sometimes I go down to North Carolina to visit my sister and he doesn't come. I come here three days a week and go to Miss Kramer two days and at night I sleep real good. You get what I'm sayin'?"

"I know you work hard, Betty, and I know it isn't easy for you and George. But we have money. I mean we're comfortable."

Betty shook her head. "You're missin' the point, Honey. Look at yourself. Are you comfortable?"

Mary stared at Betty for a moment and then said, "I'm about as uncomfortable as I can be right now. Help me. Please."

"What the man was sayin' is to make something for yourself in this world. Do your own thing, like the kids say. Let it all hang out, Mary Green. You're a fine lookin' woman with a brain and an education. You don't need money, that's true, but you do need to find something to do. Something that will make you feel good and important. The way I figure, there's not too much we can do about getting older, but we sure don't have to get dumber at the same time."

"You mean get a job?" Mary questioned.

"Right on," Betty replied. "Get a job or volunteer for something and get your ass out of this house. Maybe next time you'll be the one packing for a business trip."

They had talked for the rest of the day and then cleaned the house together. Betty called her husband and told him that she was going to sleep over that night. The two women talked into the night exploring the possibilities of what a fifty-two-year-old ex-housewife might do. By morning Mary was as excited as the day she had graduated from college.

By the time Ben came home from Los Angeles, she had written out a program for herself. They had sat together all day Saturday and discussed the plan. Mary would enroll in summer school at the University of Bridgeport and take a few refresher courses. She had been a business major. She would also take a steno and bookkeeping course in a night program at the local high school. In the fall she found a job at a large real estate office in the area and continued taking courses at the university at night. She eventually managed the office.

That was fifteen years ago. In the time since that fateful week Mary had changed her life. She was still shy, and a woman of few words, but she had confidence and a positive sense of herself. Her life with Ben had been wonderful since that week.

The business with the pool had brought back those memories, and as she built her wall of mahjongg tiles for the next game she wondered about her new friends around the table and if someday soon they might discuss their feelings the way she and Betty had so long ago.

CHAPTER NINE
A ROOM OF COLORS

The light kept changing in the room. It was a subtle change that Jack hardly noticed it at first. Now it was blue again. A pale blue, like the dresses the bridesmaids had worn at his brother's wedding last week. That thought shook him a bit because he remembered that Judy would be coming home to the apartment in an hour and wonder where he was.

As the blue faded to yellow he spoke to Amos Bright. "I have a … a girlfriend. She lives with me. She is going to wonder where I am." Amos thought for a moment and replied, "You will have to call her. Use your radio phone on your boat. Tell her that the charter will be out for a week. That will give some time to think of how to deal with her." *You're a clever spaceman*, Jack thought. He agreed to the plan. They had been in the room for a half hour. The food was more than he'd expected. Steak with French-fried potatoes, salad, wine, and coffee. If that was a sample of the treatment he would receive for his services, Jack felt better about his situation.

The room moved to a pale orange as Amos stood. "I think we can get to work now. The processing area is prepared." He motioned Jack to precede him through the door and, without thinking why, Jack turned left and walked down the hall to an orange door where he heard a faint hum coming from behind it. Amos and Jack were then joined by the two men who had been wearing the copper suits earlier in the day. They were still wearing the suits, and on close inspection Jack saw that the fabric was made of tiny hexagons fitted together without any obvious stitching. The fabric was a deeper red than copper, but definitely metallic.

Amos opened the orange door and they entered a large room that resembled a modern health club. Along the left wall were metal cabinets the shape of the cocoons. There were twelve of them. They looked like tall steam cabinets. A misty vapor rose from ten of them. The odor in the room was sweet and pleasant, like the mild perfume that Judy had worn at his brother's wedding. He put her out of his thoughts and concentrated on the rest of the room.

There was a large, square table in the center of the room—about eight feet by eight feet. Above it loomed a large conical lamp. Harry and Hal were standing at the table. They nodded at Jack, smiled, and then moved toward the first metal cabinet. The far wall was partially hidden from view by the center table, but Jack could make out what appeared to be a row of cots with blankets and pillows. Above the cots were smaller versions of the large center lamp. On the right side of the room was a huge viewing screen. It took up the entire forty foot wall, and ran from floor to ceiling. *Cinemascope,* Jack mused. A noise from the back left hand corner of the room got his attention. Through the mist he saw that two commanders, James and Bill—Shiny White and Shiny Black—had entered the room. They were met at the center table by the copper men. Although there were no words, Jack sensed that they were communicating. Amos touched Jack on the shoulder and guided him to a raised chair halfway between the wall screen and the center table. Jack climbed into it. "You can watch from here. Please don't interrupt. Any question you may have will be answered later," The silent conversation continued at the center table. Hal and Harry were in the mist near the first metal cabinet, intent on whatever they were doing. Amos Bright joined the others in the center. Jack felt as though he was on a movie set, sitting in the director's Chair, only he had no idea of the script or what the actors were going to do. He had been on a few movie sets. Judy was an actress and lately there had been several movies shot in Florida. She had had a minor role in a low-budget film last month. Jack had come to the location to pick her up one day. They were working late and he was allowed to hang around in the background until they finished. He had been interested at first, but after watching take after take, he realized how boring the process was. They were doing a scene in a bar and Judy was playing the part of a hooker. Two men were jockeying for her attention and the director wanted to play the scene in one long take from the time the second man walked into the bar until the fight between the two men broke out. It was about three minutes of dialogue. It required a tough bit of acting by Judy. She was very good. Jack watched and was proud of her and her talent. But after they had done the scene seven times, Jack could see the actors were getting tired. The last two takes had been lost because the camera had bumped into a table once and into an extra who forgot to get out of the way the second time. As those takes were spoiled the cameraman had yelled "Cut!" The director went through the roof and chewed out the grip—the man who was pulling the camera dolly. The cameraman interceded on behalf of the man and told the director to shove it up his ass because it was an almost impossible shot and move and they were doing their best. The grip was then forgotten as the confrontation between the director and the cameraman grew into a screaming match. Suddenly, the director spun away from his adversary, yelled, "Wrap it for the day!" and walked off the set.

There was a moment of silence and then the assistant director had yelled, "Wrap! Seven tomorrow. We are in the same place." The lights started to go out and as he left with Judy they passed the assistant director talking to the bar owner about what it would cost to close the bar for the night so that they wouldn't have to move the equipment and lights. All Jack heard was the assistant director saying, "Five hundred bucks? Shit! You don't do five hundred bucks a week here …"

Judy was a pretty girl. She was not beautiful or exotic, but sweet, pretty and smart. She was a child of the seventies— serious about her career and herself. The only vestige of the sixties that she carried was a mild interest in rock music. She dressed fifties and her hair and make-up were forties. These days she had a permanent and wore deep red lipstick.

The thought of that lipstick color jolted Jack back to reality, if what was going on in this room could be called reality. He was suddenly aware that the screen behind him had turned a deep penetrating red color. It bathed the room in red light. The conical light above the large center table was also glowing red.

From the corner where Jack had seen Hal and Harry working, there came a screech like the sound of chalk on a blackboard, then a loud hiss. Red, steamy mist shot out of the first metal cabinet as it opened, the two blond men rolled a jitney to it, removed a cocoon from the cabinet, placed it on the jitney and moved it briskly toward the center table.

CHAPTER TEN
THE ACTOR, THE AD MAN, AND THE POOL

Art Perlman and Bernie Lewis stood clapping as Ben approached. Joe Finley continued shuffling the cards. He had been at the meeting that morning when the final confrontation took place in the manager's office.

In a few moments they would all sit under the gold-and-white umbrella with the Antares logo shading them from the bright Florida sunlight. They would play their ritual gin game until lunch. Today would be different, however, because the gurgling sound of the pool filling would serenade them while they played. *Yes,* Joe thought, *it is a sweet sound.* He knew what it represented was winning. For Ben, it was as though he had closed a big advertising account and for Joe it was as if he had landed a juicy part in a Broadway show. For each of the retired men this morning had been a triumph.

Joe Finley had been an actor, a bartender, a salesman, a taxi driver, and an elevator repairman. He had done many other odd jobs—too many to remember. And he'd served eight years in the army from 1941 to 1949. He had seen combat in Europe but never spoke of it. He thought of himself only as an actor. That was his love and the only joy he could remember besides being married to Alma. His first wife, Dotty, had walked out on him after sixteen years of marriage and two kids. They had lived in Boston, and although they hadn't been poor, life had been without many of the luxuries that Dotty saw on television every day. It finally became too much for her and she succumbed to what Joe liked to call "Her American Dream." She met a widower. He fell in love with her. He had money and was willing to support the kids and send them to college. Most important, he was eager to give Dotty all the material things that she hungered for. Joe and Dotty had had so many fights about money that when she came to him and told him she wanted a divorce Joe just nodded and said, "Okay." That was too easy for Dotty, so she proceeded to tell him every detail of her recent adulterous life with Mr. Moneybags and outlined every detail of her future life with him and the kids. But Joe just didn't care anymore. Their life had been a struggle and arguments. All Joe could think of was Martin Luther King's epitaph. "Free at last … free at last … oh, my God, I'm free at last." He had no remorse about his two daughters leaving him, either. He loved them, but they were carbon copies of their mother. He knew that someday they would make their husbands miserable, harping on them for material possessions and luxuries.

After the divorce Joe moved to New York and rented a small studio apartment on the lower West Side of Manhattan. He drove a cab during the day and joined a small off-off Broadway theater group that met at night. He was forty at the time—a handsome man with dark hair, graying slightly at the temples, and steel-gray eyes. He was in good shape physically, and even at the age of sixty he jogged five miles every morning. But now, in Florida, couldn't even walk one mile without tiring. His present wife, Alma, came along when he was fifty-one. He had a supporting part in a long-running off-Broadway show. He managed to save a few thousand dollars and had built a pension plan in the Screen Actors Guild and AFTRA. He was a good, working journeyman actor whose future was always going to be in acting. When he turned sixty, he'd been married to Alma for four years, and he wasn't thinking of retirement. They were making plans to go to Hollywood and try for some television parts. Joe's hair was graying and his face chiseled. His eyes were penetrating blue. He had developed his craft to an extremely professional level. He was a good TV type, and he was starting to get some solid TV commercial work, too. Alma … his dear Alma, had noticed it first. "Are you feeling all right, Joe?" she would ask. "You seem tired." Joe would say that it was just her imagination. She knew she was right, and loving him deeply bothered him and pushed him to the doctor's office for a checkup. A few days later, the doctor's words fell on Joe like a lead weight. "Mr. Finley? You said you wanted it straight. Okay. You have leukemia." Joe felt as though someone had punched him in the stomach.

"Leukemia? Isn't that a kid's disease?"

"No, Mr. Finley. However, when we find it in people of your age we are able to treat it. I can assure you that you have many, many good years ahead of you. As a matter of fact, I believe we can keep you going indefinitely." Joe wondered what that meant. Life was not indefinite.

He didn't tell Alma for two weeks because the doctor was going to try a new medication. If it worked, the doctor said he could almost guarantee that Joe would be all right. But there were qualifications that went along with the treatment. "You can't push yourself," the doctor told him. "You should think about retiring to a quieter life, if possible." When the tests came back, the new medication had some effect. The doctor was optimistic. Alma met Joe at the theater that evening after the show. They went to a quiet French restaurant on Forty-Ninth Street. They ordered mussels and a good white wine. After a while, he told her what the doctor said. He had been upbeat and positive, but she could see that this dream of Hollywood was fading. She reached across the table and touched his hand. "I love you," she said. "So very much." From that day on she was all that mattered to Joe Finley and he to her.

Watching Ben Green approach to the sound of applause brought Joe back to from his reminiscing to his own performance this morning.

They met early at Ben's apartment. Mary Green made breakfast for them. She sat at the table listening while they went over their plan. Joe brought all the props. He was wearing the pinstriped suit, a white shirt and red tie. His wing tip shoes were polished to a dull shine. His hair was trimmed and neat. He had even trimmed the hair in his nose and ears. His nails were manicured and buffed.

Ben had the attaché case, the I.D., and the papers. It was amazing that Ben was able to get it all done so quickly. Ben had a friend who owned an ad agency in Miami. The guy owed Ben a favor. He never said what the favor was, but it must have been a biggie because there was a messenger at Ben's door at six A.M. that morning with the papers.

They rehearsed one more time, finished their coffee, and shook hands. Ben left the attaché case on the breakfast table and headed for Shields' office. Joe waited five minutes and followed. When Joe arrived at the office, he found Ben waiting in the reception area.

Joe gave no sign of knowing Ben. He spoke to the secretary. "Good Morning, I'm Mr. Bonser from the Attorney General's office. Is Mr. Shields in?" He flashed the I.D. that Ben had given him earlier. The woman became very nervous. "Well, sir, uh, Mr. Bonser, uh, let me just check. Uh, will you have a seat?"

Joe started to sit and then said, "In case he forgot, we have an appointment."

She smiled and made her way to the back office. Ben Green leaned forward to peer into the office as she opened the door a crack and slithered inside. Both men had trouble controlling their laughter.

When the girl returned, Joe got up and went over to the desk. "Can he see me now? I've got a very busy schedule today."

She spoke to Joe, but was looking at Ben Green. Her voice was only a whisper. "Mr. Shields says he doesn't recall having an appointment with you. Could you make it another time?"

Joe's voice boomed. "You tell Mr. Shields that either he sees me now, or he sees me in federal court."

With that, Ben Green jumped up and rushed to the desk, yelling, "He's in there, isn't he? Goddamned son-of-a-bitch! I'll kick his ass all over this goddamned office!" Before the girl could stop him, Ben rushed into Shields' office. Joe followed and stood in the doorway. Shields was backed against the wall of his office underneath a large mounted tarpon. Ben loomed over him, threatening to stuff Shields down the fish's mouth.

Joe moved toward the desk and took out the I.D. card again. "Mr. Shields, I'm Mr. Bonser, ADA from the Attorney General's office. We spoke the other day regarding a complaint from a Mr. Green."

Ben spun around. "I'm Ben Green. Goddamn, I'm glad to see you. Now we can put this rat in the slammer." He loosened his grip on Shields and moved over to shake Joe's hand.

"I'm glad to meet you, Mr. Green," Joe said. "We don't want our new Florida residents to think that just because they are new to the state we don't pay attention to their complaints. A senior citizen is still a citizen and a voter." Joe smiled the politician's smile that he had used in *The Last Hurrah,* when he had played the mayor of Boston in an off-Broadway production. He then sat down and opened his attaché case and took out the papers they had prepared.

"Mr. Shields, I hope we can settle this matter amicably." Shields moved slowly back to his desk and sat down. Joe handed him the papers. As he read, a defeated expression grew on his face. Ben and Joe knew they had won.

What they didn't know was that Shields was under strict orders from the "owners" to keep the people in Building A happy. They didn't want any publicity, and they certainly didn't want to get involved in federal court. *Hell,* Shields thought to himself. *I'd take this old fart to the Supreme Court before I'd fill the pool.* He put the papers down on his desk and looked up. The ADA Bonser wasn't a young man. Shields would get no sympathy from him. He decided to make it short and sweet. "Mr. Bonser, I'm sorry for the confusion. I'm sure Mr. Green here just misunderstood. Actually, we are filling the pool today ... yes, today." He buzzed the secretary on the intercom and told her to find Wally Parker immediately and have him come to the office.

A few moments later, when Wally walked into the office, he moved to the opposite side of the room from Ben.

"Wally, you know Mr. Green. This is Assistant District Attorney Bonser. I want you to begin filling the swimming pool right now." Wally looked confused, but he said, "Okay." He turned to leave. Joe Finley stopped him.

"Just a moment, Mr. Parker. Mr. Shields, I'm sure you don't mind if I go with Mr. Parker and observe. Just for the record. I'm sure Mr. Green would like to come along, too."

Ben Green looked at Joe Finley, then at Shields, then at Wally, and said, "You people all give me a pain in my ass. Don't patronize me, Bonser. Just get out there and do your damned job. I have to take my nap, but when I get up, that damned swimming pool, our pool, had damned well be filled or I'll blow the freaking thing up!"

Then Ben left the office.

CHAPTER ELEVEN
ROSE'S TEARS

Rose could see the four men from her terrace. Bernie and Arthur were applauding Ben Green as he approached their table. She noted that Joe Finley didn't applaud. Seeing the card table brought back a vision of her daily bridge game at Sunset Village and thoughts of the friends she left there. She would adjust. She always had. Early in her marriage she had been unhappy. Her mother, who had come from Russia, told her daughter that happiness was not a right in a marriage. If one had it, then one was lucky. A woman had to adjust to a man's ways. *Well*, she mused, *Mama was certainly right. My marriage to Bernie Lewis has been just that, a series of adjustments.*

Her thoughts were interrupted by the phone. She left the terrace and took the call in the kitchen. "Hello?"

"Hi, Mom, it's Craig. How are you?"

"Wonderful, darling. And how are you and Beth and the children. How *are* the children?"

"Just great, Mom."

"That's wonderful."

"How's Dad?"

"He's fine, dear. He's out by the pool playing cards with his cronies."

"It sounds like you really are settled in there. I can't wait to see the place."

"Yes, dear, and we can't wait to see you. Just two more weeks and three days."

There was a pause on the phone and then Craig spoke again. "Well, uh, that's why I called, Mom. There's a problem. I won't be able to get down this time. It's business. I won't bore you, but we have to redo some of the fall line, and then I'll be at the factory after that to set up the run … you know it's all the details and …" His voice trailed off.

Rose was crying.

"I'm really sorry, Mom. We were looking forward to the trip. The kids are really disappointed. I'm tempted to send them without me, but I know after a day or so they would drive Dad crazy."

And that bitch you call a wife would put me in the hospital, Rose thought. She composed herself, but she didn't wipe her tears as they dripped slowly down her face. As she spoke again, she tasted their salt. *These are the tears of our affliction,* she thought, recalling the Passover story of Moses and the Exodus. "Listen darling—business is business. We understand. When do you think you can get down?"

"Well, Mom," Craig answered, "you know the problem is the kids and school. The next vacation they get is in four months. We'll plan for that, but it's right in the middle of our busiest season. We'll talk … work something out"

Rose took a deep breath. "Fine, darling. Let us know. I'll call you on Sunday."

"Okay, Mom. Love to Dad. Be well."

He hung up. She deliberately replaced the receiver in its cradle, fighting the impulse to slam it down. She reached toward the roll of paper towels, pulled off a piece, and dried her tears. She then put her foot on the garbage-can lever, opened the top of the can, and dropped the towel with a flourish. *Adjust,* she thought, *then readjust. Is that a life?*

When Rose Charnofsky met Bernard Lefkowitz, she was seventeen years old and stunningly beautiful. Her eyes were brown, large and innocent. Her long dark hair reached to her waist. Her figure was slender but carefully hidden. The Charnofsky family was a very proper family that prided itself on high morality. They were Orthodox Jews. Her father was an extremely religious man. After all these years it was hard for her to remember him. Once recently, when she had gone to visit an aunt in Miami Beach, she had vividly remembered her father.

Rose's aunt was well past eighty. She lived in a small apartment hotel on Third Street, off Collins Avenue. It was a neighborhood filled with old people, old houses, and old hotels. Rose found it depressing. Yet, to those people it was part of the good life they had found in America. They were all immigrants from worlds Rose could not imagine. She had, as a child, heard all the stories about the Czar and the anti-Semitism and the pogroms, but it seemed so far away and foreign to her that she never believed much of it was true. When the atrocities of the Nazis were revealed after World War II, she watched the old people nod their heads and understand. She had been horrified and furious. They had been complacent and accepting. To them it had seemed only natural that Jews should be murdered.

This old aunt, Aunt Ruth, had been one of those who accepted it all. As Rose climbed the stairs to her aunt's efficiency apartment, the scent of heavy cooking was in the hallway. It brought back a vivid memory. Suddenly it was the odor of Friday night at home. The modest, three-room apartment in Brooklyn was spotless. Her mother had spent the entire day cleaning and cooking. Her father was home early. Dinner was early. Conversation was sparse. Then he was off to synagogue, but the smell of Sabbath stayed behind.

Aunt Ruth's hallway was filled with the same smell, and for a moment Rose expected her father to open the apartment door. When Aunt Ruth opened it, Rose was startled back to reality. She embraced her aunt and drank in her love. Then, uncontrollably, Rose began to cry. The tears were not for Aunt Ruth, nor for her father. They were tears for the pain that her ancestors had endured; for the courage they had to leave their homes and to find a new life in a foreign land. They were tears of understanding, because no matter how poor they were, Rose realized those people knew they were safe. They had been delivered. They too had adjusted. The fact that Rose couldn't quite face was that the tears were also for herself. She had also spent her life adjusting, but to things that were, by comparison, unimportant. Her affliction was self-imposed pity. Perhaps it was the times; perhaps it was the burden of being first generation in the promised land; perhaps it was because her suffering was so small compared to what the old people had experienced. In any case, the tears flowed and a part of her opened to let out love that she had not clearly felt or expressed before.

CHAPTER TWELVE
PROCESSING BEGINS

The cocoon had no cover, hinge or door. Instead, it was peeled away by the two copper men. The room remained flooded with red light. As the layers were peeled from the cocoon, they disintegrated at the instant they were no longer attached to the cocoon. It happened in a flash, and there was no apparent trace of the material after that. There was something about the process that gave Jack the feeling he was in a massive darkroom watching technicians develop a huge photograph.

Amos Bright telepathed to Shiny Black—*It goes well. The first is normally an expendable, but I think we will have it.*

Shiny Black answered aloud. "No reason to doubt. The process had proven itself before in the Cenedar Quadrant."

Hal interrupted. "True, Commander No Light, but Cenedar is an ammonia ice planet. I recall no time-test of cocoon in an oxygen-hydrogen medium."

The conversation was terminated by Commander Shiny White, known as Commander All Light. "Your kindness, please! It is peeled. My sensors indicate moisture. Some condensation, I believe. Check me, No Light."

The Shiny Black turned his face toward the cocoon on the table. It was now almost the shape of a man. He telepathed—*I concur. Some moisture has entered. But it is not harmful and the soldier is not spoiled. If the others are like this, we will require more time for the drying than anticipated.*

The copper men were removing the last of the covering. In the red light Jack could see a man, or at least the shape of a man, lying on the

50

table. It did not move as Commanders Shiny Black and Shiny White moved around the table examining the body. Finally, Jack was able to see the full figure. It was a human form, with a few variations.

Jack did not notice the lack of genitals at first because he was shocked to see that the body had no eyes. There were sealed slits that wrapped around either side of the face to where ears should have been. He remembered Shiny Black's face when he had taken his human face off on the boat. This man also had no nose or mouth. And there was no hair. Then Jack noticed the lack of penis and testicles. At that point the room began to hum and pulsate.

Before Jack could react, Amos was at his side, helping him down from the high chair. "It's getting late, Jack, and we have work to do. I think it might get uncomfortable for you here. Let's go out."

Jack followed Amos to the door. Just as it was closing behind them, Jack heard a shrill piercing sound coming from the room. Then it was silent. "Part of the process," Amos said. "I promise that you will see it all very soon. This is the first and we must test it very carefully before we process those we have and release others. They have been here for a long time."

He took Jack to another room with a blue door and opened it with a key. "This is your room. I will come for you in the morning. Please rest and don't worry, but by all means contemplate what you have seen and learned today. There is much more that you will learn in the days ahead."

He closed the door and locked it. The room was not unlike a Holiday Inn or Ramada motel room, except that Jack was locked in for the night.

Before Amos Bright returned to the processing room, he stopped at another door that was red. He went in and picked up a silver case. Inside the processing room, the heat had dissipated and the group was huddled around the center table. When Amos entered he immediately felt their disappointment. *How bad is it?* he telepathed.

"Recoverable, but damaged," Hal answered. "But it may be difficult to revise the programs to overcome the damage."

"We can try," Shiny Black interrupted.

"We must," Shiny White said.

Amos set down the silver case at the head of the table. He quickly scanned the body and saw the spots. "Did the moisture do this?" he asked.

"Perhaps," said copper man one, "but it may also be from the electrical input. I will send the scout probe back to the base tonight and bring down more instruments. I believe we will lose this soldier. This development is not good news for our mission." He turned and left the room.

Amos opened the silver case. In it there were two teardrop-shaped glasslike bulbs. Copper man two came over and touched them. They began to glow. The copper man then slid his forefinger along the eye slit of the body on the table.

"You will do an insertion, anyway?" Shiny Black asked.

"We must," Amos answered. "It is procedure, even with damage."

Copper man then inserted one teardrop into the slit. The opposite side of the man's body quivered. He then inserted the other teardrop and the other side of the body quivered. "Good tone," copper man said. They all agreed. He then removed a small, red, glowing stone from under the head of the soldier and passed it to Amos.

Hal and Harry rolled a narrow table next to the center table and slid the body onto it. They then wheeled the body to the back of the room and placed it onto one of the cots. The cone-shaped light above the cot switched on and a white beam emanated from the light. It split into two beams and entered the eye slits. Another beam, blue in color, came from the cone and widened to cover the upper torso of the man on the cot. Finally, a third beam, deep green in color and shimmering, appeared and spread out to encompass the entire body.

Back at the table Amos Bright was placing the small glowing red stone, the size of a golf ball, into the silver case. Copper man two, Shiny White, and Shiny Black gathered around the case and each reached a hand into the case and touched the rock. They all telepathed the same thought—Home!

CHAPTER THIRTEEN
A MAN FROM BROOKLYN

The clear, blue water gurgled, filling the pool as Joe Finley dealt the cards. Today he was partners with Art Perlman. He liked playing with Art because Art was not only a shrewd card player, but a quiet man who didn't jump on a partner if he made a mistake. That was important to Joe. He was sensitive to criticism. As an actor he had experienced more than his share and taken it personally.

As the others arranged their hands, Joe poured a cup of lemonade from his Thermos and popped a pill into his mouth. He washed it down with one gulp and then returned to his hand and the game.

Art Perlman watched from across the table. *That is a brave man,* he thought. *I don't know how I would react to having leukemia.* Art chuckled to himself at the thought because death was not a stranger to him. He had lived with it all his adult life. However, that kind of death was quick and always for a reason one could understand. Even rationalize.

It began on the streets of downtown Brooklyn. Arthur Perlman was the third son of Abraham Perlman, mattress maker. His oldest brother, Sam, had died in World War I on some godforsaken battlefield in France. He was buried there, and no one from the family had ever seen the grave. Art's second oldest brother, Harry, attended City College. It was decided that he was going on to medical school. At that time, Art was sixteen and a creature of the streets. The roaring twenties were roaring and Prohibition was in its third year. After Sam's death, his parents had withdrawn from life in general. They spent most of their money on Harry's education. They had written Art off as a wild son who would end up badly. They were simply too tired to control him.

First generation, third born was the way Art looked back on his childhood and his eventual chosen profession. *I was just there at the wrong place at the right time,* he always mused.

The wrong place was the Brownsville section of Brooklyn. The right time was Prohibition. His first job was unloading bootleg whisky from Canada in the middle of the night after it had been off-loaded from smugglers boats onto Long Island beaches and trucked to Brooklyn. The pay was good. Art could make in a few hours what it took his father a day or two to make. On good nights he often got a bonus.

The next step up the ladder was delivering booze to the clubs. Speakeasies. He was doing that by the time he was eighteen. By then he was part of an organization that controlled the bootlegging and waterfront of Brooklyn. It was run by Italians and Jews. Words such as Mafia and Family came later. They were just gangs in those days.

About that time, his father came out of his depression long enough to take notice of his young son's ways. There was a confrontation that brought his mother to tears and brought Arthur to City College as an accounting student. His father forced him to promise to finish school and keep away from the "bums." Art kept the first part of the promise, but not the latter. He was actually encouraged to go to school by the head of the gang, Angelo Sorocco. Angelo was an immigrant. He had worked his way up and had been given a small section of Brooklyn by the "big boys." He was a good soldier and followed orders. As a result he was privy to the larger plans of the gang. He foresaw the day when educated men, who could also be trusted, would be needed by the organization. "Go to school, Arty. Be an accountant … be a lawyer … use that Jew brain of yours and I promise you we will have a place for you when you finish."

While in school, Sorocco got him a steady night job in one of the downtown clubs at the cash register. By the time Art had finished school, the Depression had begun. He was a Certified Public Accountant by day, but at night he collected the cash from fifteen gang-owned clubs in Brooklyn and Manhattan. When Prohibition was repealed in 1933, Arthur Perlman opened his own accounting firm. His only clients were the various businesses of what was to eventually morph into part of the Gambino and Genovese Families. Many of the financial dealings of Brooklyn's organized crime filtered through the hands of Arthur Perlman, C.P.A.

Death entered the picture when, at a secret meeting in Atlantic City, a new business was formed. It was eventually known as Murder, Incorporated. Arthur Perlman was spared the job of handling its finances, but he was involved in setting up the fee structure and payment methodology for its services.

He took good care of his parents by buying them a home near his own in Manhattan Beach, an exclusive section of Brooklyn. He met Bess Bernstein at a neighborhood party one New Year's Eve, and they married one year later.

He loved Bess and the home she made for him. They had one child, a son, Harold. Bess had nearly died in childbirth and the doctor warned against having any more children. Harold and the house became Bess' life. Art's life was his work.

As he sat at the card table by the pool, watching Joe Finley pop the pills into his mouth, he thought back on the day that he had to tell Bess about his work. He knew he was going to be called before a grand jury and that his books were going to be subpoenaed. There might be publicity, and although the right newspapers, judges, and politicians had been taken care of, there was always the possibility that some nosy young D.A. wouldn't get the message and snoop around his home. The Organization had authorized him to reveal to Bess whatever he felt was necessary.

She had taken it well. Far better than Art had expected. But she did pop some pills into her mouth, too. "Just to relax me," she had said.

Then later, as they sat alone in the darkened living room, her voice broke the silence with a question that made Art realize how alone he was in the world outside of his business friends. "Arthur, tell me … did you ever kill anyone?"

"What are you asking?" he had answered. "Kill? Me kill? Are you crazy?"

"Arthur," she had replied, "I am not a stupid woman. I read the papers and from time to time I see the work you bring home. Some of the names … some of the clients … I read about them in the papers. I'm not stupid. I put two and two together. Just answer me that one question. I have to know. The rest will go to my grave with me. I promise."

"Never, my darling. As God is my witness. Never." And that was the end of her questions.

"What are you, a comedian today?" Ben Green asked.

Art said, "What?"

Ben answered, "I asked you to throw a card and you say never …"

"Sorry, Ben … I was just, uh, daydreaming."

"Daydream on your own time." Art threw a king of clubs. The game began.

CHAPTER FOURTEEN
LADY ON THE LADDER

The week had passed quickly for Jack Fischer. He stood on the *Manta III's* flying bridge in the warm, late afternoon sunlight and watched the commanders bring the last cocoon of the day to the surface. By his count, that made number sixty. He figured a bit more and calculated that at this rate it would take them about thirteen more weeks to raise all of the buried Antarean army—nine hundred forty-one soldiers.

Jack was anxious to get back to the condo complex. Tonight he was going to see Judy for the first time since this adventure had begun.

He recalled how he had been locked in his room that first night. Later, he heard the key in the door and Amos Bright appeared. "I almost forgot that you have to call your girlfriend on the ship-to-shore radio. We'd better do that now."

Judy had been upset when he told her he'd be occupied full-time for a while. She did not like to be alone. Jack suggested that she have a friend move in with her. He suggested a fellow actress with whom Judy took a class. "You can work with each other on that part you're going to do at the Grove Theater," he said, and her mood had lightened.

"When will you be back?" she asked.

Jack looked over at Amos. "One week from now," Amos mouthed. Jack repeated those words to Judy.

There was a silence and then she said, "I'll see you here then. Don't bother to call. I may be out!" And she hung up the phone.

Amos apologized for the inconvenience and promised that if Judy was unreasonable he would do his best to explain to her. Jack told him that it would not be necessary.

The two copper men were lifting the last cocoon onto the deck. Hal and Harry were breaking down the equipment. Amos was giving All Light and No Light a hand as they climbed onto the deck.

The drill had become routine. Jack started the twin diesels and raised the anchor. Off to starboard, the *Terra Time* was already under way, heading back toward Coral Gables.

With a final check to be sure all were aboard and secure, Jack eased the powerful engines into gear and pushed forward on the throttle. The twin diesels responded, cutting a neat wake through the darkening Gulf Stream. Home lay ahead—a night off and the company of one very warm, female, human being. He could imagine the taste of her and his body tingled with anticipation. The title of a recently popular song, "It Ain't Love, But Baby It Feels So Good," passed through his mind, and he began to sing the song to himself.

Below deck the scene was glum. A preliminary inspection of these cocoons showed the same problem. There was corrosion and condensation present. After the discovery of water damage in the first cocoon, they had sent their probe ship back to the mother ship, parked on the far side of the Moon. It had returned that night with special power supplies and regulators as well as a high-frequency drying unit. The new equipment made little difference. They had opened all ten of the cocoons that first night and revived them before dawn. When they were done the soldiers had been removed to another room on the upper floors to undergo intensive drying.

Both commanders agreed that the removal operation should continue, but instead of removing layers of cocoons from the top of the storage area, they would penetrate the stack vertically in order to reach those cocoons stored deepest and farthest away from the water. Today's batch was from the bottom of the sealed chamber, yet still they were damaged.

We will need nutrition from mother ship tonight, Bald White telepathed to his comrades.

"Yes," they all agreed.

"I have already arranged the beaming," Amos volunteered.

Silence again. Each had closed down externals and was searching deep inside for answers. The mind was but an arrangement of atoms. With proper training and centuries of practical discipline, the Antarean beings could plunge themselves inward and reach the nucleus wherein lay all accumulated knowledge of their species. The energy controlled within the cabin of Jack Fischer's boat was immense, and now it was being directed down into the depths of the souls of these strange visitors to Earth. They knew they were up against a very serious problem. If they could not solve it, then their mission would end in failure and the Antarean reputation as space travelers and traders could be tarnished for millennia to come.

Oblivious to the galaxy-shaking problems below, Jack eased the *Manta III* down the canal and headed into the Antares dock. *Terra Time* was already docked and deserted. Its crew was smaller than that of the *Manta III* and was made up only of Antareans. There were three young men who resembled Hal and Harry and a woman who seemed to be in charge. Jack suspected that she was a commander with a female disguise. He wondered if she was bald under a beautiful wig of blond hair that imagined she wore. He thought back three nights ago when he had docked before the *Terra Time*. She had been on the flying bridge. Jack had casually sauntered over to the boat to say hello. The three boys had replied to his greeting, but the female only looked at him and then went about her business. Jack had a specific thought in mind as he bent down to tie his sneaker while she climbed down the ladder from the bridge. *I want to have a look under that dress,* he thought. *I want to see how much detail they gave you, my alien beauty.*

He still wasn't clear about telepathy and mind reading, and, of course, she knew exactly what was on his mind. Halfway down the ladder she stopped and stretched a leg for Jack over the outrigger bracket. He had a clear view under her skirt, but he was not prepared for what he saw.

Staring at him, where the flower of her femininity should be, was a duplicate of her pretty face and blond hair. The face was smiling and the lips were pursed. It blew him a kiss. He looked away quickly while adrenaline surged through his body and enveloped his groin.

CHAPTER FIFTEEN
COMPLICATIONS OF LOVE

At dusk, the Antareans completed the off-loading of the day's cocoons harvest and prepared for processing. Jack showered and dressed for his night off. He always kept a clean change of clothes on board the *Manta III*, but made a mental note to pack a bag for the weeks ahead.

Building A of the complex was alive with Friday night activity. There were sixty couples living in the building ranging in age from mid-fifties to late seventies. On Friday nights they gathered in the recreation room for dancing and socializing. Usually at least thirty couples attended. Joe Finley brought his record player and collection of band music from the thirties and forties.

As people gathered, cliques formed. Tonight the Greens, Lewises, Perlmans, and Finleys were joined by two other couples they had casually befriended. They were Paul and Marie Amato and Frank and Andrea Hankinson. The Amatos were from Boston. He was a retired stockbroker. The Hankinsons were from St. Louis. Frank Hankinson was semi-retired but still spent half the year in St. Louis tending to Frank's interest in a radio station. They were referred to as "snowbirds" because they only spent the late fall and winter months in Florida.

"Great job you guys did on the pool." Paul Amato said. Ben Green told him they were only getting what they paid for and had a right to expect. The discussion then drifted to the fact that Building B was still unfinished.

"You would think that they would want to get it completed and the condos sold as soon as possible," Bernie Lewis remarked.

They all agreed. Then Joe Finley asked Alma to dance. They were joined by the Hankinsons. Several couples were on the floor. They danced a fox trot to a Frank Sinatra song. As the couples swayed slowly to the music, the scene could have been a ballroom out of the 1940s. These couples, for the most part, had spent their lives together. They knew what love and companionship were, and although a youth oriented society had subtly pushed them to the Florida peninsula, they were content and at peace with each other. The active and hectic days of fighting for a living, keeping up with the Joneses, and rearing children had passed. The music, like their current lives, was warm and slow. Ben Green, Art Perlman, and Bernie Lewis sat observing the scene in silence. Their wives had gone to the kitchen to help with the coffee and cake.

"Look at us, Art," Ben said as he gestured to the room of slow-dancers. "It's not right to farm us out this way." Ben spoke in a sad and soft voice. It was a theme that Ben had brought up several times lately.

Art nodded. "True, my friend, but what are you going to do? It's the way of our society. They say the old, uh, I mean isn't "seniors," the term? We've had our time, they say. Everything now is young-young-young …" His voice trailed off.

"Bullshit!" Ben snapped back. "The truth is it really felt good when we were pushing that bastard Shields to fill the pool."

"Yeah." Art nodded and smiled. "That was fun. Got my blood up."

Ben moved closer. "I was thinking that we might speak to Shields about the mess over at Building B. I think we have a right to know when it will be finished."

"Good idea." Art agreed. "He won't be around over the weekend, but we can see him on Monday morning before the card game."

"Okay. But let's keep Joe Finley away just in case we need our Mr. Bonser from the Attorney General's office again."

Bernie, who had just been listening, nodded his agreement.

Sinatra's "Wee Small Hours" ended … "That's the time I miss you most of all …" The couples returned to their tables. Ben and Art huddled with Joe and told him their plan. Joe loved the idea. Bernie Lewis spoke up. "I think we ought to have a look over there tomorrow. We can get a better idea of how much work is left to do and we'll be able to confront Shields with some facts." The four men agreed and promised to meet at seven the next morning to have a look at Building B.

Amos Bright watched the lights go out in the recreation room of Building A. He turned to Jack Fischer. "They are going to bed. You can leave in twenty minutes. Let's be sure we understand each other."

Jack was prepared for the lecture. "We do, Mr. Bright, I promised to be back tomorrow morning before sunrise, and I'll be here. Judy won't know anything about this place." Bright went on anyway.

"And you'll tell her that you have a treasure-diving charter for the next few months. Make sure she knows you'll be gone for a week at a time. I don't want her to be suspicious, and I certainly don't want her coming here looking for you."

Jack resented being treated like a child. Surely Amos knew that he was sincere. All he had to do was read Jack's mind.

"Harry has brought your car over from your dock. It's parked in back. The keys are in the sun visor, and the tank is filled. Have a nice time. I will see you in the morning." Amos got up and walked to the door of Jack's room.

"Thanks," said Jack. There was no sarcasm in his voice this time. He knew the seriousness of the Antarean's problem with the cocoons. "I hope you can lick the moisture problem," he said.

Amos stopped. "Thank you, Jack. I'm not sure we can, but we have to continue trying every way we know. I appreciate your concern." He left the door open.

Ten minutes later Jack was driving out of the Antares condo complex. He drove to U.S. Route 1 and then three miles south to his apartment near the Kenwood Shopping Center. The garden apartments were set back from the street. Jack pulled into his parking space. The lights were on in his apartment and his heart skipped a beat as he pictured Judy waiting there for him. He realized that he felt very deeply about her. *Easy,* he thought as he took the stairs two at a time. *That's a marrying type of lady up there, and you are not a marrying type of guy right now.*

Judy was dressed to kill. She had the stereo playing a Judy Collins album. A bottle of Chardonnay was in the ice bucket. Two joints were neatly rolled. A plate of stone crabs with cold mustard sauce set between two scented candles completed the table arrangement. As Jack closed the door, she came toward him quickly. Her satin jumper clung to her body and shimmered in the candlelight. Before Jack could say anything she was on him and her arms were around his neck and her body was tight against him. She kissed him hard and long and wet, drawing his breath into her lungs.

"Welcome home, sailor. Welcome home from the sea." She led him to the sofa. "Sit," she ordered. She filled two chilled wine glasses and then lit one of the joints. He watched, mesmerized by her movements and the care he was receiving.

A few drags and a few sips later and Jack completely forgot the world of cocoons. Judy did not speak again until they had finished their lovemaking. He knew they would not sleep that night. He felt the desire rising in him again. Judy brought the plate of crabs and the sauce to the sofa. They ate and sipped the wine. Everything was delicious, but paled at the sight of his beautiful girl beside him.

"Now, lover, how was that?" Judy asked.

"I feel like I just died and went to heaven. You are something else, super lady."

"Well, you sounded like you were going to have a long, hard week. We've never been away from each other for this long. I really missed you. Really."

"And I missed you. A lot." Jack decided that he'd better get the bad news over with quickly. "I'm afraid we're gonna be … well, away from one another for a while." Judy watched him, expressionless. "It's gonna be a long charter. But, this could just about pay off the boat. Free and clear. I had to take it. You understand, huh?"

"Understand what?" she asked softly.

"Well"—he sipped the wine—"these folks are treasure hunters. I can't really talk about it, but … well … they are on to something and I agreed to work with them for the next few months."

"Oh, shit, Jack." Judy was immediately furious. Her eyes widened. Her jaw tightened as she clenched her teeth.

"Honey, look … it's over a thousand a week plus expenses. They might even cut me in on the booty. I had to take it!"

Then she was crying—not hysterically, just softly. "Jack. Your being away this week … it made me realize how deeply I feel about you. I think I've fallen in love with you … and now … away for two months … it hurts. It really hurts."

Jack felt suddenly smothered. Christ! The last thing he needed now was a demanding woman. The months ahead had to be filled with his new space buddies. He had promised. What if he told her that he couldn't spend the time with her because he had to work with creatures from another planet? That would go over big. Yet, he felt for her. He decided to ask Amos Bright whether he could bring her to the Antares complex. But right now he would have to deal with her present sorrow or he might lose her forever. He reached and slipped off her robe. She didn't resist. Then he bent and kissed her breast, and her neck, and her mouth, and her eyes, and on and on, until they were joined again as one.

It was after midnight. The tenants of Building A were asleep. All except Alma Finley who sat alone in the kitchen and sipped tea. Her thoughts were of Joe sleeping in the bedroom. There had been a definite change in him during the past few weeks. She noticed that he was walking slower and going to bed earlier. He was tired. The doctor said that this might happen from time to time. But this time it was prolonged. He wasn't responding to the medication. Could this be the beginning of the end? Did she have the strength to face living without Joe? Did she want to?

Alma stood up and walked out onto the terrace. It was a mild night. The air was cool. The sky above was filled with stars. As she glanced to the south her eye was stopped by a faint red line that seemed to come from the sky and pass directly onto the roof of Building B. She blinked because she thought she was seeing things. When she looked again it was gone. Then it was there again. *It looks like a laser beam*, she thought. *Maybe it's coming from the top of the building like a beacon.* Yes, that was it. An airplane beacon. There was probably one on top of Building A, too. Her thoughts returned to Joe.

The three commanders, Amos, the copper men, and the five crewmen were seated in a circle on the roof of Building B. In the center of the group was a glass, bowl-shaped object. Inside the bowl was a cluster of red glowing rocks. Each of the aliens had glasslike rods extending from their eyes into the bowl. Their human faces were off. As the red beam from the mother ship struck the bowl, the rocks glowed, and then the glow traveled up the rods into the eyes of the Antareans. The feeding lasted for thirty minutes. The crew sat in silence and ecstasy as they fed.

There was a large unfinished room on the roof. It was to be the solarium when Building B was completed. Now it was occupied with fifty Antarean soldiers sitting in neat rows of ten. They were still and showed no sign of life except the glow in their wraparound eyes. In each row nine of the beings were dressed in pale blue, skintight jumpsuits. The tenth was a copper man. Each of the copper men had a device attached to his head that protruded in front of his eyes. A red beam inside the device was split three ways. Two of the beams went into the eyes of the copper men. The third beam came out of the device and passed down the row to the eyes of the other nine soldiers. The faces of the soldiers were splotchy. The stains were dark brown, as though their faces had been made of pine and the stains were knots. The first two soldiers in the first row were stained the worst. Suddenly the beam feeding the first soldier cut off abruptly in front of him. He twitched and emitted a deep humming sound. His eyes glowed bright for a moment and then went dark.

Outside, on the roof, Commander All Light stopped feeding. He looked toward the room that housed the soldiers and then telepathed for the others to stop feeding. *We have lost the expendable. The second will go soon. I fear we will fail.*

Amos grew a bit, and silently blessed the departed soldier with the old thoughts: *Serve the Master as you did your own. You have taken your reward. Guide us if you can as you move among the stars. We love you.*

CHAPTER SIXTEEN
THE SECRET IN BUILDING B

By the time Ben, Art, Bernie, and Joe entered Building B, the Antar-eans had left for the Gulf Stream aboard *Manta III* and *Terra Time*. The first thing the intruders noticed was the air conditioning.

"A/C. That's weird," Ben Green said.

"Maybe they're just testing the unit," Bernie suggested. The others agreed.

"Where shall we start?" Art asked.

Joe Finley suggested they walk up to the second floor and then work their way higher until they were satisfied they knew enough. He was tired this morning and hoped they would be satisfied with just a few floors.

"Okay," Ben said. "Here's a stairwell. Let's go."

Ben Green led the way from floor to floor. When they came to a new landing they would split up. Ben and Bernie would go to the south wing of the floor, and Art and Joe would go to the north side. If their search turned up nothing, they would head back to the stairwell. If either team was not back, the other would wait five minutes and then look for the missing team.

At ten-thirty they were on the sixth floor. They had found nothing. Joe Finley was very tired and suggested that it was to no avail to search any farther. Ben Green disagreed but then quickly understood when Art Perlman flashed him a knowing look.

"Okay," Ben said. "Let's head down. But I want to have a look at those locked doors we found on the second floor. I'm sure I heard sound coming from behind the orange one."

They walked down to the second floor and went directly to the orange door. Ben put his ear against the door. "I hear a humming noise. How about it, Joe?"

Joe put his ear to the door. "I think you're right. Sounds like some kind of machine." Art and Bernie listened and agreed.

Ben tried the doorknob, but he couldn't budge it. "I'm going to get this door open," Ben said, "one way or the other."

"You mean break in?" Art asked.

"I said one way or the other didn't I?"

Bernie and Joe looked at each other. "That could mean trouble, Ben, you know, breaking and entering," Bernie suggested.

Ben laughed. "I told you guys last night that I was bored with this "senior's" thing, right? So I spend a few days in the clink. It's better than sitting around and vegetating. Besides, we own this place, don't we? How can you get in trouble for opening a door on your own property?"

"It's not exactly our property," Art told him. "Not until the contractor finishes the building, passes inspection and turns it over to the corporation."

"A mere technicality," Ben retorted. "You guys give up too easily. I'm coming back after lunch with tools to get this lock opened!"

They left the building and went to the pool. They had worn their bathing suits on their excursion that morning, so before playing cards they all went for a swim. Ben Green was a strong swimmer and did ten laps. Bernie and Art swam a lap each and then lolled around in the Jacuzzi at the far end of the pool. Several of the Antares tenants were at the pool. They all had warm greetings for the four men.

"We're going to name this the Pool of the Fearsome Foursome!" yelled Paul Amato. Ben waved to him.

Joe was the last into the pool. He swam a few strokes, then turned and got out of the pool. *I could have swum a hundred laps a few years ago,* he thought. *Now ...* and the expression "tired blood" crossed his mind. His blood wasn't tired. It was killing him.

They gathered at their table and played their daily gin game. As the noon hour approached they promised to meet in Building A's lobby after lunch. Joe begged off, saying he was going to nap. "If you need tools, I have some in the car," Joe volunteered. Ben told him that he had plenty of tools for the job.

They met at one-thirty without Joe, and the three men proceeded to Building B. On the way they saw Wally Parker walking in their direction. Bernie and Art suggested that they continue, but Ben, who was carrying a toolbox and his auto jack, said he would circle around the back of the building. "You guys open the back door for me," he said, and left.

Wally said a polite hello to the two men as they passed. He stopped and watched them walk toward Building B. "Excuse me gentlemen!" he shouted. "Where are you going?"

"For our after lunch walk. It helps digestion," Bernie yelled back.

There was definite sarcasm in his voice. Wally decided that all old people were senile and those two were, but seemed harmless enough. "Be careful of the construction equipment. We don't want any accidents."

"Who wants accidents?" Bernie answered "And when are you going to finish this place, anyway?"

There was anger in his voice and Wally felt he had made a mistake in stopping the old codgers. The memory of Ben Green and the man from the Attorney General's office was still fresh in his mind. He didn't need more trouble. "Right," he called out, waved, and then quickly continued on his way.

Art and Bernie laughed to themselves and detoured around the pool into Building B. When they opened the back door, they found Ben waiting for them.

The trio proceeded to the orange door. Ben put his ear to it again. "Still humming," he remarked.

"How are you going to get in?" Bernie asked.

"I saw this in a movie once," Ben answered. "We pry the back side of the door with the tire iron and I slip in the 'L' bracket so that it rests under the hinges on the other side. Then we slip the putty knife into the lock and it pops open."

"I don't understand," Bernie said.

"Just watch. You're never too old to learn."

He began to slip the tire iron into the slot at the rear of the door when. "Just wait a minute," Art Perlman said. "I think I have a better way. Without damaging the door." He took a leather packet from his pocket, unzipped it and removed a lock-picking set.

Ben and Bernie stared in amazement. "Where the hell did you get that?" they both asked simultaneously.

"Arthur Perlman is a man of many accomplishments," Art said. "In other words, don't ask!"

He slipped the lower pick into the deadbolt lock and then selected a smaller metal strip from the bottom of the lock. As he worked he flashed back to his youth and the education he had received from the "Family." He could hear Angelo Sorocco explaining the art of picking a lock just as though he were standing by Art now—*Be gentle and slow. Slip in the bottom probe carefully until you feel a click. If it doesn't click after two tries, then use the next smaller probe.* But that wasn't necessary because the lock popped almost immediately. Art pulled the probes out and, with a grand gesture, said, "Gentlemen! After you."

Although Ben was their unofficial leader, it was Bernie Lewis who went into the room first. "What the hell is this?" he whispered. The others followed immediately. They stopped in their tracks and scanned the room.

The center table was empty. All of the cocoons that had been processed the night before had been moved to the roof. The room was glowing pale blue. The fixture over the center table was dormant. On the left there was a slight mist rising from the cabinets. The cots at the rear of the room were empty and their overhead units were also dormant. The screen on the right wall was the source of the pale blue light. On the floor in front of the screen were several pieces of apparatus that the aliens had brought recently from the mother ship in order to combat the moisture problem that was plaguing the cocoons.

Ben spoke first. "It's a health club."

"A health club?" Bernie asked. "Why a health club?"

"Well, just look. Those are steam cabinets over there and the table in the center is for massages. The cots in back are where you wait for the masseuse or rest with hot towels. Believe me, this is a health club," Ben said confidently.

"*Our* health club," Art added as he walked toward the blue screen. "What the hell is this for?" he asked.

"Movies," Ben answered, sure of himself. "It's a wall TV unit. We had a smaller version at the ad agency. You can run films, or ball games, or music. We used to show porns on it, too," he chuckled.

Bernie was excited. "Hey, this is great. It looks ready to me. Those rats were going to keep it closed until they finished the building. I think we ought to go down there and chew their asses out about this." He moved toward the cabinets.

"Just a minute," Ben suggested. "Let's stop and think about this."

"Why?" Art asked. "Bernie's right. The club looks okay to me. Why shouldn't we use it?"

"I'm not saying we shouldn't use it," Ben said. "I'm only saying that it seems to me that if we keep our mouths shut about this place, we can have exclusive use of it. And no one will be the wiser ... for a while, anyway. Understand?"

"Yeah," Art agreed. "But we have to tell Joe about it."

"Of course we tell Joe, but that's all. At least for a week or so. What do you say?" Ben asked. Art and Bernie agreed. The three then went off in different directions to examine the room in detail.

Joe awoke from his nap to find Alma sitting on the edge of the bed. She was holding his hand. "Feel better?" she asked.

"Yes. That was a good nap," he answered. "And I'm hungry."

"Good," she said. "I'll fix you a ham-and-Swiss on rye. Want a beer?" She didn't wait for an answer. If he didn't say no, that meant yes. Joe got out of bed and decided to shower.

When he came into the kitchen his lunch was on the table. He did feel better, but he was still a little tired. "Couldn't you sleep last night?" he asked. "I heard you get out of bed after midnight."

She looked at him with some surprise because she was sure he was fast asleep when she had gotten up. "Just restless. I had too much coffee at the dance last night," she told him casually, not wanting to reveal how worried she was.

"How late were you up?" he asked.

Why is he pressing me? she thought. *Maybe he wants to talk about it.*

"Not too late, dear. I think I got into bed around one."

"Oh," he answered, and went back to eating.

No, she thought, *he doesn't want to talk. I'll change the subject.* "I would have gone to bed sooner, but I saw something strange over on the roof of the other building. It took me awhile to figure it out." *Good going, Alma,* she thought.

"What was it?" he asked.

She proceeded to tell him about the red laser light on the roof of Building B and how she had finally deduced that it was an airplane beacon.

"That's strange," he said. "These buildings aren't that tall that they would be a menace to air traffic."

"Maybe we're in a flight pattern," she said.

"I don't recall hearing any planes," he said, and then went back to his lunch.

"Well, anyway, it stopped after a few minutes. I'm sure there is some explanation," she remarked. "What do you want to do for the rest of the day?"

"Let's just take it easy, honey. How about a drive down to the beach?" he suggested.

"Love it," she said. "I'll go put on a bathing suit." She went to the bedroom to change, feeling good that he wanted to get out. But instinctively she sensed he was fighting off the tiredness. She promised herself to call the doctor Monday without his knowing and ask about these recent symptoms.

By the time Joe and Alma Finley were heading for the beach, Bernie Lewis was in a "steam cabinet" having a good time. It had taken a few minutes to open the cabinet. At first, Bernie had been puzzled because he was used to sitting in a steam cabinet. But he had to lie down in this one. He slipped his body in and called Art over to close the door. It took some time until they figured out how to turn it on. When the mist increased they knew they had hit the right button. It wasn't hot, but Bernie felt as though he was getting a deep massage. It felt great. He suggested that Art get in the next one and show Ben how to operate it. With Art encased next to Bernie, Ben went off to explore the other equipment.

He walked around the big center table twice. The surface was smooth, but it had some give to it. He could press his finger into the material, which resembled a shiny black patent leather. Once he withdrew his finger the material immediately sprang back to its original form. *Strange stuff*, thought Ben. He left the table and went over to the row of cots on the back wall. He lay down on the first cot and the overhead conical light went on. It began to hum and then the white light beam came out of the cone and split into two green beams. Ben jumped off the cot just before the beam reached his eyes. The overhead light went off. He yelled over to Art and Bernie, "This is weird, guys. They must have installed some of the latest equipment here."

"It might be weird, but it sure feels great," Bernie yelled back, "You ought to try this. I'm about done. Come on."

Ben went over and helped him out of the cabinet. Bernie stretched. He felt wonderfully refreshed. "Boy, I don't know what that thing is, but it sure woke this old body up."

Ben started to get into the cabinet that Bernie had just vacated when Art suggested that Ben try the third cabinet. "Maybe they're different. Let's find out. All I know is I'm not leaving this one for a while. I feel like I'm getting laid."

Ben laughed and eagerly slipped into the third cabinet. Art closed the door and turned it on. A smile came across Ben's face. "Holy shit! This is sensational! But if we tell everyone about this place, we won't get near it for a month."

"Roger that," Bernie agreed. "I bet this place would perk Joe up too!"

Knowing Joe was ailing, they agreed that as soon as possible they would bring him to their new, private health club.

CHAPTER SEVENTEEN
A HELPER IS HELPED

Although Judy Simmons had reluctantly agreed to accept the fact that Jack would be away for a week at a time, she found herself depressed and lonely the next morning. It took her two hours to clean the small apartment, do laundry and make some calls. She had exercise class at eleven and then she was free for the day. By two that afternoon she had worked herself into a state. She understood Jack's taking the job, but she convinced herself that she would not be in the way if she came along with him for a week or two. He could tell the clients that she was the mate and that he needed her aboard.

Later that evening Jack's brother Arnie called, looking for Jack. Judy told him about the charter. Arnie thought it was great news and then put his new wife Sandy on the phone. She invited Judy for dinner the next night. "I'd love that," Judy said, adding, "Maybe we can call Jack on the radio phone."

"Good idea," Sandy told her. "We'll see you about seven."

Okay, Jack Fischer, Judy thought, *you're going to invite me onto that boat next week whether you know it or not.* After that she felt better. She called her friend Monica. The two actresses got stoned and listened to music until three in the morning.

At the time that Judy and Monica were crashing on the waterbed, Jack Fischer was up to his waist in cocoons. The day's harvest had been brought into the processing room. Amos Bright was pleased with Jack's promised return and his enthusiastic cooperation. As a reward the Antarean leader told Jack he would learn more about their mission that evening.

After docking that evening they allowed him to off-load the cocoons with Hal and Harry. Jack was surprised by the texture and apparent lightness of the cocoons. They were not solid, but rather pliable and pleasing to the touch. He thought of Jell-O as he lifted the first one, nearly dropping it onto the deck. The other surprising quality of the cocoons was their warmth. He was so enthralled with the sensations that he did not notice the black commander watching him. However, shortly thereafter Jack felt him.

Treat them carefully, Jack Fischer, Commander No Light telepathed strongly, like an electric shock.

The thought ran through Jack like an electric shock. *Sorry*, Jack thought. The shock immediately dissipated.

Then Jack heard another voiced in his head. *Very good, Jack. You are beginning to telepath.* It was Amos Bright.

Hal and Harry both looked at Jack and nodded. Jack was proud of his accomplishment, but not quite sure how he did it.

Amos signaled again. *Don't think about how, Jack, just do it. Practice with us and you will come to know how to control. For now we will listen for your thoughts and send you ours. Eventually, you will be able to communicate this way at will. Your race has the ability, but you have not yet realized that and developed it. Perhaps you can teach others when we are gone.*

Although the ability to communicate this way with the Antareans was amazing, Jack also realized that he could not have a private thought without their knowing. That was unsettling, yet what could he do about it? He accepted it.

After the cocoons had been delivered to the processing room and encased in the cabinets, Jack went to his room for a shower and dinner. There were fresh linens on the bed and fresh towels in the bathroom. Maid service, he mused. By who? The warm shower felt especially good this evening. Making love with Judy last night, and through the wee hours of the morning, released a lot of built up tension. He was tired. He also wondered why Amos picked this night to reveal more of the mission to him. As he dried himself there was a knock at the door.

"Just a second," Jack called. By the time he opened the door his visitor was gone, but his dinner was on a tray placed neatly on the floor.

The menu tonight was red snapper in lemon-butter sauce, mashed potatoes, carrots, salad, coffee, and cake. *I've got to meet their chef one of these days,* he thought. The food seemed to get better each day, as though someone was getting attuned to his taste. Maybe someone was. With these folks, anything was possible.

By the time Jack dressed, ate, and got to the orange door, the group was processing the third cocoon. Amos telepathed him to enter the room. Jack thought, *Maybe I'll explain how tired I am to Amos and he'll give me a rain check.* Amos' voice filled his mind. *Go to the last cot and lie down for a moment. Don't be afraid of the light beams. They won't hurt you. Relax. Tiredness will leave you.*

Jack did as he was told. He felt wonderfully refreshed after a few moments on the cot. *The world could sure use this device,* he thought.

Amos silently agreed. *Perhaps we will leave one for you Jack,* he beamed, *but now we could use your help.*

Jack got off the cot and the beams shut down. "How can I help tonight?" he said aloud.

Commander All Light motioned Jack to the cabinets and telepathed for him to give Hal a hand. As they loaded the cocoons and adjusted the settings on the cabinet control panels, Hal explained that the cabinets began the process of tissue restoration as well as a complete cleaning and priming of all glandular activity. The process, like most of the technology of the Antareans, began from within the cocoon. There were chemicals and molecular constructions stored inside the cocoon and the body of the soldier. The process in the cabinet filtered through to the stored chemicals and started a chain reaction that was the first step in restoring life to the soldier. Hal showed Jack the various settings on the first five cabinets. Jack had not realized that the last five cabinets were different and that the cocoons had to spend time in one of the first five cabinets, and then a few moments in one of the last five cabinets before moving to the center table to be peeled.

"What do the second group of cabinets accomplish?" asked Jack.

Hal did not answer for a moment because he was checking with the other commanders to see whether he was authorized to explain that part of the process to their human helper. He received an okay from both commanders in the room. "Help me with the first cocoon and I'll show you what happens next." As they slid the cocoon from the first cabinet onto the gurney, Hal gestured to leave it for a moment. They walked to the back of the room and wheeled a fresh cocoon to the first cabinet and inserted it for processing. Then they wheeled the cocoon they had just removed over to the sixth cabinet and inserted it. Hal closed the cabinet door and beckoned Jack to the control panel. "All living matter carries some disease and decay within it, Jack. This set of cabinets cleanses the tissues, organs and blood of all such substances. It gives the soldier a perfect, healthy start to his rebirth."

Jack couldn't believe what he had just heard. "That's incredible. You mean these soldiers start over disease free?" Jack asked.

"Absolutely," answered Hal. "It's quite necessary for a mission to another planet. We never want to carry diseases for which there is no immunity on other worlds. That would be disastrous."

Like the white man did to the Hawaiians, Jack thought.

Amos' voice entered his mind. *Hawaiians?*

Yes, thought Jack. *We have a place on the Earth called Hawaii. They are islands in the middle of the Pacific Ocean. When they were discovered by the white man there were natives living on the islands. The white men brought diseases with them for which the natives had no immunity. Almost all of them became sick and died.* Jack realized that he was telepathing once again.

Amos entered his mind, saying, *That is a very sad story of ignorance. A pity. Your communicating was good, Jack, and you are correct about the purpose of the second set of cabinets. That is exactly their function.*

For the rest of the night Jack helped Hal insert and move the cocoons from cabinet to cabinet to center table. It was dawn when they finished, but Jack was not tired. Amos told him that he could sleep for an hour or two if he chose.

"But I don't feel tired," Jack answered aloud.

"Good," Amos replied. "I didn't think the beams above the cots would work that well with Earth beings. You can use the cots if you do not wish to sleep. It provides the same purpose."

To fortify himself in case of drowsiness, Jack walked to one of the empty cots and lay down for five minutes. When he got up he felt as though he could work twenty-four hours nonstop. The level of energy and well being surging inside him was a sensation he had never felt before, and one that he would never forget.

CHAPTER EIGHTEEN
WHAT HAPPENED TO US?

It was their third day in the "health club." Ben Green had tried the table the day before, but when the overhead cone turned on he got scared and jumped off the table. Ben had decided to try the table today. This time he stayed there and the feeling was quite pleasant. Ben was covered with a fine white ash. "You look like you're covered with Shake 'n' Bake," Bernie remarked. "What the hell is that stuff?"

Ben wiped some of the substance from his forehead. It came off easily and disappeared from his finger. "Beats me," he said, "except I feel very …"—he hesitated—"… dry … yes … dry is the word. Like I've been in an oven, but there was no heat."

The ash was a result of his lying on the center table for less than a minute. It could not be explained, but it didn't seem to be harmful. As Ben brushed it off his hands none of it ever reached the floor. It simply vanished in air. "I thought the dammed thing burned me," Ben said as he slipped off the table, "but my hair is still here. I don't know what this lamp does, but I do recommend it highly."

Art, who was in the first cabinet, yelled that he would try the table after he finished his steam bath.

The most confused man in the room was Joe Finley. At this moment he was lying in the eighth cabinet. He had been in there for ten minutes and was experiencing a very strange feeling. He had discovered that the control panels on the last five cabinets were different from the first five. The others had not noticed that before. Yesterday, when his friends had shown him the room, his thoughts were still on the effects of the recurrence of the leukemia he was experiencing. Tiredness was

78

definitely getting worse. *What good would a health club be to a dying man?* he thought. But because of his friends' excitement, he decided to come and share their discovery. He had spent twenty minutes in the third cabinet next to Bernie Lewis before getting into number eight. It was surprising that when he got out he felt much better. Then they all had watched Art Perlman lie down on one of the cots and allow the beams to spread over his body. He related the experience to his buddies as sensationally relaxing, so they all took a cot and shared the experience. Afterward, they went out to the pool for their swim and card game. That's when the surprises began to happen.

Ben Green hit the pool first and began to swim his normal laps. Bernie and Art dove in next and caught up with Ben. The trio swam until they realized that they were racing and that the people around the pool were cheering them on. They had done twenty laps when Bernie suggested they stop. No one was tired. They were breathing very hard and their hearts were beating rapidly. But they were definitely not tired. Then they realized that Joe Finley was nowhere to be seen. Ben shouted for him. No answer. Suddenly Joe exploded out of the water in front of them. He had swum the entire length of the pool underwater. He slid out of the pool and up onto the ledge in one graceful motion. In a split-second he was standing next to his three buddies. "Guys," he said, "I don't know what kind of equipment they put in that health club, but I feel absolutely great. I can't wait to get back there tomorrow."

The four men then sat down at their table and began the card game. No one could think straight because of the new physical feelings they were having.

Finally, Ben spoke. "Let's meet in my apartment this afternoon. The girls have their mahjong game, so we won't be disturbed. I think we have to have a serious discussion about the health club."

Art agreed. "I think we've stumbled on to something special. I can't explain. Just a feeling. But …"

Bernie Lewis interrupted. "Keep it down, guys, or we'll have the entire condominium jammed into that room."

The four men didn't notice the other phenomena that were occurring because of their excitement. Normally they played gin for two hours before lunch. On a good day they got about thirty hands completed. Today they played twice that number. For the most part they also knew what the next card was before they picked it. They also had strong feelings about what hand their opponents were playing. No one realized it, but they were reading each other's minds and thoughts. Later, they would understand why.

After lunch they met at Ben Green's condo. He had a corner apartment on the fifth floor and therefore a large balcony. The four men sat in chaise lounge chairs and sipped iced coffee as they talked about their discovery.

Joe opened the conversation. "I gotta tell you guys. I still feel super."

"Me too," Bernie chimed in. "And I'll tell you a little secret. After lunch I took Rose to the bedroom. We had a matinee. I haven't done that for, well, more than ten years, at least. And I tell you, I could have stayed with her all afternoon."

The others laughed, but they understood what Bernie was talking about. The same feelings had crossed each of their minds. Bernie was a man of action. The others felt as though they had missed something, and each made a mental note to give it a try.

"I think Joe was right this morning," Ben continued. "We have found something extraordinary. This must be very new equipment; experimental stuff. But what the hell is it? Any ideas?" Ben asked.

Art spoke next. "I don't know what the stuff is, but let's really agree to keep it quiet for a little while. If everyone in this place began to feel like I do this afternoon, and the word got out, we would have a mob scene here. The press. TV. Shields."

Joe Finley stared down toward the pool and watched a man in his seventies struggle to swim a few laps. He recalled diving into the pool that morning and swimming underwater without even taking a breath. It had felt natural. While he was underwater he had a sensation that he was a diver—no longer in a pool, but rather deep in the ocean. The water was warm and crystal clear. Below him he could see other divers, and below them objects that appeared to be long white tubes. Then the image had blurred and he had popped out of the water to greet his friends. As he watched the old man swim, he decided to withhold his experience from his friends until he understood what it meant. "I think there is a proper sequence to the equipment," Joe said. "I don't know what that sequence is, but I believe we should experiment. Tomorrow, let's give it a real thorough going over and see if we can figure out a sequence."

"How can we do that?" Art asked. "We don't know even what the damned stuff is!"

"I've been thinking about that," Joe said. "There are four of us, and as far as I can see there are six different pieces of equipment. The cabinets, the cots, the center table, and two devices near the screen wall, and maybe the wall itself. Notice how it changed color when Ben got onto the center table today? I think we should each start with a different piece of equipment and go through a particular sequence. Then let's wait a day and reverse the sequence. By that time we should have a better idea of what each one does and affects the next."

"Or visa versa," Bernie said.

"Sounds like a plan," Ben agreed. "Of course, another way to do it is to have one of us do a sequence and observe how he feels and what his reactions are. Then another can do it differently."

"That could take too long," said Joe impatiently. His voice was sharp and curt. The others looked at him questioningly.

"We're retired, Joe. What's the rush?" Ben asked. "Sorry, guys," Joe said. He paused. "You know my, uh, my problem. Well, lately I've been having some bad symptoms again. I know you noticed and I thank you for keeping it to yourselves. I can't explain it, but somehow that room is a very special place. To me it's like … like being reborn in a way. I spent twenty minutes in that cabinet and a few minutes on the cot. Do you guys know I swam the pool underwater?"

"Sure," said Ben, "we saw you."

"No," said Joe, "you saw me at the end. I swam four laps underwater … without stopping for air."

"My God!" Bernie said, standing up. "Are you shitting us? Four laps underwater? How?"

"I don't know how. That's just my point. It certainly has to do with the room, and I'm going to find out how it does and what that means.

I tell you guys, and I wasn't going to say this, but somehow I believe that the answer to my trouble, my illness, is in that room, and nothing is going to stop me from finding out."

"Amen," Art Perlman agreed.

"Amen," the group echoed.

CHAPTER NINETEEN
LOVE IN THE AFTERNOON

Alma was surprised that Joe wanted to make such an early appointment with the doctor. He was intent on getting back to the complex. He concentrated on driving. Conversation was nonexistent, so she had time to contemplate the strange actions that her husband had exhibited during the past twenty-four hours.

He had returned from the gin game just after noon. He seemed preoccupied when she had asked him what he wanted for lunch. But his request for a sizable meal surprised her. Then, when she leaned to give him a peck on the cheek he embraced her with a strength she had not felt for years. He kissed her and slid his hands around to her breasts, then bent down and kissed them through the soft cashmere of her sweater. His sudden and unexpected amorous action sent a sensation through her that nearly gave her an orgasm. She pulled away and made a joke about it, but she was actually disoriented from the surge of passion that she had felt.

Joe wolfed down his lunch and was showering when she left for the mahjong game. She yelled, "See you later, honey," into the shower. A loud, "You betchum, Red Ryder," had boomed back at her.

Puzzled, she left Joe singing in the shower.

The mahjong game had been pleasant, but there too something was different. Toward the end of the game Alma realized that the difference was Rose Lewis. Rose was a good player who kept things moving. Today she was in another world. She seemed preoccupied and distracted. Her excuse was that she felt as if she was coming down with something—perhaps the flu. The other women accepted the explanation.

Alma didn't.

As the afternoon drew to a close, Rose became impatient. Alma, still wondering about Joe's sudden surge of energy, also felt an urge for the game to end. She wanted to get home so Alma suggested that they break early so that Rose could get into bed and try to fight off the flu.

Rose's reaction was violent, especially at the mention of bed. "Bed?" she had said. "I'm not going to bed. What would I do in bed?"

"Rest," Bess Perlman suggested. "Take some aspirin and stop the fever. That's what you do in bed."

Rose stared at her for a moment, then smiled and said, "Of course. You're right. I'll do that."

Then the game broke up.

Alma returned to her apartment to find Joe sitting on their terrace sipping a gin-and-tonic. She had not seen him take a drink of hard liquor in months.

"Join me?" he had asked. "Sure." She sat down. "One silver bullet coming up," he said as he got up and went to their portable bar. She noticed that he had a martini glass on ice and a small pitcher already mixed. He poured the drink and handed it to her. "Your favorite. Straight up, extra dry and cold." Alma took the drink

"Joe, do you feel …" But she didn't have time to complete the question. He raised his glass and touched hers.

"To us and to love and to this wonderful place," he toasted. "And mostly to the woman I love very, very, *very* much."

They drank. She finished hers in one gulp and he quickly refilled her glass. "You're going to get me drunk," she protested.

"Not drunk, sweetheart. Just a little warm." She blushed because she knew what was coming, remembering the noontime embrace. And she was right.

He took her around the waist and led her to the bedroom. The bedspread had been removed. The covers had been turned back. The curtains were drawn and the radio was tuned to an FM station playing classical music. He took her glass and placed it on the night table, then turned and kissed her softly. She was floating. She vaguely remembered her husband taking off her clothes and then his own clothes. They were sitting on the bed, lying on the bed. Then they were all over the bed and each other. It went on for three hours … loving … resting … touching … loving … resting. At one point he led her to the shower and they made love there, too. It was like a dream and she dared not interrupt it. Finally, he said, "Now, darling, this old retired actor would like something rare and juicy to eat. I'm starved."

As she prepared the steaks, he napped. Alma Finley, a woman who prided herself in having control over her life and her emotions, wept some very happy tears onto the french-fried potatoes.

CHAPTER TWENTY
CONFUSED WIVES

Joe pulled into the Antares Building A parking spot. He was out of the car in a flash and headed toward the pool. "I don't want to be late for the game!" he yelled over his shoulder. "See you for lunch." Alma got out and watched him disappear around the building. *Lunch? Who eats lunch?* she thought. Not when you're married to the last of the red-hot lovers!

As Alma put the key in the lock of their condo, she heard the phone ringing. She rushed to answer and found a distraught Rose Lewis on the other end.

"Alma, I've been trying you all morning."

"We were at the doctor's," Alma said.

"Can I come over? I have to talk to someone. Do you have time? Now? Please." Rose begged.

"Of course, dear. I'll put up some coffee."

The phone went dead. *Strange,* thought Alma. *Rose is always sensitive to Joe's illness. She usually asks what the doctor said, but not this time. Something must be wrong. I hope it's not serious.* She went to the kitchen and put up a pot of coffee.

As Rose Lewis made a beeline toward the Finley apartment, Mary Green was just waking up. She reached out her hand for her husband, but Bernie was not there. She sat up. There was a note on his pillow:

"You went back to sleep and you looked so peaceful I didn't want to wake you. I'm off to play gin. See you later. Kisses."

Mary fell back on her pillows and stretched. Her body felt a bit sore, but wonderful. She felt a twinge in her lower back. Then she felt the wetness of the sheet under her. *Ben Green,* she thought, *you are a dirty old man. But great. At our age! Just great!* They had made loved twice last night and again this morning. They had always had a fairly good sex life, but this was different. He seemed stronger and younger. He was gentle and caring and patient. He was, she thought, like ... like what? Like a lover? Yes. More. A passionate stranger who knew her. She realized that she was the stranger to herself. She smiled like a schoolgirl and fell back to sleep again.

Bess Perlman did not feel like a schoolgirl at all. She sat alone in the kitchen sipping her coffee. Art had left the condo early after she pleaded with him to leave her alone. "You are like an animal!" she had yelled. "Enough already."

Last night until two in the morning, and then bright and early at six-thirty he wanted her again. "Arthur," she had begged, "Leave me alone. I can't anymore."

"But I love you," he had proclaimed.

"I love you too. But it's been a long time. I'm just not prepared for this." She had begun to cry. He stroked her head and held her close.

"I'm sorry, honey. I truly am. We'll talk about it later." He showered, dressed quickly and said he was going for breakfast at Junior's Restaurant.

Talk about what? she wondered. *What had gotten into him? He had sounded so positive and strong. Was this going to be a new thing? Was she prepared to deal with it? Did she want it? Did she need it?* There were too many questions bouncing around inside her head. She decided she needed to talk to someone. She reached for the phone, but there was no answer at Rose Lewis' apartment.

Rose related the story nonstop, almost without taking a breath. "This may seem personal and I'm sorry, but I respect you and your attitude on things ... I mean, you and I are friends. Not old friends, but I feel good about you and I have to talk to someone. So ... yesterday. It began yesterday. At lunch. My Bernie came in for lunch and it was ready for him on the table. It was his favorite—chopped liver and potato salad. A new pickle. A Dr. Brown's Cel-Ray. He didn't even see it. He ... he came at me ... he grabbed me ... not violent ... but, like a young man grabs a girl. You know?" Alma nodded. "He didn't ask. Nothing. Just took me and carried me. I said *carried* me into the bedroom and put me on the bed. I'm sorry, Alma." She began to cry.

"It's okay," Alma said softly. She was captivated because in many ways Rose Lewis was talking about feelings that she had had regarding her own husband's recent actions.

"We've been married a long time," Rose continued, "A good life. But my Bernie is a difficult man. Sex was sex. It was okay, but never a big deal. I come from an upbringing where it was never discussed. I was taught that a woman was there for a man. You know what I mean." Alma nodded that she understood.

"So suddenly, after a long time, I mean we are not spring chickens anymore, Bernie comes in and, out of the blue, sweeps me into the bedroom and undresses me and makes love to me in a way he never did in all the years we've married. He was like a stranger ..." Rose paused. "But kind."

She sobbed. Alma moved her chair close to Rose and put her arm around her. "I know what you are saying, Rose. Believe me, I know."

Rose looked up at her. "You do?"

Alma felt her eyes tear up. "Yes, Rose dear. I really do!"

"So ... I'm not finished," Rose said, gathering herself. "I called you because at the game yesterday I had a feeling that you somehow understood that I was uncomfortable. Somehow I felt that you knew."

"Yes. I sensed something was wrong, and it wasn't the flu."

"When I went back to the apartment Bernie was there. He wanted to talk, but I cut him off. I told him I didn't want to talk about it. You have to know Bernie to see how funny that is, because that's his favorite line when he wants to end a discussion. Alma ... I'm afraid. I'm afraid that after forty years of marriage I suddenly have a stranger living with me and I don't know what to do."

She looked down in her coffee. Alma took Rose's hand and squeezed it. She tried to think of something to say to her friend.

As their wives struggled and reflected on their newfound lovers, the four men had made their way to what they considered their private health club and stood around the center table planning the morning's activities.

The wall screen was its familiar pale blue. The quiet hum filled the room. A fine mist rose from the cabinets. All of the overhead "lamps" were off.

"Let's have a look at those two things over near the wall," Ben Green suggested.

The men walked over to the first device. It was just three feet tall and cylindrical in shape with a diameter of about one foot. The color was silver, but dull, and there were no controls or cables. The device seemed solid. On the top were two round white dots.

The men circled it for a moment. Then Ben reached his hand toward the dots. As he made contact, the thing hummed and glowed red. When he pulled his hand away it stopped.

"Nothing," said Ben.

"What the hell is it?" Art asked.

Ben was about to answer when Bernie Lewis let out a "Holy shit!"

The other three looked at him and then down to his bathing suit because Bernie was staring at it.

"What?" Joe asked.

"My bathing suit. This morning I went in for a dip before we met. My suit was wet when we came in here. Look now. The front of the suit is dry. Bone dry. But the back is still wet. This thing must be some kind of heater or dryer."

Ben checked the bathing suit. "I think you're right. It makes sense, too. We use this before we leave to dry the sweat."

"Or maybe before we start to dry our clothing?" Joe suggested.

In any case, they agreed they had found a dryer and it belonged at the beginning or end of the "health club" sequence.

The next device was farther down the blue wall toward the rear of the room. It was larger. In fact, it reached to the ceiling. It appeared to be a black cabinet or storage locker. It was about six feet wide and, they estimated, at least fifteen feet tall. Its depth was only about two feet. They could not see a door or opening of any kind. The men began looking around the sides and base of the cabinet for a handle or control panel.

"Here. I think I found something," Joe announced. His fingers were touching a slight bulge in the lower right side panel. "Here goes nothing," he said as he pressed the bulge.

As if by magic, the front of the cabinet disappeared and revealed row upon row of slim silver handles. Art did some quick mathematics and told the others that there were nine-hundred-forty-one of them. Fifty were missing.

Ben grasped one of the handles closest to him and pulled. He could not move it. The others each tried various handles at random, but with no success. Then Joe Finley told them to back off. He studied the contents of the cabinet for a moment and reached for the handle next to the last missing one. Sure enough, it came sliding out attached to a slim silver case.

They tried to open the case for fifteen minutes, but to no avail. Finally, Ben Green suggested that they replace it, since obviously it required a key or special device to get it open.

Joe was reluctant to give up. "It really bugs me," he said. "What could possibly be in here?"

"Maybe they're lockers for very little people," Bernie suggested.

They all laughed. Joe replaced the case in its slot. He then bent down and pressed the bulge again. Immediately, the front panel appeared and the case was sealed once again.

"I suggest we keep these two devices out of the cycle for now," Ben said. "Why don't we each start in a different place?" They decided an order. Ben would take cabinet number one, Bernie would take cabinet number six, Art would lie on one of the small cots at the rear of the room, and Joe Finley would take the center table. They would stay for ten minutes and then discuss how they felt and what they felt.

But they weren't prepared for the changes that occurred when the blue wall turned red.

CHAPTER TWENTY-ONE
SOMETHING'S VERY DIFFERENT

Arnie Fischer gave Judy a big hug that lifted her right off the ground. She squealed and laughed. "You two quit messing around. He's a married man now!" Sandy called from the kitchen.

"Sorry, honey. Force of habit," Arnie shouted back. Judy laughed again. "Want a drink?"

"Sure. Red wine?"

"Coming up."

Arnie and Sandy had been married for a few weeks, but they had lived together for three years, off and on. He was an art director at a small advertising agency in Miami and a talented commercial artist too. He made extra money doing illustrations. Three years older than his brother Jack, Arnie had a very different personality. He was solid and responsible. The difference in age between the brothers had kept them on separate paths, until lately. Arnie had missed Vietnam because of a college deferment and a subsequent career as a teacher. Jack had been drafted into the navy. He served on gunboats in the Mekong Delta and had been involved in some heavy combat. After his return to the States, or *to the world* as Jack put it, Arnie had made an effort to get close to his younger brother. Their parents were dead and, apart from one aunt in Cleveland and two cousins in California, they had no other family.

Physically, Arnie was shorter and slimmer than Jack. He was a fitness nut, so he was in good shape. Jack, on the other hand, was a five inches taller and thirty pounds heavier. Although Arnie was stronger, Jack could put a bear hug on him and immobilize his older brother. As youngsters Arnie and Jack always fought with one another. The three years difference weighed in Arnie's favor until Jack was eighteen. Jack had received his draft notice and Arnie had pleaded with him to enroll in college for a deferment. Jack had refused and the discussion quickly turned into a pushing match that wound up as a knock-down, drag-out fight. Jack exploded on his brother and broke two of Arnie's ribs and put a hairline fracture in his jaw, proving he was no longer "little brother."

"Merlot?" Arnie asked.

"Fine," said Judy. Her thoughts were far away with Jack.

"You okay?" he asked, handing her the wine.

"Sure. I just miss the bum."

Sandy came in from the kitchen and kissed Judy hello. She asked Arnie to pour her a glass of wine.

"Want a joint?" she asked Judy.

"Not now. I got ripped last night with Monica."

Arnie brought the drink to his wife and sat next to her on the fluffy sofa. Judy sat on the floor pillow opposite them.

"Tell us about this charter Captain Jack took on," Arnie said.

"He didn't really say much," Judy said, "except that it was some kind of treasure hunt and they wanted him for three months. He'll be around on weekends."

"Where are they diving?" Sandy was interested. She was an amateur diver with a scuba license that cleared her for depths up to one hundred fifty feet.

"I don't know. Off the Bahamas, I think. One of the Windward Islands. He was vague. I guess they don't want him to talk about it." She sighed. *Why am I so damned emotional?* she thought.

Sandy picked up on it immediately. "You want to call him on the radio phone?"

Judy looked at her watch. It was eight P.M. "Let's wait till after dinner." She perked up. "What's on the menu?"

"Rock lobster, baked potato, salad, and your favorite, Key Lime pie," Sandy answered proudly.

"Wow! Aren't we the gourmet bride," Judy joked. "I'm starved and that sounds great!" They went out to the Florida room, a screened-in patio with a small pool, to eat.

The day had been different from previous ones for Jack and the Antareans. They had brought only three cocoons up from The Stones. These were different from the rest in that they were larger and had a silver caps at the head and foot. Amos had telepathed that these were three group commanders. They were not commanders in the sense that All Light, No Light and the female, whose name was Beam, were commanders, but they did have special powers and training. Jack recalled the first day, when Amos had explained the structure of the little army. These commanders had ninety soldiers under them in groups of ten.

After docking and moving the cocoons to the processing room, Jack had gone to his room to shower and eat. He had just removed his deck shoes when he felt a small, sharp pain that went down his spine. Without knowing why, he put his shoes back on and went quickly to the orange door. *Something's wrong,* he thought.

Yes, answered Amos into his mind.

What? telepathed Jack. *Are the group commanders damaged, too?*

No, sent All Light. *We believe someone was here today.*

Once in the room, Jack realized that it was warm but they had not yet begun the processing. Everything looked normal. The wall was blue, the cabinets misting, the lamps off, but, yes, the room was normally cool before they began processing. Now it was warm. All the Antareans' thoughts were attuned and Jack was with them. Amos suggested a possible overload in the electrics. Hal went for the test equipment while the rest began processing the three command cocoons.

It was no wonder the room was still warm. Ben, Artie, Bernie and Joe had been in there for most of the day. In fact, they had left only an hour before the Antareans returned. The day had started with a frightening experience followed by the most wonderful feelings that these men had ever had.

Ben Green noticed the color change first. "Hey, guys, look at the wall. It's going red!" he yelled from his cabinet. Art and Joe were under their respective lamps and didn't want to open their eyes.

Bernie looked up from cabinet six. "I'll be damned. Maybe the movie is starting," he said. Hadn't Ben told them it was a wall screen?

"I hope it's a porno," Bernie shouted.

Then Art Perlman called out from the rear of the room, "Hey! Who the hell turned on the heat? It's getting like a sauna back here!"

"Ow!" Joe Finley yelled as he jumped off the center table. "Jesus! I'm burning up!"

Ben called to Art to get up and open the cabinets. Art seemed in a daze and waved Ben off. Ben screamed at him, "Art, damn it! Joe's in trouble!"

Art sat up and his lamp went off. He was disoriented for a moment, but then saw Joe on his knees near the center table and ran to him. Joe's skin was as red as a lobster under the fine white ash that covered him.

Ben yelled again, "Get us out of here!"

Art left Joe and opened Ben's and Bernie's cabinets. They slid out and gathered around Joe Finley, who was still on his knees, obviously in pain. The wall had begun to turn from red to blue.

"That damned wall must be some kind of sun lamp," Joe said, getting to his feet. "I feel like I've got one hell of a sunburn."

"Are you okay?" Bernie asked, voicing all their concern.

"Yeah. I guess. Funny," Joe said, "it was cool under the lamp. Then the wall got red and I felt heat like someone opened a furnace door. But, and this is going to sound weird, it was under my skin … the heat, that is. It was like I was burning from within."

Ben gently examined Joe's skin. He first brushed away the fine ash which, once again, disappeared before it hit the floor. He poked Joe's forearm. "Does that hurt?"

"No."

"You don't seem to be burned, but your skin is definitely red." He squeezed the forearm and then released. It was white but then immediately turned red again. "Blood," said Ben, "your capillaries are full of blood."

"That's why he's red," Bernie added.

"Of course," Art said. "It's like a super massage. It gets the blood flowing right up to the surface of the skin."

"Like a slap," Joe agreed. "I just wasn't ready for that deep a massage." They all relaxed.

"I think we should take it easy with this stuff," Ben suggested. "Moderation is the name of the game."

For the rest of the morning they rotated with the equipment. One man stood by each time, just in case something went wrong. They found that each had a different tolerance for the center table, and they could judge how long to stay on it by the color of the wall. Art Perlman was able to stay the longest. They nicknamed him "Deep Red."

The foursome passed on their gin game because they couldn't sit still. Ben suggested they go out to lunch. He called Alma and told her their plan. He also asked her to call the other wives and let them know.

Alma was relieved because it gave her more time to talk with Rose. When she called Mary Green, Mary suggested that they all come over to her place for lunch. She said she was feeling energetic and would put out a light spread. Alma checked with Rose, who reluctantly said okay.

When Alma called Bess Perlman to invite her to lunch at Mary's, Bess was also reluctant. Then Alma told her that Rose was with her and that they were both going. Bess finally agreed to join them, but still sounded distant.

The men took Bernie Lewis' big red Buick and drove over to Wolfie's on Collins Avenue. They were starved. This time of day was always busy at Wolfie's. The boys got seated quickly because they were in the line for foursomes. Most of the other patrons were in twos. After they ordered, it was Art Perlman who opened the discussion. "How do you guys feel?" he asked.

Joe Finley answered first. "Like I'm twenty-one. Did you see what I ordered for lunch?"

"Did you see what we all ordered for lunch?" Ben quipped.

"That equipment sure builds up an appetite," Bernie said.

"It's more than an appetite!" Art and Joe said together. They looked at each other and laughed.

"You a mind reader?" asked Art.

"Yes," answered Joe, "and so are you."

"So are we all," Ben quietly, looking around. "I knew you both were going to say that. I knew it before you spoke."

Bernie, who also looked around at nearby tables, murmured, "Yeah.

Me, too." He turned back to the others. "Hey guys, take a good look at the people in here." The other three were already scanning the room. "It's funny," Bernie continued. "I mean, they are our age, but they look … like old."

"They are old," Ben said. "But I know what you mean. It's like we don't belong with them."

"Yeah," Art agreed.

"What?" Ben asked, looking at Joe.

"Nothing. I didn't say anything," Joe answered.

"I thought you said something about the ocean."

"No. But I was thinking about the ocean."

Then a serious expression transformed Joe's face. "Let's stop the bullshit, guys," he began. "I'm going to say what's on all our minds. Something really different and weird has happened to us—something to do with that room and that equipment. I'll bet we all made love to our wives last night and this morning. I'll bet we all feel like kids again. I'll bet we can read each other's minds. I'll bet we are all scared and confused."

No one answered, but each knew the other's thought. *Yes!*

"Right," Joe said aloud. "And I'll tell you something else. After we finish lunch, you guys are going to drive me to the hospital. I'm going to have my doctor do a blood test. I'll bet my leukemia is getting better."

"Wrong," Bernie Lewis said. "I'll bet it's gone!"

CHAPTER TWENTY-TWO
THE ANTARES CONDO BASE

Had the Antareans known about the unwanted members of their "health club," it would have made their lives easier. Instead, they pondered the possibilities of why the room was warm. Hal, Harry, and Beam, the female commander, were busy running circuit checks on the equipment and power sources. They weren't having any luck. Everything seemed to be functioning properly.

Amos glanced at his watch and telepathed to the others that he was going to the condo office to meet with Mr. Shields. He had called the manager at home after they had discovered the warmth. He asked Shields to meet him at the office on the pretext of a change in plans for construction that couldn't wait. When Amos left the processing room and headed toward Building A, he saw the light on in the office, so he knew Shields was waiting there.

Since they had begun raising the cocoons, there had been little contact with the manager other than a telephone call each morning to keep in touch. As he walked toward the office, his thoughts went back to the time before the complex was Antarean property.

They had brought the shuttle down at night and submerged near Key Biscayne. Amos, Hal, and Harry were on board. The commanders and the rest of the crew remained on the mother ship, parked on the far side of the moon. Aware of the technology that Earth beings possessed, they had jammed the radar during their approach and made the jamming appear to be an atmospheric disturbance. Their landing was undetected. The trio left their craft submerged near a wreck and swam underwater to the beach. They emerged and shed their waterproofing. Underneath they wore casual human clothing. Using the information gathered by several probes, monitoring of radio and television, and life experiences of their agents who lived among Earth people, the Antareans had devised the plan to raise the cocoons with the least amount of disturbance to the natural order of things in Florida.

They had two viable options. The first was to bring the mother ship in, submerge it, and remove all the cocoons at once. Then leave and process on board. With this approach, because of the size of the mother ship and the need for it to remain stationary in fairly shallow water, they would run the risk of exposing their presence. It would also mean processing continually, since the cocoons were perishable once they were removed from their storage environment. If anything went wrong with the processing, or if the cocoons had been damaged in any way, they ran the risk of losing the entire army.

The second plan was to find or build a facility near the storage area and process in a normal manner, under standard procedures.

When Antares Quad Three was a thriving inter-stellar community of space trade and exploration, the Florida peninsula was sparsely populated by primitive Indians. But now, what had been sandbars and swamps then, was a thriving, densely populated state with a technologically advanced civilization. The Antareans were a resourceful race and Amos enjoyed the challenge. Plan two seemed the better choice and was to be explored.

The three spacemen walked along the beach and onto the causeway that wound through Key Biscayne. Their appearance was that of vacationers out for an evening stroll. The fact that several extremely wealthy people had residences near their location had escaped their intelligence. As they approached the mainland, a police cruiser pulled up behind them. The driver called out to them on the P.A. system to stop. Amos telepathed to the others to let him do the communicating. The two policemen stepped out of the car with their hands on their guns. "Will you gentlemen please identify yourselves?"

Amos spoke in a soft voice. "Good evening, officer. My name is Amos Bright. We're taking a walk."

"Do you live in the Key, Mr. Bright?" the policeman asked.

"No, officer, we live in Miami." He thought for a moment and continued. "South Miami, that is. Is something wrong?"

"No." He spoke to his partner. "They look okay, George."

Then back to Amos: "No, nothing's wrong. We're just checking this section of the beach. You folks watch out for the traffic if you're walking back on the causeway."

"Yes. We will. Thank you." Then he added, "It's good to know that you fellows are out watching things. Makes us feel secure. Good night."

They turned and walked away feeling pleased with their success with the first human contact.

Hal asked, "What are they guarding?"

"I assume there are wealthy people nearby," Amos answered. "In this country they get special protection."

Harry telepathed, *Why must they guard the wealthy?* Amos came back. *Because the wealthy demand it,* Amos thought back to his companions.

The next few days were spent among Earth people. The three Antareans separated in different directions. Amos went south toward Coral Gables, Hal went north toward Fort Lauderdale, and Harry went west toward the Everglades. They agreed to meet back at the shuttle in five days.

Hal and Harry arrived at the shuttle together. They took nourishment from their storage unit before discussing their findings. The north was heavily populated and all of the sections along the beach were used. They would have difficulty bringing the cocoons unnoticed into any facility. There was a possibility of some industrial property near the bay, but using it at night could draw attention. Harry found quite the opposite. There was a canal system that went west, but after a few miles of heavily populated areas he had run into a great swamp that stretched for miles. He had entered the swamp and explored it. Constructing a facility there would be difficult and time consuming. And it was far from the ocean. They telepathed for Amos but received no answer, so they rested and waited for their leader's return.

Amos Bright had found what he believed they needed. It was still under construction, but the location was correct. Two large buildings situated on a canal with direct access to the sea. The sign had stated that the Blamar Construction Company of Coral Gables was the builder. The owner was South Florida Land Development Corporation of Homestead. Amos entered the construction site and walked around, inspecting and recording every detail of the property. It took several hours. The layout was perfect. He slipped into the canal and rested until the next morning when he located the offices of the owners and telephoned for an appointment. When the secretary asked what the purpose of the appointment was, Amos had told her that he wished to discuss the purchase of the entire complex. She had told him it was not for sale. Amos thanked her and hung up. He then went to the offices and telepathically manipulated the secretary so that she wrote down the appointment for the next day. But in taking this approach Amos had violated the Antarean credo of not to interfere in the lives of the inhabitants of a planet. He would have to get clearance from Antares to proceed with his plan.

Back at the shuttle, Hal and Harry sensed Amos' approach. They were interested to hear how he had fared, but they were excited to relate the near mishap they had experienced earlier that day. It seemed they had parked the shuttle near a favorite sport-fishing ground and all day there had been boat activity overhead. Three times the shuttle had been hooked by the trolling lines from the fishing craft. The last line had been weighted. It was very strong and on a powerful boat. It had hooked onto an antenna and nearly overturned the craft. Hal had kept the shuttle righted while they picked up the thoughts of the fishermen who were convinced that they had hooked a very large fish because the shuttle had pulled back on their line. Harry went out of the ship and severed the line. Undaunted, the fishermen continued to troll over the same spot all morning. Finally, Harry went out and found a large fish. He stunned it and attached it to the line. That seemed to please the fishermen and they left after boating the fish. Amos listened with amusement, but felt badly for the fish. He surmised that many of Earth's underwater creatures were not unlike Antareans. They too lived under the surface of their planet. Someday, when the Earth's human inhabitants were ready, they would have to explain the importance of preserving life in the scheme of cosmic energy. He recalled how easy it was to find the planet because of the ambient life forces surrounding it. Planets that had high destruction, or death rates, always emitted these forces in abundance. It was the released energy of life departing from the host it had occupied. On planet Earth there was a great deal of unnatural death.

Amos contacted the mother ship that night and communicated with the commanders. He outlined his plan and requested they clear it with the council on Antares. If approval was forthcoming, he would need a probe sent down with valuables to trade for the complex. The answer came an hour later. Permission was given for Amos to "sway" the humans to his bidding, but no physical force was to be involved. He was also authorized to use the diamond valuables for trade. The council suggested that he sell the diamonds for the normal exchange medium of dollars. This could best be accomplished in a city called Amsterdam, in a country to the east known as Holland. Commander All Light was on his way there by shuttle to exchange diamonds for currency. He would bring the dollars to Amos the next morning because Holland was on a different time schedule from Miami and the commerce there began while it was still night in Florida.

All Light arrived after dawn with a single document called a bearer bond that had a value of forty million dollars. Amos was to deposit it in a bank. In a few days, actual dollars would be in the account. The intelligence also warned that large transactions such as this would draw attention of many government officials. He advised that they find a bank that would be able to withhold the transaction from public view in return for a share of the purchase price. It was to be called a commission. Amos understood. He had been involved in many bizarre transactions all over the galaxy. Since the basic drive on this planet was greed, it should not be a problem to keep the transaction private for the period of time required to retrieve and process the cocoons.

Amos chose a small bank in Coral Gables. When he entered the bank, Amos was dressed in an expensive business suit. He scanned minds until he found the person in charge. The man was seated behind the last desk in an area with five other workers. The man's name was DePalmer. To ensure control, and because he had been cleared to manipulate the Earth people as required, Amos entered Mr. DePalmer's mind and prepared him for the transaction. It went smoothly. The secretary led Amos to Mr. DePalmer's desk. The man exchanged greetings and moved right to business. Amos told him that he wished to open an account in the sum of forty million dollars. The man was pleased. The bearer bond was presented and an account was opened. Mr. DePalmer told Amos he would process the bond immediately. If all went well Amos should have funds available within forty-eight hours. The problem of keeping the transaction quiet was forced into Mr. DePalmer's mind.

"That might be difficult to do," the banker said.

"I'm sure there are ways," Amos answered.

"Well, yes, there are always ways, but they can get expensive," DePalmer replied.

"Cost is not an object," Amos stated. "I'll leave the details to you, and I trust you will use discretion."

"How much discretion?" the banker asked.

"Let's say, uh, two and a half percent worth?"

DePalmer brightened immediately. "Consider your business the most closely guarded secret in Florida, Mr. Bright."

The rest was too simple, but it was a good lesson in why certain planets in the galaxy were to be left alone. Without the ability to telepath, mind control and therefore action control, was without challenge. Amos kept his appointment at South Florida Development and bought the complex, as it existed, for twenty-seven million dollars cash. This gave the owners a profit of four million, and saved them another five million in unfinished construction and marketing. When Amos inferred that change of title could be "unofficial," the owners realized that their profit could remain untaxed this year and possibly never.

The unnamed condo complex became Antares Condominiums. The construction company was not aware of the change of ownership. They were instructed to proceed on a suddenly accelerated schedule. Building A was nearly finished at the time that the Antareans bought it, and Building B was slightly behind schedule. Amos ordered that all efforts be put into Building A and that another construction company would complete work on Building B. The contractor had complained and threatened a lawsuit. It took only half a million dollars to satisfy him. Fifteen days later the construction crews left Building A completed. Shuttles ran all that next night and the commanders, technicians, and equipment were brought into Building B.

By morning, what appeared to be a small construction crew was busy in Building B. Amos had Mr. DePalmer handle the sales office and staffing. He wanted to be sure that, at least on the surface, everything looked normal. He told the banker that for personal reasons he was not anxious to sell too many condominiums right away. DePalmer suggested they price the condos high and hire an inexperienced sales staff. Amos was amused. But they had both made the error of making Antares seem so unattractive that some buyers were sure it was a great deal. However, the success of sales in Building A did not delay the Antareans. It only meant that they would have to move the cocoons at night and with care. Overall, the plan worked well. As long as they kept Building B unfinished, they could proceed with their business. Their intelligence had been good, but had failed to understand the mentality of retired Americans and the boredom that drove them either to vegetate, or, in the case of Ben, Joe, Bernie, and Art, let their curiosity lead them to adventure.

Mr. Shields was behind his desk when Amos entered.

"Hi, Mr. Bright. Long time, no see," Shields said as he extended his hand.

Amos shook the little man's hand. "Nice to see you, Mr. Shields. I have a few things that can't wait. I'm sorry for getting you out at this late hour."

"Anytime, Mr. Bright. You're the boss."

"I'll come right to the point, Mr. Shields. My partners and I are pleased at the way you are running things. However, we did ask that moisture … uh … water … be kept out of the swimming area. I noticed that it was filled last week."

Shields had been prepared for this. "Yes, Mr. Bright. I did tell Mr. DePalmer about that. I guess he didn't speak to you. We had a problem with one of our owners in the complex." Shields shuffled some papers

103

on his desk and found what he was looking for. "A Mr. Green came in a few weeks ago and demanded that the pool be filled. I tried to stall him and avoid him, but he went to the authorities. You and Mr. DePalmer were very clear about not wanting any publicity, so I had to agree to fill it." He looked at Amos for approval.

"Yes. You did the correct thing."

Shields was pleased with himself. "Is that all?" he asked.

"No. Building B. I told you that I wanted it secured. We don't want any accidents over there since the construction has been delayed."

Shields was puzzled. "No one has been there, Mr. Bright. Wally and I keep a close watch on things. The old folks have been getting a little annoyed about the appearance of the place, and a few have inquired as to when the construction will be finished. You know those people don't walk too well, and they know it's dangerous near the construction site. I can't imagine any of them getting in there. Has there been trouble?" Shields was concerned.

Amos answered carefully. He didn't want Wally or Shields poking around, either. "No, not any trouble. We have some special equipment over there and we think someone may be tampering with it."

Shields thought a moment. "How about hiring a night watchman or a security guard service? I can vouch for the daytime, but you know there could be someone sneaking in at night."

"I'll think about that, Mr. Shields. But for now I would appreciate your keeping a closer eye on things during the day just in case some of the Building A people are wandering in."

"Absolutely, Mr. Bright. Consider it done." He made a mental note to talk to Wally the next morning.

"Good. Now I must go. Thank you again for coming in. I will show my appreciation in your next salary check."

Shields thanked Amos. The two men left the office together. Amos watched him walk to his car and drive away, then he turned toward the processing room.

A strong contact with a mind came from behind and above him. He reached a thought back in answer. Then it was gone. Amos couldn't find it. *Nourishment,* thought Amos, *I need nourishment.* He knew that there were no Antareans above and behind him. All his crew were in the processing room. He didn't hear Joe Finley trip against the chaise on his terrace as he ducked away from the railing.

CHAPTER TWENTY-THREE
CONFUSED WOMEN AND JOYFUL MEN

That same afternoon, while the men were at lunch, the ladies had their own revelations to discuss. Alma and Mary were thrilled by the sudden sexual interest of their husbands. Rose and Bess were yet to be convinced.

The menu was fruit and cottage cheese, cake and coffee. As they ate, Bess and Rose sat close together. They said little. Mary bubbled over with small talk. She had doubts about telling how wonderful things had suddenly become in bed. Her own excitement kept her from noticing how depressed and upset Bess and Rose were. Alma finally broke the ice. "Do you think that we might all continue what we were discussing this morning, Rose?" she asked pointedly.

Rose looked up at Alma and then at the others. Even Bess was curious. "I suppose so," Rose answered softly.

Alma addressed the group. "I'm going to ask a curious question, and although we have become friends, some of you may feel I'm getting too personal. So please let me know." She paused to gather her thoughts. The women were interested. "You all know that my Joe is … he uh … to put it frankly, he has had leukemia for almost ten years." Alma had never spoken about this before so she had their interest. "Lately he had been getting worse."

Mary reached over. "I'm sorry, Alma."

"Thanks. Lately, he's been tired and without appetite. This doctor thinks it might be, well, the beginning of the end. I knew this day would come, but it shook me, deeply." A tear came to her eye.

Rose Lewis looked at her with confusion. *Why was Alma bringing this up now? What did this have to do with their discussion this morning, and what did it have to do with Rose's problem?*

Alma looked at Rose. "Today you called and came over. You had a problem, and frankly I would not have been in the mood to discuss it with her if something strange hadn't happened to me … to Joe and me." They all perked up and became very interested. "As I said, Joe has been tired lately and, among other things, our …" She paused, then decided to jump in. "… our sex life hasn't been terribly active." She smiled. "Actually, its been nil. Zero."

Suddenly Mary interrupted. "Until last night? No, I mean yesterday afternoon?"

"How did you know?" Alma was puzzled.

"I know, honey. I know," she answered, "and I bet Bess can tell us the same about hers." They all looked at Bess Perlman.

She blurted out, "He's an animal! He nearly raped me yesterday and again this morning."

Rose gasped, "You, too?" They all looked at Rose.

"To all of us. Something has happened to our husbands." Alma said.

"But what?" Bess asked. "What could affect them all the same way?"

As their wives pondered their predicament that afternoon, and as the Antareans were raising the three command cocoons, the four men had finished lunch possessing exciting new knowledge. They hadn't even been shocked when Bernie Lewis guessed that Joe Finley's leukemia was gone. Somehow, they all knew. For the rest of lunch the quartet communicated silently. At one point Ben Green tried calling the waitress with his mind. He focused his eyes on to her as she walked toward the kitchen. She was about forty feet from them and moving in the opposite direction. "Watch this," he had said aloud. The three other men turned their eyes toward the middle-aged woman. She stopped dead in her tracks, three feet from the kitchen door, turned, searched the dining room for a moment, and locked her eyes on their table. Then she made a beeline for them.

"Can I get you anything else?" she asked.

"Some coffee and the check, sweetheart," Ben said, proud of his feat. After the check came they divided it, paid, and left. Bernie turned the Buick up Collins Avenue toward Mount Sinai Hospital.

Joe had called Dr. Feldman from the restaurant and said it was urgent that he see him. Because the doctor knew that Joe was coming to the end of his struggle, he was receptive to the visit. He wasn't prepared for the group meeting that occurred.

The four men entered the clinic and walked to the doctor's office. Dr. Morris Feldman was a tall, gray-haired specialist who had moved his practice to Miami in the late 1960s. He was the chief hematologist of the hospital. There was no doubt in his mind that Joe Finley's disease was progressing rapidly. He was sure it was just a matter of months. The medication no longer could contain the rampant production of white cells. The last blood test had shown that clearly. Actually, the test prior to the last had shown it. Yesterday's test had been a freak and the doctor was sure that the lab had confused Finley's test with a perfectly healthy person's. The test had shown no sign of the disease. Feldman knew that was impossible.

Now the foursome burst into his office. Joe introduced his friends. The doctor was cordial.

"Doc," Joe began, "I know you're a very busy guy, and I appreciate your seeing me so quickly. Can you take some blood now and have a look?"

The doctor was taken aback. "Mr. Finley, we have procedures here. Why the rush for a test now?"

"Well, it's really hard to say. I just think that this problem that I have … uh, *had* … is gone. I want to be sure."

The doctor was immediately convinced that somehow Finley had gotten wind of the erroneous report and it had given him false hope.

"Procedures, Mr. Finley. I'll be glad to do another test, but it will take some time for the results."

"How long?" Ben Green asked.

"Well, Mr. … uh?"

"Green."

"Well, Mr. Green, we should have your friend's results back tomorrow."

"No good," Art Perlman said firmly.

The doctor was getting annoyed. Then Bernie Lewis broke into the conversation. "Dr. Feldman? You don't remember me. I'm Bernie Lewis. Used to live in Scarsdale. We played golf a few times. Maybe twenty years ago. I was a friend of Sid Blackman, God rest his soul."

Dr. Feldman studied Bernie's face and remembered. "Sure, you had a garment business. Woolens. Sid invested some money with you. Sure, I remember. Sid was a good friend, one of the best surgeons I ever worked with."

"Well, doctor," Bernie continued, "Joe … the four of us … have become good friends here … in the autumn of our lives. We are close. You understand? We're concerned, and we know about Joe's problem. Understand that we are grown-ups and refuse to be treated like children. Being old doesn't mean stupid, and it certainly doesn't mean we can be ignored."

"I'm not ignoring you," Feldman said.

"We know that," Bernie went on, "and we appreciate that, too. That's why we would like you to do a favor, just this once, and give Finley a blood test right now. You know what to look for. It won't take but a minute. Whaddaya say?"

The doctor knew he was beaten. He smiled. "Okay. You guys wait here and I'll get a syringe." He went down to the emergency room while the boys made themselves comfortable. Thoughts flew back and forth among them without any verbal enhancement. The excitement made their hearts pound. Energy surged through each to the other.

Twenty minutes later, Dr. Feldman spun on the stool. He looked at the four men gathered around him near the microscope.

Joe spoke up. "It's gone, isn't it?"

"Yes," answered a very puzzled doctor. "It's gone without a trace. But I don't know why."

The men hugged and congratulated each other.

Joe was ecstatic. Close to crying. "I knew it! Sweet Jesus, I knew it!" He crossed himself, and prayed. "In the name of the Father, the son, and the Holy Spirit." He folded his hands. "Thank you, God!"

"Amen," said Bernie.

"Amen," they all echoed, shook Feldman's hand and started to leave.

Feldman shook his head and muttered to himself, "Amen, all right. But why? Listen, Joe," he called out, "please stop by and see me in a few days?" Joe waved over his shoulder. Morris Feldman turned back to the microscope and peered through the lens at the very normal, healthy blood cells on the slide below. He focused the instrument for a closer look. These were not only normal cells they were the healthiest cells he had ever seen. The platelets were perfectly formed. There were no damaged ones, no dead ones. The white count was normal, and the most astonishing fact was that the blood itself was clean as a whistle. There were no impurities, no bacteria, no indication of damaged cells—and above all no indication of leukemia whatsoever.

He knew he would not see Joe Finley in a few days. He suspected he would not see Joe Finley again. He was right.

CHAPTER TWENTY-FOUR
ON THE RADIO PHONE

The day had been exciting for the Greens, Perlmans, Lewises, and Finleys. The women had talked all afternoon about the new and strange energy their husbands possessed. The men had gone back to the health club and used the equipment until early evening. Thus, the room was warm when the returning Antareans had entered.

One other event had happened in Amos' absence. While the Antareans were checking the equipment for faults, Jack had suddenly felt the urge to go to the boat. Commander No Light picked up on his thoughts and communicated.

Jack didn't understand the feeling, so he spoke. "I have this feeling like I should be on the boat and I don't know why."

No Light telepathed back to Jack. *A message is there. Someone is trying to reach you on the radio phone.*

Jack then heard the operator ringing his call letters. *But that's impossible*, he thought. *The radio is shut down.*

You can hear it, anyway, thought All Light. *Go to the boat and turn it on. Beam will go with you.*

Sure enough, when Jack turned on the radio phone the operator was calling. He answered and then heard Judy's voice. "Jack, is that you?"

"Yes, honey. How are you? Is everything okay?"

"Just fine. I miss you. Where are you?"

Commander Beam shook her head and put her finger to her lips.

"I'm at sea, honey. We're working late. That's why it took me time to answer. I was out on deck. My charter people are doing some night diving."

"Will you be in this weekend?"

He looked at Beam. She shook her head no. "I don't think so, honey. These folks are on to something. I can't talk about it. You understand?"

"Yes. When will you be in?" she asked. There was disappointment in her voice. Jack looked at Beam, but this time the thought was already in his head.

"Next weekend. For sure, honey."

"What about supplies?" she asked. "Do you have enough on board?"

You are a sneaky lady, thought Jack. The commander smiled.

"Yes, Judy. Plenty. These folks travel first class. Look, let me call you in a few days. I'll have a better idea of my schedule. Okay?"

Judy was put off, but could only agree. "Okay. Hold a minute. Your brother wants to say hello."

"My brother?" Jack was puzzled.

Arnie came on the air. "Hi, little brother."

"Hi, Arnie. I gather Judy's at your place."

"Yeah. She came over for dinner. She's one hell of a girl. What she sees in you I don't know. You should treat her better."

Jack was pissed off. "Arnie, not everyone lives like you. Some of us even like our freedom." Jack was immediately sorry for the dig and he hoped that Judy hadn't heard.

"Easy, little brother. She's worried about you and misses you. That's all. Where the hell are you, anyway?"

"I told her it was sort of a secret. It's a treasure-hunt thing."

"Okay … okay. Listen, if you're going to be out on the weekend, I could run out with my boss's boat. He offered it to me anytime I want."

"Not a good idea, Arnie. These folks are pretty tight with the security. They think they're on to something big. It won't work."

Arnie gave in, but he was still curious. "Okay, Jack, have a safe trip. Let someone know how you are once in a while."

"Okay. Love to Sandy. Put Judy back on."

Judy came on the radio again. "Yes? What is it?" She was still upset.

"Listen babe. I've got to run. Thanks for calling. I'll try to call you over the weekend." Silence. "Okay?"

"Okay. But don't be surprised if I'm not in when you call." The receiver clicked off.

Sorry, thought the female commander. Jack was uneasy again. *"She'll get over it,"* he thought. Beam just nodded.

They returned to the processing room. Amos entered shortly after. He let the others know that the manager was sure the security hadn't been breached. The others said they couldn't find anything wrong with the equipment, but they still had other power supplies to check. *Let's get the command cocoons processed,* communicated All Light.

Harry and Jack wheeled the first one in and set the first cabinet controls. They put the cocoon in and turned on the cabinet. Jack walked down to cabinet number six to prepare the controls. He reached for them and stopped. Something was wrong. He had worked with them all last night and he knew how he had left them. Now the controls were set in a different mode. As the thought entered his mind, it also entered the minds of the others in the room. They all converged on the cabinet and stared at the panel. Hal telepathed that he had not touched the controls in his testing of the circuits. Neither had anyone else.

"Are you sure, Jack?" Amos asked aloud.

"Positive. This isn't something that I would forget. I'm new at this, and I know its important, so I am extra careful to do things the way Hal showed me. I know how I left these controls last night and this is different."

Then we definitely have had visitors, thought Amos. But who? At this point the first cocoon was ready to be moved to cabinet six. They would have to wait until they completed their work to discuss who the intruders might be.

CHAPTER TWENTY-FIVE

PARMANS

"Time and charges please, operator." Arnie asked.

"Four dollars and forty cents," the operator told him.

"Four forty? That's not much for an overseas call to the Bahamas."

"That call was local, sir."

"Local? Where was the boat?"

"Coral Gables, sir."

"Are you sure?" Arnie questioned.

"Absolutely, sir. Coral Gables."

"Thank you, operator." Arnie hung up.

Judy had been listening, "Coral Gables, huh?" She was furious. "Your brother is one hell of a liar!"

"Now don't jump to conclusions, Judy," Arnie defended his brother. "Maybe he's in some kind of trouble. It isn't like Jack to lie. And he sounded strange to me."

"Strange?" Judy was concerned. She had been too upset with Jack to notice how he sounded.

"Well, he seemed distant. Like he was in a hurry to hang up."

Sandy chimed in. "You people are making a mountain out of a molehill. I think he just promised his charter to keep their location secret. He did say treasure hunt, right? We would expect the same if it were us."

Good old sensible Sandy, thought Arnie.

Judy was not sold on the idea. "I think he might be in trouble. Call it intuition. I'm worried."

Arnie went to the phone. He dialed Ship to Shore Information and asked for the current number of the charter boat *Razzmatazz,* docked in south Miami. The operator gave him the number and he wrote it down. He turned to the women. "It's too late now, but this is the number of Jack's buddy Phil Doyle. They fish together all the time. He'll know where Jack is. I'll call him tomorrow."

"Good. Call me when you know." Judy got up to leave. "Thanks for the dinner, guys, and for holding my hand."

Jack and Beam walked back toward Building B. They telepathed rapidly. Jack didn't think about his new skill anymore. He just used it.

I am sorry your female is upset. She has an attachment to you.

Yeah. I feel strongly about her, too. But my promise to you guys comes first now.

We appreciate your cooperation Jack. You are being quite helpful.

Things will work out. I hope you can find a way to solve the problem with the cocoons.

Yes, it will be serious if we do not get the army to its new location in time. Where is that?

It is a brilliant planet, and most unusual. The base is carbon but evolved into a crystalline form. We call it Parma Quad Two. It is fed by the star Sirius in the constellation you call Canis Major.

That's the star after which we name the Dog Days of July and August. It's a morning star in our summer sky—the Dog star.

I understand. Beam's thoughts went to the diminutive Parma Quad Two. She had been on the initial probe mission to the planet. At that time she was not yet a commander and served the same function as the copper men—scientific and technical service. However, because of her birth and training, she knew she was destined to be a commander. The current recovery mission was her first at that rank.

Parma Quad Two had been probed for ten time periods. That totaled roughly two hundred Earth years. The Antareans knew that a life form existed on the planet. By their rules a life-form planet was studied for at least eight time periods before any contact or an actual landing was attempted.

The Parmans were an old race and highly developed technologically. Their only nourishment requirements came from their star, Sirius.

They used only the ultraviolet spectrum of its light. They were a peaceful race, yet within their crystalline bodies they possessed an ability to unleash extremely destructive force upon outsiders. But they had never had occasion to use their power in a negative manner.

The planet itself was brilliant. The entire surface had a glasslike appearance. Actually, it was a silicone "skin" constructed by the Parmans. Its main function was to filter the light from Sirius so that only the ultraviolet end of the spectrum passed through to the crystal beings below.

Parma was like a huge, smooth marble on the outside but constructed like a honeycomb on the inside.

When Beam and her party had finally been allowed admittance to the planet, the Parmans greeted them warmly. They offered friendship and a sharing of their knowledge. One of the most exciting discoveries made by the Antareans was that because of the Parmans' extreme sensitivity to ultraviolet, and their ability to extract it from all starlight; they could be, in effect, living guidance and propulsion systems. In other words, a Parman could be installed on an interstellar vehicle and guide the craft to any source containing ultraviolet light, no matter how weak or how far away. Since the Parmans were able to extract ultraviolet from the source, they could then pull a spacecraft toward it. As the distance between the Parman and the source lessened, the flow of ultraviolet light charging atoms of gasses in space increased and thus the effect increased, much like an electro-magnet that grows stronger as current increases. Beam theorized, and then proved that the Parmans who required no gases for life support could live in space freely.

Negotiations had proceeded and one Antarean time period ago the Parmans agreed to let the Antareans build a craft that utilized this phenomenon for propulsion and navigation. It was a living spaceship system capable of zeroing in on any star … any planet … any galaxy, moving toward it rapidly in a geometric progression of acceleration. No fuel was required. No guidance system was required. The Parman guides on board were the key to the ultimate space vehicle.

Jack read all of Beam's thoughts as they approached Building B. He was overwhelmed.

Jack, she telepathed, *our Universe holds wonders around nearly every star. Yours is a strong race and one that will someday travel among the stars as we now do. It will be time periods before that happens, but it will happen. The things you consider so large and important here will become small and trivial. But that which is small, actually smallest—the atoms and electrons that compose your mind will become large. Their energy is the energy of the Universe. It is the life spark. It is what makes us all exist and be part of the Universe.*

Jack understood and thought back to Vietnam and the war. He felt shame for the human race. Beam touched his hand. It was a female touch, filled with caring. Jack thought a kiss to Beam, and she returned a formless thought to him that made his body warm and caused a tear to flow. "Someday," she said aloud. "Someday Earth humans will understand what you just felt." They entered Building B and moved quickly to the processing room.

Joe Finley had been unable to sleep. He was supercharged for two reasons. First, because the men had spent several hours in the health club that afternoon; second—his leukemia was definitely gone. He felt more alive and vital than he had ever been before! And so did Ben, Art, and Bernie!

He did not tell Alma about the visit to Dr. Feldman. He wanted to tell her about his sudden cure. The men knew somehow it was the health club, but before they told their wives, they wanted to try to figure out what was the actual process. He did, however, let Alma know that he was feeling much better and mentioned that he felt the disease had gone back into remission.

They had dinner and made love that evening. Alma fell asleep. Joe could not and that was why he was on the terrace, sitting in the dark, contemplating the stars above when he noticed Mr. Shields arrive at the office. He did not know the stranger who entered the office shortly after Shields. When the two men emerged from the office later, Joe had stepped backed from the terrace railing and tripped over a chaise chair.

He had backed away because he felt he was being pulled toward the stranger with Shields and he feared he would be pulled over the terrace. He also had the crazy idea that if he fell, he would fly down to the stranger.

The noise woke Alma. She noticed that Joe was not in bed. Then she saw him crouched on the terrace. She smiled inside. That was the same position he had been in when they first met.

Alma McClain was a beautiful woman. She had never married, opting to advance her career as a journalist to a position of editor for a major New York television station's news department. They had even offered her a crack at commentator, on camera every night, but she declined. She did do the editorial comment weekly and was a celebrity of sorts in chic New York circles. This was long before the Internet and cable entered the world of news media.

She met Joe Finley at a party on Fire Island. She was scheduled to work the evening news that summer Friday, so she didn't arrive at the party until after midnight. By then things were in full swing. The first thing Alma did was make a beeline for the bathroom. Her bladder was ready to burst after the long drive and then boat ride from the mainland. It was there that she met Joe Finley. He was crouched down on the floor looking for a contact lens that his date had dropped. His date looked more like his daughter. Penny was a slim, pretty girl with long brown hair. She wore a see-through blouse that revealed how young she really was. The idea of older men and young girls passed through Alma's mind and she immediately disliked Joe Finley. He had been polite and explained the circumstances. It took a few more minutes until Joe found the lens and Alma could relieve herself. As Joe and Penny left the bathroom, Alma let them know of her discomfort by suggesting that they have their trysts in a room other than the only bathroom in the damned house.

When she came out of the bathroom, Joe was standing there. Penny was nowhere in sight. He said three things. "My name is Joe Finley. You are a beautiful woman. You are a mean bitch, too." He then turned heel and left her startled.

In twenty minutes she approached him and apologized. She then found out that Penny was not his date, but rather an attempt by their host to put them together. It wasn't working.

After that night their relationship grew slowly. Although they saw a great deal of each other, they didn't make love for six weeks. Alma began to doubt if they would ever be lovers. She liked Joe and sensed that she could love him. But he seemed removed. Distant.

His new show opened off Broadway on a Wednesday night. The reviews came out that weekend. They were excellent. Alma had made sure that her friends in the press and television covered the show. She never told Joe that she had done that. The show was good and Joe was great.

After the Saturday night performance, Alma waited for Joe in a small restaurant in Greenwich Village. He walked in at eleven P.M. He was glowing brighter than when he had read the reviews. He walked up to her, threw a ten-dollar bill on the table to pay for her drink, took her hand, and led her out of the restaurant. He had a cab waiting outside. Without a word, he took her to his apartment. She had tried to find out where they were going and what he was doing, but he remained silent, holding up his hand and smiling.

They entered his apartment. Joe turned down the lights, opened a bottle of champagne, and poured two glasses. He then gave her a glass, clinked a silent toast, and drained it in one swallow. Then he took her hand and led her to the bedroom. "Alma, I love you," he proclaimed. "Will you love me?"

"Oh, yes," she answered. He took her in his arms. They made love for most of the night. He asked her to marry him. She agreed and they set a date.

Their life had been beautiful together until the leukemia. They considered their marriage something to be cherished.

Their love had never diminished.

She watched as Joe slowly raised his body up to the railing of the terrace. She could see that he was holding on tightly. She thought that he was shaking and became frightened. Was he sick? Has he been stricken. A seizure? She got out of bed and rushed to the terrace.

"Son-of-a-bitch," he murmured over and over. "Son-of-a-bitch …"

She was quickly at his side and put her arms around him. "Are you okay, honey?"

He saw the concern in her face. "Am I all right? You bet your sweet little butt I'm all right."

Then she was crying and he held her as they sat on the terrace floor rocking back and forth. He realized that he must have given her an awful fright. He should tell her. Joe Finley rolled that thought over in his mind as they went back into the bedroom.

CHAPTER TWENTY-SIX
MEMORIES AND REVELATIONS

Early morning found Ben, Art, Bernie, and Joe at the pool. They each had an urge to go there without knowing. None had slept much last night. Ben and Joe left sleeping and happy wives. Bernie Lewis' Rose was reasonably happy, but still confused. Bess Perlman was nervous and refused to discuss her feelings with Art. They had not made love that night.

The men met at the card table. They stood there, silently, waiting for something to happen.

Ben finally spoke. "I called you all here. I used the new phone system in our brains that our health club seems to have given us."

The others understood.

"I know no one slept much last night. And I know we are not in the least bit tired. Joe is cured, thank God."

"I'm growing hair," Art Perlman announced. He bent over and pointed to a dark fuzz on his normally bald scalp.

Bernie Lewis sat down under the umbrella and put his left hand on the table. "See that, guys?" He pointed to a small scar on the side of his thumb. "I cut my hand this morning. Actually, I just picked up a glass of orange juice and it … well, I must have squeezed it too tight or something because it broke in my hand and a big shard went into my thumb." The other three men leaned closer to examine the scar. "It began to bleed and I thought that it was going to be the emergency room and stitches. I went to the bathroom to get bandages but by the time I got there it had stopped, so I ran some cold water over it to wash off the blood. When I turned off the water, I saw … well, the cut was healed."

"Healed?" asked an amazed Ben Green.

"Healed!" Bernie said emphatically. "Healed and sealed as though it had been there for years."

Bernie didn't tell them what the sight of blood did to him. It was an old story and a deeply personal matter—traumatic experiences that people carry silently all their lives.

Bernal Woolens was incorporated in 1948 in the state of New York. Bernie Lefkowitz, a tough kid from Chicago's South Side, had been through a war and survived. He returned from Europe on a packed troop ship and sailed into New York harbor in the winter of 1945. Two years of fighting and occupation in Germany had left him drained and bitter. He was discharged at Camp Kilmer, New Jersey. The first thing he did was to petition the court to have his name changed from Lefkowitz to Lewis.

His father had died when he and his brother Martin were young kids. His mother died shortly after hearing that her oldest son, Martin, was killed on Okinawa. So there was no family left for him in Chicago. He decided to stay in New York.

When he met Rose Charnofsky she was young and vital and beautiful. The woman he had dreamt of while slogging across Europe fighting the Nazis. They married. He worked in the garment center as a showroom salesman for a manufacturer of inexpensive dresses. Bernie was successful and became sales manager in a few years.

There was only one thing that Bernie Lewis never spoke about in those days—his experience of being part of the first unit to enter the Auschwitz concentration camp. He spoke Yiddish and was attached to a British unit. The sights that he saw and the deprivation that Jews had been put to so shocked and angered him that he could not speak to a German without the thought of killing coming to mind. His hands trembled and his heart raced for a whole day after that liberation. Then he worked around the clock to try to help the poor souls who had miraculously survived in that death camp.

He told Rose about the experience only after he had another experience that replaced the concentration camp as the thing that he would never speak about. That was what happened to his partner, Al Berger.

Bernal Woolens was Bernie's and Al's dream. They met in the garment center and liked each other right away. They became good friends. Al ran the business, supervised the cutters, and kept things on schedule. Bernie did the buying and selling. They were a great team.

The business grew through the prosperity of the fifties and into the sixties. Bernie and Rose had their son, Craig, in 1950. Life was beautiful; a good business, an honest partner, a beautiful wife, a son, and a new home in Hewlett, Long Island. Bernie was even thinking of buying a Cadillac.

But their business was cyclical, and the garment industry was especially prone to fads and fancies, as well as economic cycles. In late 1965, amid the Vietnam War escalation, Bernal Woolens had a setback. Synthetic fabrics were moving into the marketplace rapidly. Imports were growing. On top of all this, Al had talked Bernie into buying new equipment for the cutting room and three new trucks. The partners signed personal guarantees on the loan to make the purchases.

Unlike Bernie Lewis, Al Berger was an introverted man. He had come to America as a boy in 1932. He struggled through the Depression. Deep inside him were the scars caused by his father's fears that the family would go hungry. When bill collectors came to the door, Al watched his father hide in the basement. They had no money. His dad, Benjamin Berger, a proud man, eventually had a stroke and turned into a vegetable. He swore that he would never put himself in that position.

So when Bernal Woolens could not make its bank payments or its payroll, Al Berger, Mr. Inside, took the blame for their failure on his shoulders. He could see no way out of their financial predicaments. On a muggy summer Monday morning, Al came to the office early. He neatly arranged his desk papers, then sat down and typed a letter to his partner. The quiet Polish immigrant, Albert Berger, who was born in Warsaw and escaped the Holocaust, pried open the elevator door, carefully hid the tool he had used, and then jumped down the shaft, landing on top of the elevator fifteen floors below.

Bernie had to identify the body. It had torn through the top of the elevator car and a sharp edge had ripped Al's body open. The elevator was filled with blood viscera.

After reading the letter, Bernie realized that Al had killed himself to save the business because they had insurance on each other's life. He explained in the letter that he would make it look like an accident and even suggested that Bernie sue the building and buy the mill they always dreamed of owning.

Bernie destroyed the letter. He followed Al's instructions and bought the mill in the quiet countryside of eastern Pennsylvania. He named it Berger Mills. Al's wife and family always remained partners in the firm.

The night after the suicide Bernie went home and told Rose about Auschwitz. He cried and railed and beat his fists on the walls. Rose knew his tears were brought on by Al Berger's death, but she said nothing. From that day on, when the subject of Al Berger came up, Bernie Lewis had only one answer: "I don't want to talk about it!" And he never did. It was only the sight of blood that brought Al Berger and the secret sacrifice he made to the front of Bernie Lewis' mind.

"Let's cut the bullshit." Art Perlman said. He sat down at the card table. "This health club of ours isn't a health club at all. It's the goddamned Fountain of Youth and Mt. Sinai Hospital rolled into one."

Ben Green was half listening as he followed another train of thought. "I feel like I'm in a science fiction movie," he blurted out.

Joe Finley laughed. "We are, my friends. We most certainly are!"

They stared at him and asked him to explain.

"I'm an actor, right? so I know about movies. The things that have happened to us are impossible. But in the movies the impossible always happens. That place … that room in Building B is not, to put it mildly, not human."

"How do you know?" Ben asked.

"Facts. Here they are. My leukemia is gone. Art is growing hair. Ben swims a hundred laps in the pool. Bernie slashes himself and the cut heals in a minute. We are all trotting around like young studs trying to be young bucks with wives again. We can read each other's minds and thoughts. We can project our thoughts into other people's minds."

Joe Finley had their attention as he rattled off their accomplishments. "Now I'll tell you the weird stuff!"

"All that's not weird enough?" Bernie asked. "I mean we have …" Art

Perlman spoke.

"Wait," Joe interrupted. "You remember when I told you that I was under the water for four laps? Well, there is more to the story. I didn't understand … couldn't bring myself to tell you before. While I was underwater I had the feeling that I was in the ocean. I could see the bottom … and … I wasn't alone. There were others swimming below me. They were down deep, yet I could see them. They didn't have diving suits. They seemed to be pulling caskets or tubes out from under large stone slabs."

"Not caskets or tubes, Joe," Ben Green interrupted. "They were bodies."

"Bodies? How do you know?"

"Because I saw the same damned thing two days ago when I went for a swim. I decided to try your underwater feat. It was lunchtime, and the pool was deserted. I stayed down for fifteen minutes. Hear? Fifteen minutes! I saw the same thing. They were bringing up bodies. I thought I was hallucinating."

"Okay," Joe continued, "that's number one. Now listen. Last night I couldn't sleep so I was out on the terrace. It was late. After midnight. I saw a guy come out of B and meet our old friend Shields. They went into the office and had some kind of powwow. When they came out I suddenly felt … don't laugh … I felt like I could fly."

"Holy shit!" Bernie Lewis put his hand to his mouth.

"I had to drop to my knees and crawl back away from the railing because, I swear to Christ, I was about to take a header down to the parking lot."

"What do you think that was all about, Joe?" Art asked.

"I think that place belongs to someone who doesn't live here."

"You don't mean here at the condo?"

"I mean here on this mother-loving planet!"

CHAPTER TWENTY-SEVEN
DISCOVERIES AT THE DOCK AND POOL

Operator, I'd like to call the vessel *Razzmatazz*. It's registered in the name of Mr. Phillip Doyle, Coral Gables."

Judy waited patiently as the ship-to-shore operator searched out the number.

"Please make note, that number is 22-4851-CG-11. I'll connect you. Just a moment."

The line crackled a bit and she heard Phil Doyle's voice.

"The old man of the sea, here."

"Phil? This is Judy Simmons. Jack Fischer's friend."

"Oh yeah. Hi, Judy. How're ya doin'? Is something wrong?" There was concern in his voice.

"No, Phil. I'm just trying to raise Jack and I seem to be having trouble. Have you spoken to him?"

"Not for a week. No, almost two weeks. He told me he had some kinda special charter."

"Well … okay. Thanks. If you see him, please remind him that he has a girlfriend who's lonely."

"How about dinner with me? Jack hasn't been at the dock for a while. Matter of fact, Jimmy Patras told me he thought he saw Jack's boat over at the condo with the strange name. Ya know. Like a star?"

"Where is it, Phil?"

"At the end of Red Lake Canal. I got it. Antares! Yeah. It's called Antares."

"Why would he be there?"

"Well, maybe it's not Jack. Just a boat like the *Manta III*. Or maybe that's where his charter lives." There was a condescending tone to his voice. He was covering up for his buddy in the male tradition.

"Thanks, Phil. How's the fishing?"

"Good in the Stream, but lousy over by The Stones."

"Nice to talk to you. Hey, maybe we can have that dinner if the louse keeps me hanging on too long."

"Anytime, sweetheart. Anytime."

"Bye."

"Bye."

Judy slammed down the phone. She was furious. Minutes later she was heading toward the Antares condominium complex.

Wally Parker noticed the pretty young girl in the convertible as she parked in the visitors' lot. She wore tight jeans and a well filled tank top. *Probably a granddaughter of one of the old fogies*, he thought, as Judy walked toward the pool.

Bernie Lewis looked up from his gin hand. The sight of Judy Simmons filled his eyes. He was immediately interested. He locked on her mind and guided her to their table.

"Can we help you, young lady?" he asked as Judy stopped next to them.

"Uh, maybe." She was looking into the face of an old man, but the eyes were bright and burning right through her. What she felt was strange and extremely sexy. She smiled, with as light adrenaline rush. *Dirty old man,* she thought.

"Well, what is it, sweetheart?" Art Perlman chimed in.

He too had that look. Judy gathered her composure.

"I'm looking for the boat dock. A friend of mine is supposed to meet me here with his boat."

"Boat dock?" Bernie looked at Ben. "We have a boat dock?"

The construction at Building B blocked access to the canal and the residents had not been aware there was a completed boat dock. The overall condo plans showed the dock, but Tony Stranger had told them all that it would be the last facility built.

"Oh, the boat dock," Art said. "That's not finished yet."

"That's strange," Judy said, "because my friend told me he docked here regularly."

With that, Joe Finley stood and suggested that they all walk over and check it out. Bernie offered Judy his arm. Art took the other side. Ben and Joe brought up the rear.

"Stay out of trouble," yelled Paul Amato, the former stockbroker from Boston. "You guys are too old for that."

"Says you, old man," Bernie shot back. They headed for the rear of Building B.

After the discovery that the processing room had been visited, the Antareans decided to keep a few back in the room to watch their equipment.

The rest went out early at dawn on the *Manta III* and *Terra Time*.

Amos Bright, the two male commanders, and one copper man watched with interest as the four men and the very pretty girl climbed over the construction obstacles at the rear of building B.

Where are they going? thought Amos.

To the dock, answered copper man.

But why? They were told it was not built. Also, that young girl is not a resident here.

Copper man concentrated. He reached for the hand of the two commanders. They formed a triangle and copper man's eyes glowed.

The triangle broke. He thought to the others. *She is Jack's friend. She is searching for the Manta III. Somehow she thinks it is here. The others are among those who live here. They are taking her to the dock.*

How could she know Jack was here? thought Amos.

She does not reveal that, answered copper man. *Something else. The four men with her ... they are very hard to read ... two of them block as we do ... the others remain clear, like a commander.*

Amos stared at the four men with special interest.

Rose Lewis was on her terrace serving coffee to Alma and Mary. The three women were in their bathing suits catching the morning sun. They had decided to meet and continue their discussion about the changes in their husbands. Bess Perlman would join them later. She had to visit her sister, who had suffered a stroke and was in a nursing home in North Miami. She watched as the four men and the young girl disappeared around the back of Building B.

As Rose was turning to tell the others about what she had just witnessed, Bess Perlman turned her blue Olds on to the 163rd Street Causeway. She drove slowly and ignored the horns and shouts of other drivers. No one could accuse her of reckless driving. No one could accuse her of reckless anything.

Her life had been careful and quiet. Before Arthur Perlman there was the good life in Manhattan Beach in Brooklyn. Her father was a judge of the State Court of Appeals. He was an honorable man with political connections. He was also second generation and totally Americanized and assimilated. Her mother was a gentile and considerably younger than Judge Bernstein. Bess had her mother's looks and her father's intelligence. She was a beautiful girl. She met Arthur Perlman at a New Year's Eve Party at a friend's house. The Bernstein sisters, Bess and Betty, were extremely popular girls.

After Art had revealed his mob connected business to her, Bess understood why her father had avoided them socially after their marriage. He had disliked Perlman from the beginning, but he never gave Bess an acceptable reason. Actually, his resistance to Art had driven the two closer. Judge Bernstein was civil to Art Perlman, but nothing more.

Then the business with the hearings and the Mafia hit the papers and Bess understood. The thing she never knew was that her father was deeply involved in Arthur's business and had been on the "Family" payroll for most of his career. Art never had told her, and he never would.

However, she was not thinking about her Brooklyn past today. Her concern was for her widowed sister, Betty, lying in a nursing-home bed, unable to speak or move. Bess visited her at least once a week, even though most of the time there was no communication. The State of Florida had moved Betty to the home because they had judged she would never respond to therapy. Prior to that she had been in a hospital.

The Perlmans had enough money to take care of Betty, and Art had suggested that they get a special nurse to live with Betty. Bess had refused. For some reason, when it came to her family, she didn't want to use Art's "dirty" money. It was personal and only between them. He never argued with her. Deep down he knew that she knew about things that could put several people in jail for a long time. He didn't ever want to aggravate her to the point where she might tell what she knew out of spite. So he kept quiet and she looked after her sister as best she could which meant getting Betty Medicaid eligible.

The home was a modest three-story building west of Biscayne Boulevard and north of 163rd Street. She parked the Olds and walked up the stairs to the main entrance. There were a few old people sitting on the porch. They were expressionless. One man, who looked to be well over eighty, kept dabbing his mouth with a wet handkerchief held in his right hand. His left hand rested immobile in his lap.

As she opened the door a tiny old woman using a walker stood in front of her. The woman motioned toward the door and Bess understood. She held the door as the woman tried to go outside.

Then a voice boomed out from behind the woman. "Mrs. Poland! Where do you think you are going? Stop right there." A heavy woman, fiftyish, who looked as if she had come directly from a Gestapo recruiting poster, put an arm on frail Mrs. Poland. Bess watched the old woman flinch in pain as she was grabbed. The matron pulled Mrs. Poland around and pointed toward a doorway. "You go in there. I'll talk to you later."

Mrs. Poland looked back at Bess for a moment. She had a tear in her eye, but she nodded a thank you.

Fear for her sister gripped Bess. She didn't realize the matron was talking to her.

"Can I help you?"

Bess looked away from the old lady directly into the eyes of the matron. "Help me? I don't think you could help anyone."

The woman ignored her sarcasm. "Are you here to visit someone?"

"Yes, my sister. Mrs. Betty Franklin."

"Oh … that one. She's on the third floor. Room 303. Take the elevator over there." The woman gestured, turned, and left.

As Bess walked toward the elevator the smell reached her senses. It was the sweet odor of the old, mixed with disinfectant and rotten cooking. It made her even more afraid.

The door to room 303 was shut. Bess turned the knob and the door swung open. The room was dark. She reached for a light switch and found it didn't exist. Her eyes adjusted to the room. There was a faint light coming from a small window where the shade was drawn. Then she saw an overhead light with a string hanging down. She pulled the string and the light went on. *I didn't know they made ten-watt bulbs,* she thought to herself, because the light made little difference in the illumination of the room. It was just as well.

Her sister, once the most beautiful girl in Brooklyn, was lying on a small, old hospital bed that resembled a crib. The sides were up. She lay on her back. Her eyes were open, staring at the ceiling.

Bess touched her hand and bent to kiss her sister on the forehead. There was a slight response and a sound. Not a moan, nor a cry. It was a whine—a whine of a hurt puppy. Bess leaned over the bed and cried. Tears rolled from both the sisters' eyes in that darkened tiny room, so far from Brooklyn and the wonderful days of youth.

The four men and Judy got around and past the construction materials and equipment and found the path leading to the dock. Copper man joined hands with the commanders again and read the minds of the quintet on the dock. He also listened to their words.

Ben Green trotted onto the dock and checked the two slips. "I'll be damned, young lady. You were right."

Joe knelt to examine the bumpers along the dockside. "This place is being used, all right. These bumpers are worn."

Art Perlman checked the other side. "These, too," he shouted.

"Two boats?" Ben muttered to himself. Then he noticed the tractor and flatbed parked behind some bushes near the path. He walked over to examine it. The others read his thoughts and turned to look.

Copper man gasped audibly. "They telepath," he blurted out.

Yes, thought Amos and the commanders simultaneously. *They telepath. But they are Earth dwellers, and we know they are yet unable to telepath. Yet these can!*

Commander All Light broke into the minds of the others. *Clear,* he ordered. *Quickly.* But it was not quick enough.

Ben and Bernie caught Amos' thoughts at the same time. They looked at each other.

"You get that?" Ben asked.

"Loud and clear," Bernie replied. "Like being tuned into a radio station. Who was it?"

Judy didn't notice the strange behavior of the four men. She was focused on being here when Jack returned. She would come back tonight, but now she was wasting her time. *Manta III* was out somewhere on the ocean.

The men walked back to the car with Judy. She asked them to keep an eye out for the *Manta III* and told them she would be back later. She left them her phone number.

Above the parking lot, in the Lewis condo, three very angry wives guessed what their husbands were doing—taking down the phone number of a pretty young girl.

"The last of the red-hot lovers," Rose quipped.

"Letches," Mary added sarcastically.

Alma watched. Joe didn't really seem interested in the girl. He was looking left and right as though he was searching for the source of a sound. Ben joined him. Art opened the car door for the girl. Bernie helped her in, but abandoned her quickly, not even closing the car door.

Then the four men made a beeline toward Building B.

"Maybe not red hot letches," Alma said softly. "Something is going on."

The doorbell rang, interrupting her train of thought. When Rose opened the door a very distraught Bess Perlman was standing there. Her eyes were red and she seemed to have aged ten years.

Marie Amato had sat by the pool with Andrea Hankinson. Their husbands came out of the pool and toweled themselves. Paul Amato had yelled a remark at the four men as they took the pretty young girl behind Building B. Now the group had returned and the girl was leaving. Marie looked up and saw Alma and the other wives watching from the terrace. Then the men had moved quickly to Building B again. She also noticed that the handyman seemed to be following them.

"Those old men are getting stranger each day!" Marie said.

"I'm glad you said it," remarked Andrea. "I think they have flipped."

Paul Amato smiled and chided his wife. "Can't you let a couple of old guys have a fling? They aren't hurting anyone."

Marie attacked immediately. "Not hurting anyone? Did you see their wives watching them?"

"No. Poor old guys. Haven't got the sense to play off the grounds."

"You're impossible. A chauvinist. Think of how humiliating it must be for their wives."

CHAPTER TWENTY-EIGHT
WHO ARE YOU?

The calm water broke as Hal and copper man two popped to the surface. They swam rapidly to the *Manta III*. On board, Jack prepared to weigh anchor. Harry had ordered him to do that after receiving a telepath from Beam on the *Terra Time*.

The message was clear—return to base immediately.

Terra Time was already under way off to the *Manta III's* port side.

"What's wrong?" Jack asked.

"The commanders called. We must return to the dock immediately. They do not say why."

With all aboard, Jack revved the engines and turned toward the coast in *Terra Time's* wake.

Back at Building B, Hal spoke to Amos. "Why did you call them in?"

Amos didn't answer as he mulled over what might have happened. *They are like us, yet they are not Antarean. I do not know their kind. They have powers. Could they be Ferons? But we know of no Feron expeditions in this quadrant. They use their powers quickly so they understand. Now they come.* He gestured for all to move back to a dark corner of the processing room.

A moment later the four old men popped the lock on the processing-room door and entered their "health club."

Rose saw Bess was distraught. "Bess. Come in, dear." Bess leaned against her heavily and sighed. Alma and Mary came to help.

"What happened, Bess?" Rose asked when she had settled Bess on the sofa.

"We should all die quickly in our sleep." Bess sobbed and said to no

134

one in particular. Her voice was weak. "I went to see my sister today at the new nursing home. It's a nightmare. She's in a room like a closet. Alone. Just lying there in the dark. She can't speak. She can't ask … Alone … all alone … oh, God …" Bess cried. Her three friends let her cry, knowing she would feel better after the tears.

Thoughts flew around the processing room like bees outside a hive.

Where are they?

Who are you?

You command nothing!

I see them in the corner.

How many?

Four.

Four.

They are human.

Of course I'm human.

What are you doing here?

We ask the same. This is our club.

Club?

Oddly enough, it was Ben Green who overcame the confusion. He reached deep inside his mind and blocked the chatter. Then he shouted "Shut up!" aloud.

There was silence. Amos moved out from the corner of the room into the blue light emanating from the wall screen. He spoke aloud to Ben Green. "May we speak?"

"Of course."

"You've been in this room before, haven't you?"

"Many times. It's our health club."

"Not so."

"Then what is it?"

"That I cannot say yet. Will you talk with me first?"

"Watch it, Ben," Bernie cut in. "These guys don't live here."

The commanders moved into the light. Copper man stayed back.

"Holy shit!" Art Perlman exclaimed. "Look at those two!"

Ben looked at the commanders. Then the four men felt them, but only briefly. Again thought flew, but this time only among the four men.

Watch it.

Ow!

Block them, guys.

Suddenly Bernie Lewis grabbed his right arm. *Hey, that hurts!*

The commanders were directing mild energy at them. What happened next was not expected.

Joe Finley started it. He turned to the commanders and thought a punch at them. All Light hit the floor. No Light doubled up in pain. Ben had thought a punch in the stomach at the Shiny Black at the same time that Joe had mentally hit Shiny White. Amos spoke again as he stared in disbelief at his hurt commanders. Copper man was frantically sending a message to Beam for them to hurry back.

"May we please talk?" Amos asked again

"I thought that's what we were going to do." Ben answered.

"Tell your buddies that that shit won't work with us," Art added. "And if they try it again we'll really kick some ass," Joe warned.

"I am sorry. It won't happen again."

The commanders got up slowly.

"May I have a moment to see to my friends?"

"Go ahead, and tell the other guy back there in the shadows to step out here where we can see him."

Copper man moved into the light.

"Good God!" Bernie muttered, rubbing his arm. "Look at that one. He looks like a piece of plumbing."

A few moments later Amos guided the commanders onto one of the cots. The copper man helped. The lamps above the cots came on and the commanders rested. Their faces glowed as the beams hit them.

"Are they okay?" Ben was concerned.

"Yes," Amos answered, "but I am not sure why they were hurt."

"We did it," Joe told him.

"I know. But their powers are strong. Now they are weak. I don't think you made them weak. Let us talk."

Amos moved toward the large center table. The four men met him there.

"Let us speak with verbal language. If we use thoughts then I fear we may hurt the commanders more. It will be less confusing."

Ben agreed. "Who are you?" he asked.

Amos considered his answer carefully. His thoughts were totally Antarean now and deep within. No one could read them. *What shall I tell these Earth-humans? They have used the equipment and gained powers that they do not understand. Yet they can use them. The other problem is worse. We are weakened. Have they done this? Or is it an outside force? If I tell them who we are, how will they react? What will they do? Do they know how strong they are? Do they know how weak we are at the moment? I wish Jack would get here. They would believe him. He is one of them. He is the only one they will believe.*

CHAPTER TWENTY-NINE
FOREVER CHANGED

Amos Bright has told you the truth. I swear it." Jack had just finished an explanation. Ben Green, Art Perlman, and Bernie Lewis stood at the center table staring at Jack Fischer. They believed him.

Joe Finley had moved over to the cots where the commanders were resting. His thoughts went to a copper man and Hal. *Will they be okay?*

Your concern is welcome. Yes, they will be fine.

"Well, what can I say?" Ben began. "It's fantastic. Amazing! What does one say to people from another planet? Welcome?"

"We thank you," Amos responded. "That is a good start."

"But what are you going to do about your army?" Bernie asked, concerned.

"That is a serious problem that we must solve, but right now ..." Amos hesitated, "... now we have a greater problem."

"What now?" Jack asked.

"Something has weakened us. We are losing abilities. Normally the commanders would have been able to protect themselves. But they could not. And I don't know why."

As they talked, Beam moved around behind the group at the center table. One of her functions was that of medical officer. As the men and the Antareans talked, she scanned them. She discovered two interesting facts. One was that Amos, Harry, Hal, the copper men, and the commanders were experiencing a molecular breakdown of the protective shield that they wore. It was a super-thin spacesuit of sorts whose main function was to keep their bodies within a specified temperature and atmosphere. That explained their weakened state.

138

The second fact was fascinating and unique. As she scanned the bodies of the aging Earth men, she realized that by some accident of nature the processing equipment meant for the cocoons was transforming them into a condition that would make them super-human on this planet and perfect space soldiers. She kept these thoughts blocked, storing them in her mind to discuss later with Amos.

Beam moved around to the commanders on the cots. She transferred her knowledge to them at close range, much like one might speak to a baby. Her thoughts were soft and whispered.

Commander All Light got up and moved to the center table.

Amos moved aside to give him space.

"I am All Light, commander of our expedition. I apologize for our foolish attack. Your response was deserved. It will not happen again."

The four men understood and gave their apologies too.

"When we were here, that very long time ago, and left our cocoons buried, Florida was a primitive place. Now it has changed. Our intelligence is good, but it seems we have overlooked some rather important facts."

Amos could not read All Light's thinking. All of the Antareans gathered around the table. Everyone listened as the commander continued.

"Jack has seen our real faces and bodies. What you see now are coverings to appear Earth human. Later we will show you. The coverings are so that we may work among you. I am sure you understand. You will not find us ugly. We are humanoid, too."

Commander No Light picked up the discussion. "The covering we have serves another purpose. It has, underneath, a thick skin-like substance that allows us to keep our bodies at the correct temperature and pressure—an environment like our home planet, Antares. Beam is our medical officer. She is a commander, too. She has discovered our problem."

Beam stepped forward and continued. Bernie Lewis wondered what a female Antarean really looked like. *If she was anything like the attractive blond woman facing them now*, he thought, *he'd like to take a trip to Antares himself.* His thought was heard by everyone in the room.

Beam smiled at him and continued. "The protective skin is four molecules thick. Normally, that is enough. At least it was when we came here before. Now your atmosphere has changed. It is breaking down our protection. The molecules are being changed by several caustic, carbon-based chemicals that were not in your air before."

"We're not only killing ourselves with bad air," Bernie muttered. "We also screw it up for visitors from outer space." No one laughed at Bernie's joke. "Sorry," he shrugged.

"It has taken three of your Earth weeks for our protection to deteriorate," Beam went on. "We can visit our mother ship and obtain new skins, but they will last only for the same period. Then we will have no protection left."

"Jesus," Joe said.

"That's a damned shame," Art added.

"Is there some way we can help?" Ben asked.

"You do not have a technology capable of making these skins," Amos answered. "And we do not have the material on board that can accomplish the task."

"What temperature and pressure do you require?" Bernie asked. "In Earth terms."

"We need one hundred forty of your Fahrenheit degrees under five hundred of your pounds per square inch pressure."

Jack Fischer now understood why the room had been so unbearable for him when the cocoons were opened. Although each soldier had a protective skin, it had to be activated when the last layer of the cocoon was peeled away. For that instant the room pressure and temperature were brought to Antarean conditions -thus, the red wall and the feeling of being hit with a shock wave.

"But Commander, when we release the soldiers from the cocoons you simulate those conditions in this room," Jack said. Then he realized that he might be telling the Earth men something that the Antareans didn't want them to know. He didn't continue, but the four men understood what he was trying to say.

Beam spoke again. "There is another matter we must discuss." She looked toward Amos and whispered thoughts about the conditions of the humans who had used the equipment. The four men strained, but could not read her.

"I will convey what Beam has discovered," Amos began. "Before I do, we will need to agree on a method of private conference. I am sure that you dwellers will understand that we wish to remain undetected by any others of your race. It would be disastrous to our mission, and to the delicate religious and societal balances in your world, if our existence was known."

Joe Finley was way ahead of him. "Mr. Bright, I think that we need to talk among ourselves as much as you do. The solution could also show good faith. I know that if I don't want to listen in on your thoughts, I can block them. Each time I try to do it, it gets easier. I am sure you can do the same."

"Yes," Amos concurred.

"Well, then let's agree not to eavesdrop on each other."

Amos liked this man. "Agreed." Then he continued. "You four men have used our equipment. We know that this has affected you in certain ways, shall we say? Mr. Finley has been cured of a disease. All of you are extremely healthy and energetic. Our readings show that other changes have occurred in your bodies and minds that are of great interest to us."

"What other changes?" Art asked.

"You have become, or are becoming, capable of …" Amos paused because he was about to break one of the cardinal rules of contact with other planet's beings. "Capable of accepting the programming scheduled for our cocoon's regeneration."

A surge of adrenaline coursed through Ben Green's body, and the others.

"What exactly does that mean?" Ben asked.

Amos decided to tell them everything. He had broken the rule. There was no turning back. Only the copper men resisted. Beam, Harry and Hal were neutral.

"Our Galaxy … our Universe … is vast. In time, your race may learn to travel through space. They will learn to survive other environments. They will learn to be with other races. In time. Much of what is required for space travel and for communication with other beings depends on the full development of you brains and nervous systems. Your race is barely one-tenth of the way to that goal. But that is not true of the four of you."

Amos was telling facts the four men had only begun to suspect. They listened intently.

"You have become superior to your fellow Earth dwellers, and you will always be that way. We cannot reverse the process that has altered your bodies and minds."

"My God!" Jack Fischer gasped. His expression was one of exhilaration.

"God of us all!" answered Amos Bright. "Wondrous!"

CHAPTER THIRTY
WHO'S WATCHING WHO?

Judy left her exercise class at five P.M. and drove to Arnie and Sandy's apartment. She had called them earlier to say that she had found out where Jack was. They asked where, but she said she would tell them in person. As she drove she thought about those four old men who had helped her. There had been something weird about them. They were obviously well over sixty but she sensed something about them that was exciting, even sensual. What Judy didn't know was that they found her exciting, and the feelings that she had about them were due to their newfound ability to telepath their own thoughts and physical emotions.

The four wives had spent the afternoon together. Their first goal was to calm Bess Perlman and promise to help her find a way to get her sister out of the home. They made a pact among one another and that brought them closer to each other. They spent the rest of the afternoon trying to understand what was happening to their husbands.

The four men spent their afternoon on the *Manta III*. It had been decided that the Antareans would remain at the complex to discuss their problems while the Earth men used the privacy on Jack's boat to have their meeting. By separating it would make the blocking of thoughts a little easier. It was also imperative that the Antareans set the processing room to the proper atmosphere and pressure to feed and regain some of their strength. That would help, but they knew it was only a temporary measure.

With the excitement of the day, Amos Bright had forgotten his conversation with Mr. Shields the night before. But Shields had not forgotten. He remembered Mr. Bright telling him that his appreciation would be shown in his paycheck.

Shields had called Wally Parker at home early the next morning and told him to be in by eight A.M. They met in the office and Wally had spent the day secretly watching the four men while they were on the condo property. Wally had been aware of the fact that his employer, Amos Bright and several of his friends used Building B from time to time. His instructions were to never go into the building. Therefore, when he saw the four men leave the young girl in the parking lot and go into Building B, he had stayed outside, pretending to inspect the shrubs that were in tubs, waiting to be planted along the path leading to the main door of the building. He had watched the two boats arrive and tie up. His curiosity piqued as the crews from both boats ran to the back door of Building B and disappeared inside.

Later, the four old men and the boat's captain had boarded the *Manta III* in silence. Wally watched the sleek cruiser back out, turn, and proceed slowly up the canal. Then he watched Building B for a sign of the others. After twenty minutes he walked back to the office to report to Mr. Shields on the strange happenings at the unfinished Antares building B.

Dr. Morris Feldman sat in his office waiting for Dr. Fred Breedlove. He had called his colleague and asked him to come to the hospital at five-thirty. The Finley case was on his mind all day. He couldn't shake it. How had this miraculous recovery occurred? But it was more than a recovery. He looked at the microscope slide again. Joe Finley's blood was amazing. No disease, not a hint of foreign bodies. Perfectly formed platelets. He was sure there was something else, but he couldn't get a handle on it. So Fred Breedlove would have a look, too, because Fred was the top, *numero uno*, when it came to lab work in hematology. Fred would find the answer.

Frank Hankinson didn't comment about his wife's take on Ben Green and his friend's being with the pretty young woman. He knew Ben was not the kind of man who would flaunt an affair in his wife's face. He also knew that the other three men were solid citizens. No, something else was going on. Frank's background as a reporter before becoming a partner in the St. Louis radio station pushed him to decide to do a little investigating of his own. So when he saw Wally spying on the guys and then make a beeline for the office, Frank excused himself from the Amatos and his wife and followed Wally into Shields' office.

CHAPTER THIRTY-ONE
A TRIP TO FOREVER

Bernie, Art, and Joe sat quietly as the *Manta III* passed the sea wall and turned north toward Miami Beach. Ben Green was finishing his conversation with Mary on the ship-to-shore. "It's a business deal honey. Nothing more. All we want to do is check out the boat. We were going to surprise all of you, so don't say anything to the other wives if you can help it. Just tell them it's business and we're going to be late for dinner. Bye, love."

He switched off before she could respond. He felt guilty knowing Mary would tell the others the story so at least they wouldn't worry when their husbands were missing. Ben didn't know that the women had seen them talking to the young girl in the parking lot that afternoon. Now Mary was convinced that the men were going to meet the girl and her friends to practice their newfound sexual prowess.

Ben stood next to Jack Fischer. He had taken a liking to the young charter captain. "You must have had quite an interesting time these past few weeks."

Jack, glad to be among his own kind for a change, chuckled. "Interesting isn't the word, Mr. Green. It's been downright weird. But, to tell you the truth, I have never been so excited in my life. These are good people ... or whatever, and they sure know a lot about things we can't even imagine. It's screwing up my private life a bit, but I really feel honored to be part of all this."

Ben understood and agreed. Now they were part of it, too. But how much of a part? That had to be decided this night. He asked Jack to excuse them. The men went out onto the fantail. It was time to begin.

Ben spoke first. "I would like to preface our discussion with my personal feelings about who we are, where we are, and why. If you don't mind, I've been thinking about this little speech since Mr. Bright told us what we have become and what we will remain being. We've become very close in the past few weeks. I consider you guys my best friends … well, after my wife, that is. I want to tell you about my feelings. They are just what I think, given the fantastic things we've learned today. Just bear with me, please."

"Go ahead," Joe said. Bernie and Art nodded their agreement.

"I never thought of myself as an old man. Never, that is until we moved down here and were cut off from business, from the hustle of the big city, from the day-to-day action that we call work. That happened and I began to feel old, and more. I began to feel useless. Tired. Bored. The spaceman called us superhuman. Ten times more ability than the rest of our human race. Well, let me tell you that I sort of always felt that way … Maybe not ten times better, but I certainly knew I was and am a capable man. But for some reason, today particularly, that attitude seems ridiculous. We live in a society that tells us that old is useless … old is being finished … old is being unable to make a contribution any more … old is ugly … old should be out of sight at a place like Florida. Retire, they say. You earned it, they say. And we believe it! Bullshit!"

The other three men listened and felt Ben's anger as their own.

"I don't know what I really feel now except I am more alive than I have been in quite a while. It's not only the physical awakening. We know the room did that. It's also a mental reawakening of that part of me that used to be there. I don't ever want to lose it again. I guess what I'm trying to say is that we have been touched by something special. A miracle? God? Who knows? I feel like we've been singled out. Made unique for a reason, and I don't want to blow it."

Art was staring out at the setting sun. "What don't you want to blow, Ben?"

"The greatest, most important event to take place on this earth since the birth of Christ."

Bernie Lewis stood and walked to the stern. He was deep in thought. Joe Finley got up and walked out to the ladder that led to the flying bridge. He began to climb slowly. He too wanted to be alone for a moment. Ben's words had shaken him; awakened him to the core.

A quiet settled over the boat. The hum of the diesels and the slapping of the bow onto the calm canal water mixed with the evening cries of gulls and pelicans to create a background for thought.

Twenty minutes later Jack heard their minds come alive and call to each other. They gathered again in the cabin.

Art Perlman spoke first. "Jack, we know you have some ability to read our thoughts. But you are nowhere as advanced as we are, because we have used the Antarean equipment. We would like to be able to speak freely here and know that you will respect our desire that what is said tonight be kept confidential."

"Sure, guys. But they can read my mind, so they may pick up some of my thoughts by chance."

"We'll take that chance." Ben said. "You know things about them that we need to know."

Jack began to feel as though his brain was community property held by the Antareans and these four old men. But he also felt like a middleman, an intermediary, and that felt good.

"The way I see it," Bernie said, "is that we are in a negotiation. A business negotiation."

"A contract." Art added.

"Exactly," Bernie replied.

"Before we get to the terms, can we agree to go all the way with these people?" Ben asked.

Joe Finley held up his hand as though he were in a classroom trying to get the teacher's attention.

"What is it Joe?" Art asked.

"When you say all the way, exactly what do you mean?"

"I mean that Mr. Bright exposed two problems to us and, I believe, inferred the solution to both rested on our cooperating with them."

"I have no problem helping them operate the room and helping them to conserve their strength. We can certainly do that," Art responded.

"You miss the point, Artie," Bernie interrupted. "The man, Bright, and the shiny white, uh. Commander All Light told us something else."

"Correct," Ben agreed. "They don't think they can get the army up and running. It was spoiled is what they said."

"Water damage," Jack chimed in.

"Right. Water damage. So in addition to helping them," Ben continued, "I think they were saying that the four of us, and people like us, would or could … replace their army." There was silence.

Jack throttled back and stopped the boat. "Holy shit! You mean they want to take you guys into space?"

"You got it now, Jack."

"I wonder where," Joe said softly. "I wonder what kind of place. And what would we do there?"

Art Perlman began to pace. "To tell you the truth, I feel like I could fight a whole army myself, but well, we've been to war. I'm too old and too smart to be a soldier anymore."

"Wait a minute, gentlemen." Jack got their attention. "Last night I was alone with the female commander, the one they call Beam? She's the one who examined you guys while we were talking. Anyway, she told me a little about the planet where the army was supposed to go. It was called Parma Quad Two. It's near the Dog Star, uh, the one we call Sirius. But it wasn't for war. This is like an army of education … something like that. The inhabitants of the planet are quite advanced technologically and have agreed to let the Antareans onto their world."

Ben interrupted. "You say for education, not war?"

"Right. These beings on that planet, Parmans, are crystals. Like rocks, but they are alive and they feed on ultraviolet light. The Antareans want to use them as spaceships or on their spaceships. It's all beyond me, but what I'm trying to say is that I don't think this army is for war as we know it. These Antareans don't make war."

"That's good to know," Ben said.

"This planet is near Sirius, you say?" Art asked. He was on his feet.

"Yes."

"That's not like going to Detroit," Bernie said.

"Not even Beverly Hills," Joe quipped.

"Not even Disney World," Art said. "We are talking about nine light years. That's, uh, I think something like fifty-three trillion miles from here. That's pretty far, guys."

Ben leaned back against the bulkhead. "So are we talking about a trip to forever?"

CHAPTER THIRTY-TWO
TO REPLACE AN ARMY

The room was glowing bright red. The atmosphere was humid and thick. The entire Antarean expedition crew laid on the cots with the overhead lamps turned on full. They communicated silently with one another, each projecting thought without interruption; each absorbing the previous thoughts into one pattern; each building on the pattern until it became one thought for all.

Shall we block out their thoughts?

We promised.

We should.

Agreed and done.

They are good men.

I like them.

Strange that their race rejects them because they have age.

It is common in primitive societies.

Not always. The Sengs in Galaxy Outer Seven revere their old ones and ask them to rule.

True, but the Sengs are descended from the First and are closest to Touching.

True.

These are not Sengs. They are dwellers who call themselves human beings. I will trust them.

And I.

Will it be right to take them to Parma Quad Two?

That is the mission.

Then you are sure the cocoons are useless?

I am certain.

We must replace them deep and secure in the undersea chamber.

For another time.

If the dwellers agree, can we program them in time?

I believe we can.

We have only four of them. We need nine hundred forty-one!

Where will we get them?

We will task the four to find them.

They must be old like our four. Of that I am sure.

Explain.

The processing will not work the young dweller tissue like Jack. I am not certain why. But the chemistry is clear.

So they must be old human beings.

There are many in this area.

They gather here before they die.

We will need to make commanders of some of them.

Yes.

Shall it be these four?

They will tell us.

Remember, this is an army of nines and threes. We will need more than four commanders.

Amos will speak with them. Beam will assist.

Agreed. Agreed by all.

Now feed and prepare for new skins.

The Antareans rested as the overhead cones fed them and prepared their outer skins for the trip back to the mother ship. As they rested an entire row of Antarean soldiers died. Their glowing eyes dimmed slowly until they went dark.

CHAPTER THIRTY-THREE
SPYING AND CONVERSATIONS OVERHEARD

Mary Green told the other women that Ben had called and that the men were going to be late. She had not told them about the "business" deal, because she didn't believe it, and she knew the others wouldn't, either. However, she felt that perhaps after a drink or two she would work up the courage to tell them exactly what Ben had said. Buying a charter boat, indeed! The ladies met at Alma Finley's car. They decided to have dinner out as long as their husbands were going to be home late. Mary suggested that they treat themselves to the fancy French Restaurant that had recently opened in Coconut Grove.

Bess was quiet as they drove north. Her three friends had been helpful. She felt hope in that she was not alone in helping her sister. She was considering asking Art for a loan to pay for private nursing care. Blood money or not, all she knew was that Betty had to be out of that horrible place as soon as possible.

Judy Simmons was angry and let Sandy and Arnie know it in no uncertain terms. "Your brother is a lying jerk. He's been in Coral Gables all of the time."

"Are you sure, honey?"

"Don't 'honey' me, Arnie Fischer. I am positive."

Sandy tried to calm her but Judy wouldn't have it. "I didn't see the *Manta III* but he was there all right. Some men told me that two boats were there. I also spoke to Phil Doyle on the *Razzmatazz*. He tried to cover up, but he let it slip that Jack was seen over at that Antares Condo Complex too."

"Look, Judy," Arnie tried to reason, "maybe he's really tied up with these people and they want him to keep things secret. It's a treasure hunt. You said that. Maybe he's just doing his job."

"He knows he doesn't have to lie to me. He knows I'd keep my mouth shut. It's people diving for stuff, not some damned covert CIA action!"

"But maybe it is. Did you ever think of that?"

That stopped her for a moment. Then she looked them both in the eye and, in a slow and deliberate manner, said, "Maybe it is the god-damned CIA. If it is, then I really want to know. Because if he's hooked up with them I don't want to see him ever again! Now are we going, or not?"

They took Arnie's car and drove toward the Antares complex.

Frank Hankinson had been trying to call Ben Green since seven P.M. It had been a strange afternoon. Perhaps Ben could answer his questions. Wally and Shields certainly didn't know the whole story.

He had followed Wally into the office at five-thirty. The secretary was gone and Wally was in the inner office with Shields. Frank had decided to wait and listen.

"Mr. Shields, the boss is playing you for a sucker."

"What are you talking about?"

"Well, I followed those old fogies like you told me. They left this morning and came back about one. They went into Building B."

"I knew it. Damned, I knew it. Mr. Bright was right."

"Mr. Bright knew they were in there!"

"What? Bright knew?"

"That's right. They went in for a few hours and then came out. Then they met some young chick by the pool and took her down to the dock."

"The dock? No one is supposed to go to the dock!"

"Yeah, well they did. Before they went down I saw Bright and a few of his strange buddies watching from the rear door.

They didn't stop them. And since you told me just to watch, I didn't stop them either."

"So what happened?"

"It was weird. They checked the dock out. Then suddenly they all jumped up—not the girl. Just the old guys. They looked up at Building B and hustled the girl away. It was like someone yelled for them to get off the dock. But no one yelled. Anyway, they took the girl back to her car and then came back to Building B."

"Did you follow them in?"

"No sir. You told me to stay out of there. I hung around for about an hour. Then I saw the two boats come in and all of those weird people also make a beeline for Building B like some big emergency."

"Maybe they caught the old farts. You don't think they would hurt them, do you?"

"No. About an hour later Mr. Bright comes out the back door with the four old guys and the captain of the *Manta III* charter boat. He walks them down to the dock and they take off in the boat. Then Bright goes back to the building. I hung around for a while and when nothing more happened, I came right here."

"Was Bright friendly with them?"

"Like old buddies. Especially with the big guy who reamed us about the pool."

"Green."

"Yeah. Oh, also, you know who was with them? The guy from the D.A.'s office."

"You mean the old lawyer who pushed us to fill the pool?"

"You got it. He's one of them?"

"Son-of-a-bitch! What the hell is going on here?"

"Beats me, boss."

Wally sat staring at Shields. Outside, Frank Hankinson understood by the silence that the conversation was over. He knew he had information that his friend Ben needed. No need to speak to the men in the office now. He quietly opened the office door and left. Instead of going home, he walked around behind Building B and made his way to the dock area. As Hankinson approached the dock, copper man number one turned off the cone above him.

"Someone approaches *Terra Time.*"

"See who it is."

He left the processing room and went out the back door toward the dock. Frank had boarded the *Terra Time* and was in the lower cabin when copper man one quietly came aboard. Suddenly, Frank froze in his tracks. He was awake and aware, but couldn't move. Then he felt himself turned around and stood facing the strange-looking man.

"Who are you, and why are you on my boat?"

Frank felt his vocal cords release and he could talk. "Hank ... Hankinson ... Frank Hankinson is my name. I live here."

"Why are you on my boat?"

"No harm meant. I was just looking ... looking for my friend."

"Who is that?"

"Ben Green. Do you know him?"

"He is not here. He went out on our other boat."

"Oh. Do you live here? I mean if you don't mind my asking? I don't think I've seen you around."

"No. I work here. On the construction."

"Oh, I see . Well, I hope you guys finish soon." Frank felt the unexplained grip on him loosen. But he was not completely free to move. The stranger, who remained in shadow, backed away and swiftly went up to the deck above. Frank then shuddered and he was free. He moved toward the door to the deck but his steps were ponderous and slow, as though his feet were filled with lead. When he finally came on deck the man was gone.

He stood for a moment and then distinctly heard a voice say, "Please get off my boat!"

It frightened him because the voice came from inside his head, yet was as clear as if someone was shouting at him. Frank jumped off the boat and headed for home. It was then that he realized it was almost dark and what seemed like a few passing minutes on the boat must have been at least an hour. He had to talk to Ben Green as soon as possible. He was sure that Ben was in trouble.

CHAPTER THIRTY-FOUR
A FOREVER DECISION

The *Manta III*'s running lights played on the calm water of the canal as the cruiser slowly made its way toward the Antares dock. Ben opened his mind and reached out for the Antareans. Commander No Light answered.

We are decided.

And so are we.

Are you rested?

Enough to meet.

Where shall we gather?

Ask Jack to take you to his room. We will find you there.

Good.

All the Antareans, as well as Art, Joe, and Bernie, heard the message. Jack got most of it.

Ben had put things in perspective. In a word, they were talking about forever. How do you leave your home, your life, your planet, forever? It had been only a few years since the people of Earth were able to view their planet from space. It was just becoming familiar. Now these four elderly men were talking seriously about leaving Earth and most likely never seeing it again.

It is human nature to rise to an occasion when either opportunity or circumstances dictates action. None of the men could deny the excitement and wonder they felt. They were mature—able to weigh their emotions against the facts that faced them. But still, it was a most fantastic thought—to travel through space to a distant star and live with a totally alien life form.

Once they began to discuss it, they could not control their minds. The excitement was too much. Their deepest thoughts were laid bare for the others to see. Yet, in an almost magical way, it was just that phenomenon that allowed them to reach their final conclusion. Bernie's mind opened first. He could not help himself. Visions of Auschwitz and the horrors of that experience burst upon the minds of the others. They turned to him in disbelief, and then immediately understood. Joe Finley cried. Art Perlman put his arm around his friend. Ben gritted his teeth in anger. Then they saw the bloodstained elevator car and the torn body of Al Berger. They gathered Bernie Lewis' pain inside themselves, and so forever after his burden would be lighter.

Joe Finley had few secrets. He had faced death-dealing cancer bravely and then had seen it removed from his body. For him there was little doubt about what he owed to the Antareans. But there was more than just a debt. He was filled with the idea that they would be explorers—the first humans to venture to other planets; to meet other beings. To learn, and as Amos Bright had said, to teach as well. He told the others that as far as he was concerned, he had died on planet Earth from leukemia. His future lay in the stars.

Ben opened another line of reasoning to the group. His excitement came from the challenge. He was a bitter man and although the others had suspected his anger at a society that forces its aged to retire, they let him vent his feelings. He was born again in a way that was different from Joe. He looked upon this as a business discussion. They were needed. He was needed. The Antareans were depending on them for help. And most exciting, they would return for a meeting and negotiation of terms that would determine their future; their destiny. He believed that to deny this opportunity would be to admit that old age made one useless. And he was far from useless.

The last to open up was Art Perlman. He knew that he must, and that it must be the truth, but he was not sure how the others would react to his past life and deeds. He had no strong feelings one way or the other about the Antareans and their problem. He wasn't excited about traveling in space or about being useful to others. He was a selfish man. That was what he told his friends. They were surprised and silent. Ben asked him to explain. It came out slowly, in dribs and drabs, in disconnected thoughts and memories of tawdry deeds. The ugly story of Art Perlman's life flowed into their minds as the blood from the hundreds of contract victims had trickled onto the streets of America for decades. He related his part in this and they were shocked. The mild, quiet accountant was a mobster! He was a facilitator of crime.

It was Art Perlman's revelation that took the most time to discuss. At one point Art and Bernie nearly came to blows when Bernie asked Art about his involvement in the garment business. He asked whether Art might have been involved in a manipulation that caused Bernal Woolens its financial trouble. Art denied any knowledge of those activities. Bernie read Art's mind through to the thought that Art's friends did, in fact, control a larger part of that industry, especially the trucking and union organization.

Ben became the mediator and calmed them both. Joe Finley suggested that the burden of Art's life was really his own business. If Art was satisfied with his position today, then so be it. If Art didn't want to help the Antareans, that was his business. Certainly it was not their place or desire to pressure anyone to leave the Earth against his will.

And then, Art Perlman found the answer that satisfied himself.

"Joe," he said, "you are right. You can't ask me to leave the Earth against my will." Then he paused a moment to gather a thought. "It's kind of the same situation as when I was in the business. I couldn't leave against their will. Once I was in, I was stuck for life. You may not believe it, but for many years I did want to get out. To leave it all. But you never can, you know. I knew too much. To this day I'm sure they watch me. They sort of drop in from time to time. A note. A call. An unannounced visit. It will never end."

"It can now," Ben said.

Art stared at the big adman. It was a cold, penetrating stare. They were both, in their own ways, extremely tough men.

"Yes Ben. It can. I know it will. I'm in."

They were agreed. Bernie Lewis made it official by placing his hand on top of Art's and then moving both hands toward Joe. Joe and Ben got the idea.

Four old men stood on the deck in a circle, hands joined in the center, and silently swore an alliance to forever. Then they began to discuss their wives and families. And as Bernie added, "Where the hell will we get nine hundred forty-one old farts to be a galactic army?"

CHAPTER THIRTY-FIVE
CONFRONTATION AND QUESTIONS

T hat's the girl," Wally told Shields. "The one who the old men took down to the dock." He was pointing toward Judy as she led Arnie and Sandy Fischer from the parking lot toward the dock. Shields and Wally cut across the rubble-strewn, would-be lawn of Building B to cut them off.

"Can we help you folks?" Shields asked, standing on the path to block their way.

"I don't think so," Judy told him. "We're meeting a friend on the dock. He keeps his boat here."

"No one keeps boats here, miss. The dock isn't opened yet."

Arnie stepped forward in front of the two women. "Who are you?"

"I'm the manager of this place, and to put it directly, you people are trespassing."

Arnie got the hostility in the manager's voice, so he tried to be diplomatic. "Look, friend, this young lady was here before. Her boyfriend is a charter-boat captain, and apparently he is running a charter for some people who live here. She is supposed to meet him this evening."

"Well, mister," Shields answered, "I don't know where your young lady got her information, but our dock isn't finished and, like I said, there are no boats here, charter or otherwise."

"Do you mind if we have a look?"

"Yes, I mind. Like I said, you're trespassing. Wally, please show these people to their car."

Wally stepped forward and gestured to Arnie that it was time to leave.

"Can't we discuss this?" asked Arnie.

"The boss says leave," Wally told him. "There is nothing to discuss. Why don't you have the young lady call her boyfriend on the radio? I'm sure she is mistaken about our dock. Let's go."

Wally watched the car clear the gate and walked back to meet Shields. "They're gone. Funny, she didn't argue with you. She was on the dock today, you know."

"Yeah, well, she didn't see any boats down there, so she's not sure. What she didn't know was that there is no way I could call the police. The boss would have a fit."

As they spoke, a slightly dazed Frank Hankinson came up the path from the dock toward them. They stepped back along the shrubs, but he was distracted and never noticed them.

"That guy looks like he saw a ghost," commented Wally.

Shields watched Frank for a moment. "Maybe he did." Then he turned toward the dock and listened. The faint hum of diesel engines grew louder. The *Manta III* was docking.

After they drove out of the Antares complex, Judy, who had been silent up to now, spoke. "Arnie? Can you get your boss' boat tonight?"

"Not tonight, but you can bet I'll have it tomorrow after work!"

They drove for a few more minutes before Sandy spoke. "Please let's be careful. I don't want to get Jack in trouble, and that place gives me the creeps."

Mary ordered a second round of martinis with her escargots. The ladies were quiet and Bess' depression hung like a cloud over the table. *Now is the time,* thought Mary. "Ben told me that the boys are thinking of buying a fishing boat," she said quietly.

"A what?" Rose Lewis asked.

"A fishing boat. That's where they are tonight. Out on a fishing boat to try it out."

Alma was smiling. "Joe would get seasick in a bathtub. What would they want with a fishing boat?"

"To have parties with … you know, like that girl they were with in the parking lot today," Rose exclaimed.

"What girl?" Bess asked, suddenly interested.

"Oh," Alma said, "it was before you came back from seeing your sister. The boys were talking to a young girl in the parking lot. We saw them from my balcony."

"Talking, my ass!" Mary said. "They were behind Building B with her and they took her phone number."

"My Arthur did that?"

"Your Arthur was the one who wrote down the number."

Bess was angry. "So the sex maniacs have decided to go outside for their action."

"Let's not jump to conclusions girls," Mary suggested.

The martinis arrived, and the ladies paused for a moment to take a much needed sip.

"It may be innocent," Alma told them. "Perhaps the girl has something to do with buying the boat." Alma was proud of her logic, but as she looked around the table she saw that her story had convinced no one.

"Maybe," Mary then agreed. "I didn't think of that. I suppose it's possible. All I can say is that Ben has some explaining to do. I don't like surprises!"

"I'll second that," Rose announced.

The other two reluctantly agreed, and the rest of dinner was spent discussing how to help Bess get her sister to another nursing home.

Jack docked the *Manta III* smoothly. Ben tied the fore and aft ropes to the dock cleats. The five men headed toward the back door of Building B. Wally and Shields crouched behind the shrubs and watched. Ben sent the message to the others. *That creep Shields and his henchman are hiding in the bushes. What should we do?*

I'm going to stop and tie my shoelace. You think ahead to Bright and tell him they are out here but I'll see to it that it's not for long. As Joe Finley telepathed to Amos Bright, Ben Green knelt on the path and faked tying his shoelace. When the others had entered the building, he turned toward the bushes and sent a mental jolt into Wally's stomach. The handyman fell over in pain. Shields was stunned as he watched Wally roll over in pain. Then Ben sent him a kick in the ass. Shields jumped up yelling and flailing his hands at thin air, trying to hit whoever kicked him. Then Ban gave them both a pounding headache. Both men turned and ran toward the parking lot, got into Wally's car, and took off.

Ben Green chuckled to himself and headed toward Jack's room.

CHAPTER THIRTY-SIX
THE NEGOTIATION

It was the beginning of a night they would remember always. Amos, All Light, No Light, and Beam were in the room when Art, Bernie, Joe and Jack arrived. Copper man two stood outside the door. Ben followed a few moments later.

They greeted each other out loud and kept their thoughts blocked inside. Joe felt a sad presence.

"I sense some of your soldiers have died. Is that true?"

"Nine more a short while ago," All Light answered. "We have said the words for them."

"Serve the Master as you did your own." Joe said.

"You have taken your reward," Art continued.

"Guide us if you can as you move among the stars," Bernie added.

"We love you." Ben finished the words.

"Thank you," answered all the Antareans.

Ben spoke directly to Amos. "We have come to some decisions, but no final conclusion until we have more information. And, of course, speak to our wives."

"Understood. How shall we proceed?"

"Let's talk about this army business first. Exactly what kind of army would we be?"

Amos and the commanders once again, but in more detail, explained about the Antarean base on Earth and why they came to evacuate it, leaving the army buried in their cocoons. The damage to the cocoons was not foreseen. This army was one of many operating throughout the Milky Way galaxy. It was one of the reasons why the Antareans have

165

survived so long and why they were universal travelers. This particular army was formed and trained for diplomatic service. That was why they were on Earth to begin with.

The Antarean base here was a diplomatic center as well as a trading center for their Galaxy. The role of the army was that of service, translation, education and supplying comfort to the almost endless variety of visitors who came to the base in this quadrant. They were not a fighting army. Their purpose was not war. Antareans and all of the advanced galactic beings put war far behind them millennia ago.

When Amos finished his description of the army, Ben spoke. "We know that your equipment can do things to our bodies so that we are able to travel in space. But from what you describe, this army has very special skills and knowledge that we don't possess. How do we learn?"

"It will require programming and training. We have the methods to accomplish that task. Beam has assured us that your brain and nervous system is quite capable of assimilating the knowledge."

"And exactly how many soldiers do you need again?" Joe asked.

"Nine hundred forty-one," No Light answered.

"Who will command?" Bernie asked.

"We will make nine commanders," All Light said.

"How does that work. I mean what's involved?" Art then asked.

Beam understood his concerns. "It will require special training and some, well, changes to part of your nervous system. But only to those chosen for command who, of course agree to assume that rank."

"Surgery?" Art asked.

"Special implants and one small device that activates a portion of your brain," she answered.

"Brain surgery?" Bernie was also concerned.

"Yes. You might call it that. In what you call the medulla. Your brain's center. It must be enlarged and attached directly to certain nerves. It's quite safe. I assure you. I've already prepared the programs should you choose to …"

"Safe? Screwing around with the brain is never safe!" Ben was adamant.

"But," Amos said, "you men have been screwing around, as you put it, with your brains for the past week yourselves. The procedure Beam speaks of is as safe as what you have been doing accidentally."

Mary Green heard the phone ringing as she entered the condo. She answered the call in the kitchen. "Hello?"

"Hi Mary. It's Frank Hankinson. Is Ben there?"

"No Frank. He's out with the boys for a while. Can I help you?"

"No. It's okay. Can you ask him to phone me when he comes in?"

"Sure. But he may be late."

"Tell him no matter when he comes in. I'll be up and waiting. It's important."

"Is everything all right, Frank?"

"Yeah. No problem. It's business. I have some information for him."

"Okay. Bye. Oh, Frank. Is this about the boat?"

How did she know what happened to him on the boat? "The boat?" he asked sheepishly. "What boat is that?"

"Oh, nothing really. I thought it was something else,' she said quickly. "So, I'll have Ben call you. Bye again." She hung up.

Mary felt better. Frank sounded evasive so she was sure he was involved in buying the boat. He almost let the cat out of the bag. She guessed it was supposed to be a surprise of some sort. She called the other wives and told them. They all felt better.

The discussion continued for over an hour in Jack's room. Ben was in his glory. This was an actual negotiation, but he wasn't pitching a new advertising account. It was their life and future that was being discussed. They were coming to final terms, all of which would depend on their wives. And of course there was the eight-hundred pound gorilla in the room—if a deal was struck they would have to find nine hundred thirty-three more seniors willing to leave Earth, possibly forever.

Ben summarized the discussion. "So this is where we are. We will most certainly help you with the immediate problem of your protective skins. We will work with you to get the remaining cocoons reprocessed and put back securely under the stones. We will absolutely keep all of this secret and help in any other way we can. As far as becoming your army, if it were up to the four of us you would have no problem. But this is about the most far-out thing that has ever happened on Earth, so I am sure you will understand our need to proceed with some caution—for ourselves and for your sake too. Step one will be our wives. I think that our plan for tonight is good … perhaps a bit unfair to the ladies, but certainly dramatic. If they are convinced, then we will be able to turn to raising the rest of the army. We have some ideas to explore in terms of how to do that efficiently and keep it under wraps for as long as possible. The last thing we need is the authorities or media getting wind of it. Let's all think positively. Any questions?"

Bernie, Joe and Art had none. Neither did the Antareans.

"Then we will see you in an hour in the, uh, our health club."

The four men headed home, and the Antarean party went to the processing room to prepare for visitors. As he walked down the hallway, Amos took a moment to discuss how they would handle Shields and Wally Parker tomorrow. The old men's positive attitude had invigorated the Antareans. Beam couldn't wait to play her role in the plan.

CHAPTER THIRTY-SEVEN
MAGIC TRICKS

The four couples met at the deserted pool. It was after 9:00 PM. Each man had returned home to an argument. Each had played innocent. They did not argue, but rather quietly took a verbal trouncing from their wives. The only one who ran into unexpected problems was Art Perlman. Bess broke down and told him about Betty. He immediately offered to pay for private nursing. This time she didn't refuse, but didn't accept, either. At least she knew that if she and her friends solve the problem, then Art's money could. It relieved her burden.

Ben Green called Frank Hankinson as soon as Mary told him about the urgency of Frank's call. Frank didn't want to talk over the phone but Ben said it was too late to meet that night. They would meet by the pool at nine the next morning. Frank kept asking if everything was okay. Ben assured the snowbird that things were fine. After the conversation he telepathed the strange call to the other men.

As the four couples sat in the dark around their husbands' card table, the four women waited for their husbands to announce their purchase of the fishing boat. Their expectations could not have been further from the truth.

"Tonight is going to be a very special," Joe Finley began. The men had chosen him to speak first. "We ask that you lovely ladies allow us to present, to tell you, actually to show you something absolutely wonderful that we have discovered." The women looked at each other and smiled knowingly. "Please hold your questions." Joe then raised his hand dramatically and, with a flourish, continued. "First, I would like you-all to reach over and touch Art's bald head."

Each woman slid her hand across his scalp.

"You got a transplant?" Bess asked.

"It feels fuzzy. Like a baby." Mary.

"Next, Mr. Green will perform his famous aqua-show."

With a flourish, Ben stood, kicked off his loafers and took off his pants and shirt, revealing a bathing suit underneath. In one swift movement he ran to the head of the pool. Joe invited the women to poolside. Ben dove into the water and swam four laps underwater in just thirty seconds. He leaped out at the spot where he began. Bernie threw him a towel. Joe asked the ladies to sit down again. Mary shouted to Ben to see if he was okay. He wasn't even out of breath.

"How in God's name did you do that, Ben?" she asked.

Joe interrupted her. "No questions yet. Please. Now, for our third trick, oh, event Mr. Bernard Lewis will take center stage."

Bernie stood and took a sharp penknife from his pocket. He placed his hand on the table and slit his palm in one quick motion.

Rose screamed.

Alma jumped up. "This isn't funny. Are you crazy? Have you all gone mad?"

Calmly, Joe Finley answered, "Ladies, we asked that you hold your questions. Please watch Mr. Lewis. This is his favorite trick."

The women looked back at the table and watched Bernie wipe away the blood. There was no cut. It had healed.

"They went to a magic store," a relieved Rose Lewis deduced. "Just little boys with some new tricks trying to give us heart failure so they will be free to play with their young cuties."

Joe sat them down again. He put his arm around Alma. "My dearest, alas I have no tricks to show you myself." He was the talented actor again and had the audience in his grasp immediately. He flashed a thought to the others: *Am I overdoing this?*

Do what you feel, they flashed back.

"No tricks, because as you know I am not a well man." Alma was shocked. The other women were embarrassed. He held Alma tighter, as if to say, "Bear with me."

"But I do have of trick of sorts. You see, a few days ago, Art was bald,

Ben got headaches underwater, and if Bernie had cut his hand like he did, we would all be in the emergency room getting ready to donate blood. Except they wouldn't take my blood because it was full of white cells. My leukemia."

"Oh, Joe," Alma whispered. He put his finger to her lips.

"I said a few days ago all that would have happened. My trick is to tell you all that it is gone. My disease is completely and irrevocably gone. Vanished … finito … kaput. I am well again and always will be."

Alma threw her arms around him and hugged him. The other women wiped tears from their eyes.

"When?" Alma asked.

"Why?" Mary asked.

"How?" Bess asked.

"What is going on?" Rose asked.

"That, dear ladies, is what we've been trying to discover for the past several days," Ben said. "Now, without any questions, we would like to show you the answer."

He stood, as did the other men. Each took their wife by the hand and the group moved toward Building B.

"Are we going to the dock?" Mary asked.

"No, not the dock," Ben said so that everyone heard. "We are going to the damnedest health club you ever saw."

"Run by some pretty far-out attendants!" Joe added.

CHAPTER THIRTY-EIGHT
WE ARE ANTAREANS

Arnie and Sandy Fischer sat at their kitchen table sipping coffee, speculating about Jack's mysterious behavior. Sandy was sure there was a logical explanation. Arnie, knowing his brother could be flaky at times, wasn't convinced.

Judy, alone in her apartment and feeling deserted, smoked a joint and called Monica. She spent over an hour complaining about Jack. Monica listened patiently and tried to soothe her friend's anger.

Shields and Wally Parker sat at the bar of a small local chop house and waited for Tony Stranger, the worst salesman in Miami, to join them. They ordered their third drink but still hadn't decided how to deal with the weird events at the Antares Condos. They were hoping that Tony, devious man in his own right, might have some ideas.

Frank Hankinson was more confused than ever. He watched the four couples at the pool area from his balcony. Although it was dimly lit, he saw the women touch Art's head and go to the pool to watch Ben swim. The screams filtered up when Bernie cut his hand, but Frank didn't see it. Then there was some hugging and kissing and the four couples walked toward Building B. He felt left out of what appeared to be a private party.

"It's cold in here," Bess commented as they walked down the hall toward the room they were told was a health club. No one answered her.

The orange door was slightly ajar when the group reached it. Ben halted them for a moment. "What we are about to show you is, to say the least, different. So please keep an open mind, and trust us. That's important because we're going to ask you to, well, sort of do some

things. I promise nothing will hurt you and the results will be terrific."

The women looked at each other warily.

"Lead on," Alma said. "Enough talk. Show us this great mystery."

The wall was blue. The center table was bathed in soft green light. On the left, all of the cabinets were misting and opened and inviting. In the rear of the room four of the cots were turned on and bathed in green light.

"What?" Mary Green asked, startled. "Did you say something, Ben?"

"No," he answered. "That was Mr. Bright."

"Who?"

"Amos?" Ben called out. "You there?"

Amos stepped into the light of the center table. He was wearing what appeared to be a pale blue, one-piece jumpsuit. The men were surprised by his appearance. They were used to seeing him in ordinary human clothing. His face was in shadow.

"Yes, Ben, I'm here. Before we go any further, we thought that it would be better to do this introduction properly. We have removed our outer camouflage, so to speak, so that you will all see us as we really are."

"Do you think they are ready for that?" Art asked.

"Ready for what?" Mary asked.

"We think it is the best way," Amos said.

"Who is that?" Bess asked.

"Okay, ladies," Joe said. "Here's the God's honest truth. We found this room by accident two weeks ago. We thought it was a health club, so we began to use the equipment. Well, it isn't a health club, and the equipment you see in the room is not ... well not really ..."

"Not of this Earth," Bernie interrupted. "It belongs to that gentleman and his friends." The Antarean crew gathered behind Amos at the table. They were all in shadow.

As Bernie spoke, Ben urged the women toward Amos at the center table. All their faces were in shadow, too.

"Who did you say they are?" Rose asked nervously.

"They are visitors," Ben said. He felt uneasy. He wasn't sure that revealing their actual faces to the women at this time was such a good idea.

Amos read him and telepathed a calming word to him. *The sooner they see us, the faster they will become used to us. It is better this way. We have much experience in these matters.*

"Look, girls." Joe said firmly. "These folks are from another world."

"What?" "Oh, my God!" "You guys have lost it!" "This is getting nuts!" The women blurted out all at once.

"Hold it and listen," Joe said, raising his voice. "I'll say it again. These people are from another world. And again, so it sinks in. These people are from what we call outer space. They are from far away. Another planet in our galaxy. You know? UFO's. Roswell. All that stuff is true."

At that point the group at the center table moved into the light. Bess screamed. Alma grabbed Joe's arm. Mary stared and began to shake. Ben held her. Rose Lewis moved away from the rest, and with clarity and courage that none of the women had, she approached the Antareans. It was a magical moment. She reached the near side of the table and looked at each of the Antareans individually. When her glance came to Beam, she stopped. "And you. Lovely creature, are a female. Yes?"

"Yes, Rose."

"You are beautiful."

"Thank you."

She was. The men had not seen them all together like this, nor had they ever seen Beam as she really is. There was a difference. No doubt that she was female.

The shape of her eyes was different from the others. They wrapped around her head and tapered to a fine point past where the temple would be. At that point there was a faint red spot. It began there and ran down her neck, circling back and joining at her throat. Alma thought of a ruby-throated hummingbird. Joe read her thought and agreed silently to her. She looked at him, wondering how he got into her thoughts.

Bess reached out her hand to Beam. Beam reached for Bess. Her hand was attached to an arm that was longer in proportion to a human arm. The hand had four fingers, three of equal length and a longer thumb. When her hand reached Bess', the three long fingers appeared to divide and become six that enveloped Bess' hand.

"Oh!" Bess exclaimed, feeling the warmth and friendship that Beam passed to her. "How very pleasant! I can feel your welcome."

After that display the others needed no convincing. Beam didn't come from a magic store. Not with a hand like that.

The three other wives approached the Antareans and exchanged greetings. Ben handled the introductions. All Light and No Light, commanders of the highest grade, were shy with the women. Amos explained they were showing respect. Historically, the females of species encountered were treated in this manner because they were usually responsible for the bearing and nurturing of the young, and the continuation of a race or species.

Alma marveled at the physical makeup of the commanders. They were smaller than the others. Their heads were larger and appeared to have appendages growing out from the sides and rear of their skulls. The two side bumps were red in color and glowing. The bump in the rear was white and kept expanding and contracting, as though it were breathing. Their arms were long and tapered, with hands similar to Beam's. Their legs were short and stumpy, and their feet were flat and spread duck-like on the floor for support. Their skin appeared cream-colored and translucent with a slightly visible, complex circulatory and nervous system beneath.

Hal and Harry had shed their blond, beach-boy covering. They had no bumps on their skulls. Their eyes wrapped around their heads and glowed like the others. They were a bit taller than the commanders, but much shorter than they had appeared when disguised as humans. The copper men were still metallic. But now their heads were Antarean.

Amos, whose stature and eyes were larger than the rest, had a long bump extending from between his eyes over the top of his skull and down his back.

They had no visible mouth, ears, nor nose.

"The copper men, as you call them, are soldiers in the sense that you use the word," Amos stated. "They are specially suited for combat, should it be necessary, and thus have the metal skin. We ask that you do not touch our skin, only our hands if we extend them."

Then he turned to Ben. "Shall we show the ladies the equipment?"

"Good idea. Let's start with my wife." He motioned Mary to follow him and thought to Hal and Harry for their help. " "How's your back today, honey?"

"Stiff as always. Why?" Mary asked.

As the others gathered at the first cabinet, Ben helped Mary into it while he explained that she should relax. Harry set the dials and they enclosed Mary in the cabinet. It turned on and the mist began to rise.

"Hmm …" she said. "Now that feels good." Mary smiled.

While she relaxed and enjoyed the sensation, Bernie Lewis took Rose's hand and guided her to the second cabinet. Amos opened it. "Rose, when was the last time you could bend and touch your toes?"

"Are you kidding, Bernie? Longer than I care to remember."

"Try this cabinet. I guarantee you will be as supple as Nadia Comaneci in a few minutes."

"But will I be as young?"

Amos thought a smile to the human men. Alma Finley heard the thought, although she didn't know where it came from or why.

As Joe and Beam were guiding Alma to the third cabinet, Joe had a thought. "Alma is physically quite healthy, so I propose we show her a different piece of equipment."

Beam picked up on his idea. "Good. Put her on the second cot. I will adjust the lamp." They took Alma to the cot and as she lay down, Beam reached up to the lamp's controls. The lamp turned on and its beam descended down to Alma and spread over her body in a pattern that duplicated her nervous system.

"Relax," Joe told his wife.

"That tingles," she said, "but it feels wonderful."

Bess stood apart from the rest. She somehow knew that a miracle was taking place and was surprised at how easily she, and the other women, accepted the strange happenings.

Art came to her side. "I know what you are thinking."

"How can you know that?"

"Because I can read your thoughts. This stuff isn't just for the body. It affects mental powers, too."

"Can it cure Betty?"

"Well … yes. I believe it can. But don't get your hopes up too high. We have more to discuss after you all see what this place can do."

Amos Bright listened to the conversation between the Perlman's. He came over to them. "Let me be alone with Mrs. Perlman for a moment, Arthur. I think I can answer her questions."

Art moved away.

"Place your hand on my forehead, Mrs. Perlman."

Bess put her right hand on the bump between Bright's eyes. She felt her hand drawn to and adhered to his skin. His eyes glowed for a moment and her body shook. Then it relaxed. "Oh, God," she said softly. "How absolutely beautiful!"

Then his eyes glowed again, brighter this time, and Bess saw her sister sitting up in bed in the dingy Nursing Home room. Betty was smiling. Amos Bright's skin released her hand.

"Can you do that?" she asked.

"What you saw we did together. Now your sister rests comfortably. She is not cured, but she feels us. I have given her rest. You have given your thought of love. She knows we will help her."

"Thank you. Thank you so much." She reached up to kiss his cheek, but he pulled away and offered his hand instead.

Mary and Rose were moved to the second set of cabinets to complete their treatments. Alma was up and around and having the time of her life reading everyone's thoughts. Joe kept sending her thoughts of love and she began to get embarrassed because she knew that everyone could feel her loving responses to him. They were like children with a fabulous new toy.

Suddenly Alma felt a jolt to her body. Then sadness. She was confused. Panicked.

"A leader is gone in the second group," Amos announced. "That is what you felt."

"They will go quickly now unless we replace them in the cocoons very soon," Beam said.

"Gone? Someone died?" Alma asked. "I felt someone leave. I was sad."

Joe came to her. "It was one of their army up on the roof."

Then he thought to the commanders. *I think we should do what we have to as quickly as possible. The ladies will believe.*

All Light directed Harry and Hal to remove the two women from the cabinets. Immediately, Mary knew her backache was gone forever.

Then they watched Rose Lewis get out of her cabinet and proceed to stretch her arms in the air. Then she bent and touched her palms to the floor.

"Wow. Did you guys see that? I'm fifteen again!"

They all gathered at the center table.

"You women now believe who we are," Amos began. "Allow me to tell them why we are here and what has happened. Then we may discuss the future." He told the Antarean story to the four wives.

It was dawn when they all came to an agreement. The hardest part was to figure out how they would tell their children that they were leaving Earth.

Unlike the assumption their husbands had made, Amos assured them they could return for a visit sometime in the future.

Bess agreed only on the condition that Betty could join them. Also, Bess did not want to be a commander. However, she was sure that Betty would.

The only person in the room who was disappointed was Jack Fischer. Beam had explained that because of his age, he could not go with them. The equipment and processing would work only in human bodies that had reached a certain stage in the aging process. The muscles, tissues, organs and bones of the older Earth people had begun degenerating. It was only at a stage of fairly advanced aging that rejuvenation and change would be effective.

When Amos felt Jack's disappointment, he went to the charter captain who had been so helpful to the Antareans and whispered a promise. "Keep our secret and help us with the tasks ahead. We will return one day when you are old enough to join us." The promise of eternity, for doing only what he would do anyway, cheered Jack immensely.

CHAPTER THIRTY-NINE
THE FIRST RECRUIT

Energized, the four couples sat in the Greens' apartment and discussed their commitment to the Antareans. They marveled at how radically their lives had changed, and how calmly they accepted the situation and made their decision.

"We are really going into space!" Rose Lewis kept repeating her feelings. "I keep picturing Neil Armstrong stepping foot on the moon. It all looked so forbidding and cold and barren."

Bernie looked at her as though she were a stranger. He couldn't recall her ever being so alive and excited. The others let her go on. She was expressing all of their thoughts.

Alma helped Mary with the coffee and Danish. It was nearly eight o'clock in the morning. "Remember, you have to meet Frank Hankinson in an hour," Mary reminded Ben.

"Right, Hon. I think we should start recruiting as soon as we can. He can be the first."

"My sister is first," Bess reminded everyone.

"Right," Joe told her. "So, how do we decide on whom to approach?" he asked. "We have certain criteria that will narrow the list, but nine hundred forty-one is a lot of people."

"Old people," Art said.

"Exactly," Alma said. "I figure if we get everyone in Building A, assuming they are all old enough, we would have about one-hundred-thirty. So we should all start making lists. Time is short."

The ladies were in their element, approaching the task as though it was to be a large party. They quickly gained control of the logistics.

"It's like a big wedding reception," Rose said. "I think each of us should make a list of all the people who we think would be old enough, and whom we think would like to go. Assuming we all have about the same number of friends and family and people like that, I guess that would give us about a hundred or more."

Arthur did some fast calculating. "So that leaves about seven hundred more people to find. I think we're gonna have a problem."

Rose and Bess spoke at once. "I can think of …" They laughed.

"Go ahead, Bess," Rose deferred.

"Well, I was thinking of the nursing home where my sister is. If there was some way to get those people out of there …"

"We could buy it," said Art.

"And how do you explain the disappearance of all those people?" asked Ben.

"We don't," Art answered. "We won't be around to be asked."

They all laughed and agreed.

"I had a little different idea," Rose said. "A few months ago I went to see my Aunt Ruth down on Collins Avenue. There must have been hundreds of old people down there living a meager existence. Maybe there is a way to organize them. Aunt Ruth knows a lot of them and they sort of look up to her."

"I know we all have good ideas," Ben said, "but a word of caution. We have to remember that if the word gets out and the authorities get wind of what's happening, there won't be any space trip for anyone. So let's be real careful of how, and who, we approach. Okay?"

Everyone understood and agreed.

They spent the next hour planning during breakfast. Each of the women took a piece of paper and began making their lists. The men added a name now and then. Within the hour, much to their surprise, the four couples had over two hundred candidates. They also knew that it was going to be tricky identifying and convincing the rest of the people to complete the army.

Meanwhile, Commander No Light communicated the situation to the Antarean Council. "We are assured that these dwellers can be trusted, and that they will serve well on Parma Quad Two. It is our belief that others of their age will adapt. But until we have completed the return of the cocoons to their resting place, and secured it, and have gathered and processed the replacement army, we suggest no communication to the Parmans about this situation. We must be on our way to Parma Quad Two before that is confirmed. We will send a probe with a history of what has transpired here."

No Light knew that his superiors would understand when they knew all the facts, but for now, detailed messages that spoke of interference with life forms, and radical changes in plans, were best presented in person. He paused in his communication to consider the coincidence of the damaged cocoons and the ability of the aging dwellers to adapt. He had traveled in space for a very long time. Coincidence and purpose had often been partners in his experience. These events served to strengthen his conviction that there was a universal plan, guided by a force that they believed in, but did not comprehend. It was referred to as The Master.

Above, on the roof, the second row of soldier's eyes flickered, then glowed bright, then dimmed slowly until they were dark and life passed from them. He reported the event to the mother ship and uttered the prayer for the departed.

Now they would have to move quickly to replace the remaining soldiers in cocoons and back under the sea. He slid from the center table and went to the cots where his companions rested. He turned off the lamps above the cots. The Antareans awoke and went to work.

Tony Stranger sat in his car in the bank parking lot, waiting for it to open. He mulled over the story he would present to Mr. DePalmer. Shields and Parker had been vague about what was going on at the complex, but through their drunken muttering, Tony was convinced that something had seriously scared them. It wasn't his business, or so he told them, but he knew that he would make some good money when they opened Building B. So he was interested. He also saw the possibility of getting rid of Shields and managing the complex himself. He had gone along with the two men and told them he would find out what he could from Mr. DePalmer because DePalmer had hired him. What he didn't tell Shields and Parker was that he would keep the information to himself if it proved to be useful. He had a feeling that this was going to be his lucky day. He flushed with excitement as DePalmer's car pulled into the lot.

Judy awoke to the ringing telephone. It was Arnie reminding her that he would have the keys to his boss' boat by late that afternoon. Sandy and he would pick her up at 4:00 P.M. She agreed and then went back to sleep. The events of the previous day and too much grass had knocked her out. She felt she would need her strength later.

Frank Hankinson sat by the pool as the four men walk toward him. He wondered why Ben had brought the others. "Hi, guys," he greeted them.

Ben smiled and reached out his hand. Frank extended his, thinking that to shake hands was a rather formal thing to do. The men read his feelings and communicated to each other to put him at ease.

They pulled over some lounge chairs in a circle and waited to hear what Frank was so anxious to say. "Look, guys," he began, "it may be none of my business, but there have been some weird things happening around here. Weird to me, that is, because I'm an old reporter, who has a nosy nose."

The men listened calmly.

"When you guys took that chick down to the dock yesterday, I was sitting here. I was kind of interested so I kept an eye on you."

Joe Finley tried to keep it light. "Dirty old men, huh?"

"No Joe. I mean I know you guys and, like I say, it's none of my business. But the caretaker, Parker, he was following you real sneaky like."

Art thought to Bernie: *How did we miss that?*

"Anyway, he was onto you guys for some reason, so I kept watch. I don't like the guy. After you came back with the girl and then went back to Building B, I was interested enough to hang by the pool. Parker watched for a while, then went to the office. I followed him. He met Shields there. I listened to their conversation."

"Did they speak about us?" Ben asked.

"Yes. And boy, were they pissed. But also confused. They kept talking about some guy named Bright and how he was Ben's buddy. Also about a man from the D.A.'s office being with you."

Joe laughed. "The infamous Mr. Bonser!"

"Yes, that's what Parker said. Bonser from the D.A."

Joe explained that it was a long story, but not a problem. He thought that would satisfy Frank.

"Well, I'm glad that's okay. I thought you guys had some problem with the D.A. or something."

Ben reassured him that it was part of the swimming pool scheme and not a problem with the authorities.

"Good. But … well, that's not all. After I left the office …"

"Did they see you?" Art asked.

"No. Anyway, I went down to the dock."

"Dock? You know about the dock?" Bernie asked.

"Now I do. I didn't before, but they were talking about it so I thought I would have a look. They were pissed because no one is supposed to go down there. Then when Parker said you guys were buddies with this Bright fellow, Shields was confused and sort of annoyed. Like he should have known this Bright guy knew you. Anyway, I went to have a look at the dock."

"And?" Ben asked.

"There was a boat down there. A real nice cruiser. *Terra Time.* I guess I shouldn't have, but I went aboard to have a look and uh …" He paused to gather his thoughts because he wasn't sure how to explain what had happened to him.

Ben read his thoughts. He was about to recruit his first soldier. The others agreed.

"Frank, how long have we known each other?"

"Since we all moved in here." Frank wanted to get on with his story. "You guys want to hear the rest?"

Ben smiled and put his hand on Frank's shoulder. "Well friend, to tell the truth, we already know."

"The guy told you?"

"No, you told us."

"Me? When?" He was confused.

"Just now."

"No I didn't. Are you nuts?"

"No Frank. We want to tell you who you met and what you saw and why. It's difficult, and it's the first time we have had to do this, so bear with us. I promise you the most fascinating day of your life."

"Are you guys okay? I mean … you're talking weird."

"We're more okay than we have ever been in our lives. Please listen and try to believe us. First, let me ask you how old you are."

"Fifty-eight."

"How is your health?"

Frank looked at the four men facing him and smiled nervously. "My health? What are you selling? Life insurance?"

"No, Frank. Humor us. How's your health?"

"Okay, I guess. A little arthritis. An ulcer. Wear and tear. You know … your're getting old too."

"Good."

"If you guys think that's good, you are nuts. The aches and pains … nothing good about that."

"I know. How about your business?"

"What about it?"

"Well, do you like it? How long before you retire?"

"Sure I like it. I've been in the radio business all my life, just about. I built that station up from nothing to the fifth biggest in St. Louis."

"Do you think you'll keep working at it, or will you retire?"

"I'll retire. To tell you guys the truth, it's not as much fun as it was in the old days. Then I was a reporter and D.J. and engineer all in one. It was exciting. Now? Well now it sort of runs itself. I don't get the chance to get my hands dirty anymore. Maybe that's the way it should be … " His voice trailed off. It was a sore point with him. He had had a hard time adjusting to growing old, and had really not yet accepted the fact that he was no longer young and energetic. What bothered him the most was the arrogance of the young people. They were always telling him that he wasn't "with it" and didn't understand the youth oriented society and today's marketing techniques. *This is a country that worships the young. You have to cater to them," they told him.* Deep inside he always said "bullshit" to himself, but they really got their way and ran the business. All he did was own it.

The others read his thoughts and knew they had their first recruit. Ben repeated those thoughts out loud.

Frank was struck dumb. "How the hell did you do that?"

"Do you really want to know?" Ben asked.

"Yeah, I really want to know. And quick—before I lose my mind."

Ben laughed. "You won't lose your mind. I promise. Not only that, but I am about to give you the biggest news story you ever had."

"And eternity to boot!" Joe Finley added as he reached over and squeezed Frank's arm.

Ten minutes later Ben and Frank headed toward Building B to see the "health club" while the others returned to Ben's apartment.

Shields had a hangover. He sat with Wally in his office and sipped black coffee. The secretary banged away on the typewriter in the outer office. He motioned for Parker to close the door because the typing was jangling his nerves.

"You think Tony will get some answers for us, Mr. Shields?"

"I think Tony Stranger is an asshole. But he knows DePalmer, and the banker is Bright's buddy. I'll give him till noon."

"And if nothing comes up?"

"If he has nothing for us, then I'm going to take matters into my own hands and find out what the hell is going on here. I am the manager. I have a right to know."

"Right. You're the boss."

"Yeah, boss. Meanwhile, you snoop around and keep an eye on those old farts. Check back with me later."

Wally left the office in time to see Ben and Frank walk toward Building B. He had a funny feeling in the pit of his stomach. It was fear of Ben Green. He made believe he didn't see them and walked in the opposite direction toward Building A. His maintenance office was there. He would lay low for a while; maybe even catch a nap.

Mr. DePalmer excused himself and left Tony Stranger sitting at his desk. He went to the head teller's desk, out of sight of Stranger, and telephoned Amos Bright.

"Mr. Bright, this is John DePalmer at the bank. I'm fine. How are you? Good. The reason I called is that Mr. Stranger, the salesman I hired for you, is here at my office. He seems to have some information regarding the B building. He says that you are beginning to occupy the building and he wants to know why he wasn't hired for the sales office."

"I appreciate your call, Mr. DePalmer, but Mr. Stranger is wrong about Building B. We are far from completing it."

"That's what I told him, but he says he knows that it is occupied."

"How does he know that?"

"He won't say, Mr. Bright. I know you like to keep things quiet over there, and I have tried to fulfill your every request."

"Yes, Mr. DePalmer, I'm very pleased with the way you have handled things."

"So I thought you would want to, uh, deal with Mr. Stranger, rather than have him nosing around and bothering people over there."

"You are absolutely right. Have him come by this afternoon to see me. And thank you again, John."

"Yes sir, Mr. Bright. Good-bye."

Tony Stranger wasn't surprised that Mr. Bright wanted to see him. In fact, he was quite pleased and felt sure that he would be making big commissions shortly. Now all he had to do was make up a story to tell Shields and Parker. He wanted some time to think it through so that he could move right into the manager's job after Building B was sold out.

He drove a few blocks from the bank and pulled over to a pay phone. He called Shields.

"Ralph? It's Tony. How's your head this morning?"

"Larger and pounding. What did you find out?"

"Well, my friend at the bank tried to put me off, but I pressed him. He told me they were ahead of schedule on the construction and didn't want to open the building for sales before the season began. It seems some of the people in Building A have lined up their friends for apartments in the new building, so they are pushing Bright for a date. He's being nice to them and humoring them along. Understand?"

"Yeah, I understand. But he could have told me when I saw him the other night. I hope he doesn't blame me for those old farts poking around."

Tony thought to himself: *Thank you, Ralph Shields. You just gave me the ammunition I need to get you fired.*

"No Ralph. I'm sure he doesn't blame you, or Wally. I'll keep in touch. Let me know if anything happens."

"Yeah. Thanks for the call. See you."

Shields hung up, leaned back in his leather armchair, and closed his eyes. He needed a short nap.

As Wally Parker and Ralph Shields napped, the world, their world, was changing radically around them. They would never know what hit them.

CHAPTER FORTY
POSSIBILITY OF FAILURE

Phil Doyle held the *Razzmatazz* against the current in the channel. He had no charter today and was going to bring the boat over to the yard in Miami to get the throttle adjusted on engine number two. He entered the main channel and was running toward the sea when he caught sight of the *Manta III* coming out of the canal that led to the Antares complex ahead of him. He cut the engines and turned toward shore so that Jack Fischer would not see him. When he was sure the *Manta III* was well down the channel, he started up and eased out to follow his friend's boat. The throttle adjustment would have to wait.

It had been a long night for the Antareans. A probe craft had arrived with material for the cocoons. They worked all night and well into the morning repacking nine soldiers and a leader. *Terra Time* and *Manta III* carried the precious cargo of ten cocoons back out to The Stones. There was sadness and frustration on both boats.

Jack tried to cheer the Antareans as he read their thoughts. "You guys haven't failed. You couldn't help what happened to the cocoons. And you're going to get a great army here. Humans can do the job. You'll see."

"Thank you, Jack," All Light answered. "It is not that we are unsure of the humans. It is that we are returning our own to another long rest. We would much prefer for them to be among us."

"Sure. But now you know about the pollution so when you come back you'll have the right equipment."

"To lose just one is tragic."

"I know and I'm sorry. But at least you found out in time and can protect most of the army." He said his piece and then kept his mind on running the boat. Their loss upset him, too. He liked the Antareans, but until now he really didn't think of them as people. They were outsiders from another world. Aliens. Now he knew they felt sadness and loss just like human beings. He knew that must be a universal trait, and it lifted his spirits a bit.

As the *Manta III* cleared the breakwater and turned south toward The Stones, Hal, looking like a beach boy again, climbed the ladder to the flying bridge. "We have someone following us, Jack."

Jack turned and looked behind toward the breakwater. The *Razzmatazz* was back there. "That's Phil Doyle, my fishing buddy. He's probably got a charter. You think he's following?"

"Yes, we do."

"Let me give him a shout." Jack turned the bridge over to Hal and slipped down the ladder and went into the cabin. He keyed the mike. "This is KAAL-9911 to *Razzmatazz*."

"Hey there, Jack."

"You following me out today. Phil?"

"I thought I'd have a run near The Stones. Is that where you are heading?"

"Yeah. But the fishing has been lousy over there. I may head south."

"Judy called me the other night. She was looking for you."

"Yeah, I know. We spoke after that."

"Well, I hope I didn't cause any trouble. She's a nice lady."

"No problema."

"Are you okay, Jack? I mean, is everything all right?"

"A-okay." There was an uncomfortable pause. Jack keyed back on. "Look, Phil, I haven't been ignoring your calls. It's just that this charter is sort of special. They don't want a crowd around. Dig?"

"I got it, buddy. I just wanted to be sure you were okay."

"I appreciate it."

"Roger. I'll take your word for it about The Stones. I'll take these folks over to the Stream. See you later."

"Roger, Phil. Good luck."

"Thanks. Over and out."

Jack climbed up to the flying bridge and took the wheel from Hal.

"You sure no one else is on that boat?"

"There is only one human aboard. Why?"

"Nothing, I guess. He made like he had a party on board, that's all."

"Do you think he suspects something?"

"He was worried that I was in trouble of some kind. My girlfriend called him looking for me. I think I convinced him otherwise. Maybe he was embarrassed that he was following me, so he made like he had a charter."

"Do you believe him?"

"Yes."

"Then we will not worry about it." Hal left the bridge as Jack turned the bow toward the morning sun, headed southeast for forty minutes and then steered toward The Stones.

Ten cocoons were going back to sleep for a while and the rest down there would be resealed to protect them from the polluted ocean.

Frank Hankinson listened quietly to Ben all the way through Ben's explanation of the processing room and was prepared properly for Amos Bright to remove his face. Then the Antarean and the two humans sat in the half-finished Building B office where five deck chairs from the *Terra Time* had been placed. Frank was concerned.

"Gathering nine hundred some-odd people is no small task, Ben. Have you formulated a plan?"

"Nothing firm. We're open to ideas."

"Well, we are certainly in the land of the old, so we know the bodies are here. The problem is that as people begin to disappear you are going to have the cops poking around. Maybe even FBI."

Ben was pleased to hear the "we" coming from Frank.

"Your nation is large," Amos said. "Could you not gather a few dwellers from each city?"

"That would take too long," Ben answered. "We have to be out of here, according to your schedule, in no more than five weeks. It's a logistical problem."

"And," Frank offered, "we don't want to kidnap people. Somehow we have to expose the proposition to each one, or at least a couple at a time, so we don't blow the lid off this thing. Just one negative person could cause a problem."

"There has to be a simple way to do this," Ben said.

Frank thought for a moment. "Let me try something. The Amato's from Boston are good friends. Suppose I set up a little question and answer session with them and see if I can develop the conversation to the point where they admit that this situation would interest them. I'll keep it on a fantasy level. Then I'll hit them with the fact that I'm talking about reality. I make my wife part of it so she will be just as surprised. If I can get them to bitch about the boring life they have now, maybe they will be more open to the proposition."

Ben nodded. "I think you're on the right track, Frank, but remember what you said—we can't afford a failure or the cat is out of the bag."

Amos listened silently to the two men. Raising the army on Earth was going to be difficult. This was precisely why the rules about interfering with alien societies were so important. The Antareans had thrust a problem upon human beings that they were not prepared for. He knew that by mind suggestion alone they would raise the army, but it was a serious moral issue. The men had used the term kidnapping. He read that thought as the stealing of a human being against its will. These older dwellers had respect for individuals. But he also knew that there were factions in this society that had little respect for individuals—shunning the old, the poor and the injured ones that they called unfortunate. In addition, there were other nations, societies, and religions that had no respect for individuals or their freedom. So much of the development on Earth was still primitive and violent. He would have to let the old men work it out by themselves as best they could, leaving the failure to raise the army a possibility. In that case they would return to Antares humiliated. And who knew how the Parmans would react? Would they believe Antarean promises in the future? Would they once again close the Quad Two to outsiders?

CHAPTER FORTY-ONE
WEIRD SEX, A CASTING CALL, AND SPIES

Tony Stranger parked in the far corner of the lot. He didn't want Wally or Shields spotting his car. He then cut through the brush and construction at the side of Building B and around to the outside door that led to the office. It was locked. The windows were dirty so he could not see if anyone was in the office. Mr. DePalmer had told him to meet Amos Bright here at three o'clock. It was three on the nose.

Beam sensed Tony's approach. She decided to make him wait a moment while she read his thoughts. As he cast a shadow through the dirty glass, she read his anxiety. Then she probed deeper and found his greed. *So*, she thought, *he is out to get Mr. Shields and Mr. Parker in trouble. Well, Mr. Stranger, we have different plans for you.*

Tony was surprised to see the beautiful woman open the door and greet him.

"Mr. Stranger? I'm Laurie, Mr. Bright's assistant. He'll be a few minutes late."

Tony was taken by her stunning looks. She was tall and slim with soft blue eyes. Her body was full and round. The top three buttons of her silk blouse were open and revealing. Blondes in Florida were a dime a dozen, but blondes like Laurie were rare anywhere. He came on immediately. "That's fine, dear. I have time."

She smiled coyly. "Come in, please."

He entered the office. Beam, now known as Laurie, set the room in his mind. In reality it was still an unfinished office with the five deck chairs from *Terra Time* scattered about and a small bridge table against one wall. But Tony saw it as a plush office with a large and inviting couch. He even heard soft music and sensed the faint smell of very expensive perfume in the air.

"You been with this outfit long?" Tony asked.

"I work for Mr. Bright in his other ventures. I'm just filling in over here for a few weeks."

"Terrific!"

"You used to work for Mr. Bright, too?" she asked innocently.

"I sold the entire Building A for him."

"Oh, yes. I recall he was very pleased about that. You must be a wonderful salesman."

Tony beamed with pride. "I do my job. I do lots of things well." He stared at her and smiled lasciviously

I'll play him a little more, thought Beam, enjoying the game. It was rare that they were authorized to manipulate others beings this way. It was enjoyable.

Tony began to make his move. "You people really fixed this place up nice." He moved toward the imaginary couch. Beam projected pure sex to him. He felt a rush pulse through his body. Now Beam was ready.

Later, when Tony discovered semen in his underwear, he was confused. He knew he had made love to Laurie, better than he had ever made love before. But then Mr. Bright had come into the office and caught them in the act. That was a colossal screw-up. But Tony felt he could approach the man in a few days after he cooled down. God, she was beautiful. It was worth it.

Beam and Amos had a good laugh as the salesman had stumbled around the bare room attempting to put on his pants, which, in fact, were already on. He had never taken them off. Beam had projected the entire affair into his mind. As he tried to dress, imagining himself naked, Tony had pleaded with Amos that it was just one of those things. Animal and magnetic attraction. Laurie had just left the room, which Tony thought was a bummer, considering he was bare-ass naked and she wasn't there to support his story.

"I don't know how it happened, sir," he pleaded. "She was just here and I was here and then suddenly it was happening."

"I don't care to hear about it, Mr. Stranger." Amos said sternly, playing his part. He was cool and aloof. He kept the images of the office in Tony's mind.

"What about our meeting?" Tony was panicked.

"Meeting?! Mr. Stranger, in view of your attitude regarding my office and my employees I don't think we have anything to meet about, do you?" His word seemed final.

"Okay. Look, I understand you are upset. I'll call in a few days. I'm really sorry. Please believe that." He moved toward the door.

"Yes, Mr. Stranger. You do that if you wish. Now please leave."

The work out at The Stones went slowly. It was one thing to open the seals and bring out the cocoons, but a much more difficult task to replace them, particularly because they had been removing the last few squads vertically to assess the water damage to the cocoons at the bottom of the vaults. Now they had to replace the bottom cocoons first, which meant they had to remove some of the top layers, set them aside on the ocean floor, replacing the resealed cocoons, and then set the top layers back in place. It would take most of the day and early evening to put the ten sleeping soldiers back in place. After that, the process of sealing the vault, draining it of all the polluted sea water, refilling it with purified water and then sealing it again was daunting. But it had to be done to protect the army until a re-equipped Antarean rescue mission could be launched.

Phil Doyle had heard uneasiness in Jack's voice. After the *Manta III* was out of sight, he steered the *Razzmatazz* north toward the boatyard in Miami with all intentions of getting the throttle adjusted. It was a mild day. If Jack Fischer wanted to keep things to himself, that was his business. But if he was in trouble, well, Phil would have to think about that. The problem might have passed out of mind if the radio hadn't suddenly crackled with the familiar voice of Jack Mazuski, chopper pilot, freelance fish finder and all-around lunatic. "How about you worm drowners this morning?"

Phil keyed the mike. "Good morning, Maz. *Razzmatazz* here. I'm heading up to the North Miami yard. Where are you?"

"Over at the pad. I thought I might have a peek around to see if the sailfish have moved in yet."

"When are you going up?" Phil asked.

"After lunch. Will you be out there?"

"No. Things are still slow for me." An idea popped into Phil's head. "Want some company?".

"Sure, Doyle. Grab some Jack Daniels and we'll go for a ride."

"Okay. I'll go back to the dock and cab it down to the pad. See you about one." Today was not the day to get the throttle adjusted.

"You got it, baby. Don't forget the booze. I'll bring the cups. Over and out."

"Roger. Out."

Phil knew that after a few shots of Jack Daniel's, Maz would fly his chopper to Europe if he asked. So going over to The Stones would be no problem. Perhaps he could get a better idea of what Jack Fischer was up to. In any case, Jack wouldn't know it was Phil spying on him, just Maz looking for sailfish. He opened the throttle as much as he dared and moved back to his dock.

Judy awoke to the ringing phone. It was after one. She had slept all morning. The voice at the other end was unmistakably her agent, Carole Kress. The affected drawl and lisp of the aging agent and den mother always bothered Judy a bit.

"Good morning," Judy said sleepily.

"Morning, dawling? It's the middle of a glawious day."

"It is? What's up, Carole?" Judy was not in the mood for chit-chat.

"Cwanky, awn't we? I just cawlled to tell you that you have … that is, that I got you … an awdition faw the Flawida Powwa and Light Commerciawls … that's all."

"Oh? Hey, that's great." Judy was honestly excited. The local power company always did a pool of several TV commercials each year. It meant several thousand dollars to whomever got the job.

"Gweat, you say? I think it swoperior."

"Do you think I have a chance?"

"Absawlutely. They woved your pictawes."

"Great. Where and when?"

"Well, sweethewart, the only time they can see you is tonight. At the agency at six. Be there with bells on, heah?"

"Yes ... oh ... a problem."

"What cwould pwossibly be a pwoblem?"

'I have an appointment late this afternoon."

"Well, bweak it, honey, bweak it. This only comes along once a decade faw you."

"How long do you think I'll be?"

"I hawve no idea ... as lawng as they want. They have to make a chawice by Monday."

It was Friday. The trip on Arnie's boss' boat would have to wait a day. This was more important. "I'll be there. Like you say, with bells on. Tell me about the part."

"Spowkespwosen ... faw *all* the commerciawls."

"Holy shit! That's the big tamale! A gold mine!"

"Now you gwot it, howney ... go to it."

"Okay, Carole ... and thanks."

"I'm on the case, dawling. Be your nawtraul self and you hawve it made. Ta ..."

"Bye. Talk to you later."

Carole was gone. Long ago Carole had read that agents in Hollywood always got off the phone abruptly when they had no more to say. She had practiced the ploy until it became instinctive. She had no idea how much that pissed off the advertising people, but, oddly enough, as a ploy it still worked. They treated her with respect that few agents in Miami received.

Madman Mazuski lifted the aging Sikorsky EA-155 slowly off the pad and swung to the southeast, up, up over south Miami, over the inland waterway, up, up over south Miami Beach, up, up and out over the blue-green water of the Atlantic. Phil Doyle poured their third Jack Daniels into the paper cups that Maz had supplied. The Madman belted his drink down in one smooth gulp. "Fill 'er up one more time, old *Razzmatazz*, old buddy."

"Just remember you're the pilot."

"I'd better remember or we both go into the shithouse." He laughed, making Phil even more uncomfortable. "Have another drink, Doyle. You're uptight today."

"Yeah, well … just keep your eye on the road."

"No sweat."

Jack Mazuski had served with the 101st in Vietnam. In those days he had flown a Medivac chopper and then had been transferred to a carrier for search-and-rescue operations. The reason this rare occurrence happened was that he had seen a downed F-105 from the carrier *Hornet,* in the My Tho River in the Mekong Delta. He was on his way to make a pickup north of the river. The Viet Cong were firing at the pilot as he scrambled out of his fighter where it ditched in the shallow riverbed. Mazuski had swooped down over the V.C. throwing hand grenades out of his small chopper. Then he turned up over the river and hovered the chopper on the far side of the plane, allowing the pilot to jump aboard once he had set the destruct devices. It was a crazy and heroic action. Maz then took the pilot with him to pick up the wounded soldier, which had been his original mission. Against regulations, he brought both his passengers out to the carrier. He was ordered to do so by the pilot, who turned out to be a wing commander and a full colonel. Maz got a Distinguished Flying Cross, two Clusters, a recommendation for a presidential citation, and mention for a Congressional Medal of Honor. In addition, the colonel had Maz transferred to the carrier for the remainder of his tour. Maz trained search-and-rescue pilots on the Hornet and continued to fly missions. But he never got the Medal of Honor. He used to say, "No sweat. I got back to the world alive and that's enough for me."

The chopper chugged its way out over the Gulf Stream. The greenish-blue water turned blue and they knew they had reached their destination.

After an hour in the air they had spotted six sailfish and a marlin. They directed five boats that were out on the Stream to the locations.

"Nota lot out here today, but those boats will cover the gas today, anyway." Maz was semi-drunk, but steady.

"Want to take a little detour?" Phil asked.

"What you got in mind, Bro, Bermuda?"

"No such luck. I want to have a look over at The Stones."

"Why?"

"Well," Phil lied, "the fishing has been lousy over there for a few weeks. I think it may be a big shark or a mess of them. Something's screwing up the fishing."

"Jaws, huh? Okay. Let's go have a peek. But that will require another bourbon."

Phil gladly poured.

The work aboard *Manta III* and *Terra Time* continued to be slow and tedious. Six of the ten cocoons were in place. Two were in the works below, and two remained on deck. Both were on the *Manta III* as the helicopter's rotor noise caused Jack and Hal to look up toward the north. Hal saw it first. "There's a helicopter coming this way."

"Coast Guard?" Jack wondered.

Hal gave his attention to the sound. He then telepathed to Harry on *Terra Time*, asking him to zero in on the chopper and triangulate thoughts. Jack picked up their conversation but it became too painful for him to listen in on their intense thought waves. Their rapid thoughts, translated into his brain, were at speeds that became a high-pitched whine. He tuned them out and watched. Hal broke it off as the chopper came into view.

Looking up, Jack spoke. "It's the Madman."

"You know the pilot?"

"Yes. He spots fish for us from time to time. He's harmless."

"He is not alone. Your friend from the boat this morning, Mr. Doyle, is with him."

"Phil? Damn him!"

Hal knew he could not interrupt the commanders working below on the ocean floor. He sensed danger. There were two cocoons on deck. Turning quickly from the aircraft, he jumped onto the deck and yelled to Jack, "Help me with these, quickly!"

Jack caught on fast. "Over the side?"

"Yes. Quickly, before they come too close."

It was too late. In the chopper, the Madman saw and recognized the *Manta III* immediately. Then the *Terra Time*. "Hey, Phil, that's your friend Fischer. I don't know the other boat."

"Right," Phil said. "I wonder if he's catching fish."

"Don't look like he's fishing to me."

"Let's have a closer look."

Maz swung the whirlybird in closer. They came in above the *Manta III* from the west, out of the sun. It was an old combat pilot trick. "They won't see us right away." The Madman was slurring his words.

Phil leaned over and peered out of the bubble. "What the hell is that?" He was watching Hal and Jack dump a cocoon over the side.

Mazuski hovered the copter and turned so that he could look down onto the *Manta III*. As he did this, Hal and Jack lifted the second cocoon and carried it to the stern of the boat. "Looks like some kind of buoy."

"More like a big white torpedo."

The Madman dipped the chopper so that both men could look out of the front of the bubble. Two of the copper men popped to the surface, grabbed the cocoon and disappeared below the water in a matter of seconds.

It was at this point that Harry, the Antarean on the deck of the *Terra Time*, reached out with his mental powers and froze the minds of the two men in the helicopter. The Sikorsky began to spin out of control.

"No!" Jack shouted aloud. "Don't hurt them!"

Hal mentally took over the controls of the copter while Harry kept Jack Mazuski and Phil Doyle frozen in time.

"Let them go," Jack shouted. "They're my friends."

"They saw the cocoon," Hal said. "They will tell others."

"Listen Hal," Jack pleaded. "They don't know what they saw. I'll talk to them tonight. I'll straighten it out. I promise. Don't hurt them!" He was emphatic.

Thoughts passed rapidly between the two Antareans. Then the shiny white head of All Light broke the surface of the water below the hovering aircraft. Hal telepathed to the commander. A tense moment passed. Finally, the commander ordered the Antareans to release the intruders and their helicopter.

Above, Madman Mazuski jolted awake. "What happened, Doyle?"

"I don't know, but let's get the hell out of here!"

"Roger that!" Maz was sober. The chopper took off at full throttle to the east.

Arnie was disappointed when Judy called to say that they would have to put off their spy mission until the following morning. Sandy was ambivalent. She still felt that Jack was simply doing his job and protecting his clients. Arnie felt differently. He called his pretty wife and told her he had to work late. Then he was going to go over to the yacht club and get the keys to his boss' boat. In fact, he already had the keys. If Judy and Sandy wanted to wait until tomorrow, that was their business. He was going to have a look tonight.

CHAPTER FORTY-TWO
THE GERIATRIC BRIGADE

Joe, Art, and Bernie had returned to the Finley's condo. Their wives, plus Mary Green, had gathered there after a quick shower and change. Each woman had a neatly printed list. The names totaled over three hundred. Bess had estimated that there were at least fifty men and women at Betty's nursing home. Rose Lewis had called her Aunt Ruth and casually, in the context of their conversation, asked how many people she really knew on Collins Avenue. Aunt Ruth had guessed over a hundred. Most of them were living on the edge of poverty.

Art calculated again. With the people in the building, plus the lists, plus the nursing home, plus Aunt Ruth's friends, it gave them a total of nearly eight hundred. Now they were cooking.

"Maybe we can count on everyone in this building knowing at least one other couple," Joe suggested.

"That's good thinking," Bernie said.

"And that makes one complete space army," Rose added.

"More like a geriatric brigade," Alma Finley joked.

Joe laughed at his wife's joke. Then he nodded. "Yeah. Geriatric Brigade. I like it."

They spent the rest of the morning and early afternoon discussing how to contact the people on their lists. It was decided that someone from each family would have to make a trip back home to speak to some of the people in person.

Bernie was on the phone making plane reservations when Ben Green and a rejuvenated, mind-reading Frank Hankinson reached to ring the doorbell of the Finley's condo, they didn't have to. Joe had sensed their approach and opened the door. He startled Frank.

"What the … How'd you know I was…"

"We just do," Joe said. "You have to get used to being a superman."

"I guess so. You startled me."

"Sorry. Come on in. How did it go, Ben?"

"Fine. As you can see, Frank has joined us."

They entered the apartment. Ben waved a hello to Bernie and then Frank and he went into the kitchen where the ladies were gathered. "Welcome Frank to the army."

"We have a new name for our army." Rose announced. "Your wife conceived the title. We are now known as the Geriatric Brigade."

Ben roared with laughter. "It's Perfect!" he exclaimed. "I love it."

Art gave Ben and Frank the count and their projection for completing the Antarean requirements for personnel. Ben and Frank agreed with the assessment, but they were skeptical about getting the total cooperation of all the people in Building A. Frank explained his plan with the Amatos. It might serve as a litmus test. Meanwhile, the women would book flights, pack, and head for their respective hometowns as soon as possible. Perhaps even that night.

CHAPTER FORTY-THREE
THE MIND READER

Frank had not expected to convince his wife and the Amato's so easily. It was at their usual Thursday night card game. His wife, Andrea, and their guests wanted to play cards but Frank seemed to want to talk about some nonsense to do with the B building and the manager. Frank got them worked up and annoyed, then stopped abruptly stating, "Are we going to play cards, or what?" The game was bridge. The cards were dealt and then Frank began to recite what cards the three had in their hands. At first they were sure he had stacked the deck, so Paul Amato shuffled and dealt again. Frank, smiling, repeated the feat. "Isn't that a bitch?" he asked them.

"How the hell do you do that?" Paul Amato demanded. The Boston stockbroker was impressed.

"I can read your minds."

"Bullshit!" Paul said. It's some kind of magic trick. Damned good one.

"You want to see it again?" Frank asked.

"No. I believe you. But *how* you do it is the question."

The women were silent. Andrea was embarrassed because she thought Frank was showing off. She liked the Amatos and she was afraid they would get angry with Frank.

"So you're embarrassed about this, Andrea?" Frank asked his wife. She was shocked. "I'm a mind-reader, too," he boasted, enjoying his powers for the first time.

"Okay, smartass," Paul said, "I'm thinking of a number."

"2,347.66" Frank responded immediately.

"Jesus H. Christ!" How in the hell did you know that?

"What in God's name is going on here, Frank?" Andrea asked.

"Okay. Okay. I'm sorry about the theatrics. I couldn't help myself. Let's put the cards aside and I'll tell you one hell of a story ..."

It took a half hour to tell it all. When Frank finished he asked the question. Andrea, and Paul and Marie Amato looked at each other, smiled, nodded and told Frank they would be delighted to join the Geriatric Brigade. So the four couples became six. They all gathered in the meeting room for the Friday night function to plan how to spread out among the other people from Building A and size up the chances of activating more recruits.

CHAPTER FORTY-FOUR
WHAT GIRL?

Ralph Shields was in jail. Wally Parker was in the hospital. It had been fun. True, it had to be done, and she never did anything halfway, but Beam felt guilty. Somehow, she would have to make it up to the two men before she left.

Beam had gone to Wally's office in the basement, where she knew he was sleeping. She knocked to awaken him. From that point on she had mentally seduced him under the guise of Laurie, Mr. Bright's assistant. As with Tony Stranger, physically nothing happened. But Wally was sure he had gone to heaven as the beautiful young girl appeared like magic and began to make love to him.

At the same time, Amos Bright stormed into Shields' office and, in an uncharacteristic manner, reamed the manager for allowing his employees to turn a respectable residence into a brothel. Shields begged ignorance. "What are you talking about, Mr. Bright."

"I'm talking about that damned Wally Parker and my assistant shacking up in the service office, that's what I'm talking about!"

"Wally? Shacking up? With who?"

"My assistant, Mr. Shields. A sweet young girl. He must have given her drugs."

"Wally? Drugs?" Shields was sure Amos Bright had made a terrible mistake. Wally drank a little, and went out with a woman now and then, but never drugs, and certainly never young girls. He had never seen Wally with a woman under forty.

"Please, Mr. Bright. Let me check it out."

"You'd better do something, Shields. And now!" Amos stormed out of the office, chuckling to himself. He felt a bit weak and knew he had better get back to the processing room for an hour under the lasers. Beam would take care of the rest.

Shields knocked hard on Wally's door.

"Wally, open up!" He could hear Wally moaning in ecstasy and the sound of a female laughing.

"Not now, boss. Not now."

"You open this goddamned door, or I'll break it down!"

"Bug off, Ralph. I'm busy!"

Shields reached into his pocket for the master key. Wally had double-locked the door from the inside. Beam heard the key in the door and released the inside lock. AS Shields burst into the room, Beam gave him the image of Wally naked with a sixteen-year-old girl. "Oh Christ, Parker! Are you out of your mind!"

All Wally could see was his angry boss staring at his lovely, unexpected date.

All Shields could see was Wally raping an innocent young girl.

Beam then had Wally pronounce a loud and abusive "Screw you, Shields!" and the rest took care of itself.

The police arrived within minutes, brought by a call from Amos Bright, before he lay down to rest and feed.

They discovered a crazed Ralph Shields sitting on top of an unconscious Wally Parker, punching away at the caretaker's face, which by now was a swollen, bloody mess. Shields babbled incoherently about a kid being raped as the two Dade County officers lifted him off the larger man and cuffed him. One of the cops then called for an ambulance and a backup unit. Within fifteen minutes the Antares complex was quiet again, minus two of its key employees.

Beam found her way back to the processing room and lay on the cot next to Amos. She, too, needed rest and food. They had ten more cocoons to process that night. After that the humans would begin their own unique processing and the Antareans would have to prepare the way. There would be little rest for any of them for a while.

CHAPTER FORTY-FIVE
PROCESS TO COMMAND

After feeling out other resident of Building A, but revealing nothing, the six couples arrived at the decision to begin recruitment by sending the women back to their home cities since it was the women who kept the social and family contacts. There were only a few old business associates whom the men had who might be potential soldiers. That could be handled with an invitation to visit in Florida.

By morning Bess, Mary, and Alma were already in New York City. Andrea Hankinson was on the morning Eastern Airlines Flight to Atlanta where she would catch a Delta flight to St. Louis. Marie Amato would be on the noon plane to Boston. Rose Lewis, whose mission was to lower Collins Avenue, Aunt Ruth, and the ghetto of the old and forgotten, took the red Buick.

The men gathered in the Green's condo. They sat and assessed their inquiries from the Friday night social. About half of the occupants of the condo had been there. Of the thirty couples, eleven were definitely out. They were in their fifties, active in business, and part-time, snowbird residents of the Antares complex. They were too young anyway. And they tended to stay apart from the permanent residents. That left about fifteen couples, not counting the six couples that made up their own group.

Each of the men had chosen two or three of the couples as targets and had spent time talking about the life in Florida, their feelings about being retired, their families, and how they looked at the future. They were laying the groundwork for the more complicated conversations that would come later.

Initially, the men told people at the social that they were forming an exciting senior citizens corporation that would start a business in which all the residents could work and contribute their talents. It was exciting to the older people. Retirement in most cases was forced or a result of illness. Some of the people had spent their lives at jobs they hated, scrimping and saving for the glorious days of retirement. The big payoff they called it. Now they found it was boring and isolated. The new business was going to be done with federal funding based on a new law attached to the new Social Security bill pending in Congress. The plan was in the early stages of development awaiting the passage. Once the funds were available, the men lied, they wanted to be ready to apply immediately. So the planning had to take place now. Arrangements were made for each of the men to call on their chosen neighbors that morning.

Ben Green left the meeting in order to meet with Amos and Beam.

A probe ship had come down early Saturday morning. Joe Finley had seen it as he left to drive some of the ladies to the airport. The small probe, glowing slightly blue as it descended directly onto the roof of Building B, was barely noticeable. Joe saw it and pointed it out to the women because he felt its arrival. His senses, now more tuned to the Antarean world, than the human world, were able to pick up the guidance sent out to the probe by Amos and Beam. In fact, Joe pitched in and helped a bit. It amused Amos to feel Finley's powers join their own. It also felt good to know there was help for them on this planet.

The probe had brought replacement spacesuit skins for the Earthbound Antarean rescue party. They would last a month or so depending on how long they were exposed to the caustic atmosphere and waters of south Florida.

Amos and Beam were rested and refreshed when Ben Green arrived at the processing room. The new suits were working and the atmosphere in the processing room had been brought up to a point that both humans and Antareans could tolerate. The large wall glowed pink, the pressure was about three Earth atmospheres. The temperature was a warm one hundred five degrees Fahrenheit.

"We will probably be bringing some volunteers in today," Ben said.

"Already? Good news." Amos Bright was pleased to see activity so soon.

"How many do you anticipate?" Beam asked.

"Hard to say … figure on twenty or thirty."

"We will need your help with the equipment. All others are working at The Stones." Beam said. "They have not yet put on the new skins so they must work slowly and will not be back until late tonight."

"Joe and I will help. Bernie and Frank will be available late this afternoon. Art will be back tonight."

Ben was concerned. "There isn't any danger out there, is there?"

"No," she answered. "Only that they will be very tired when they return. They will need the cots for a while, and we will have to bring the room to Antarean atmosphere while they change skins." She thought for a moment and a message passed between her and Amos that Ben could not read. It was transmitted in a different language.

"What was that?" he asked.

"The language of the Parmans," Amos answered. "Soon you will know it."

Ben paused for a moment. "I wanted to ask you about something. We have sort of decided on who will be our commanders. When do we begin making, uh, doing the changing to become commanders?"

"That will be done last," Beam said. "I will have a schedule programmed by tonight so that we can process the people as you bring them. They must understand that once this begins they cannot roam about outside anymore. Since they will come in mostly as couples of male and female, I will program that one of them can be out of this building for a short period of time for one day. This time can be used to finalize their business transactions and gather any possessions they may wish to transport."

"Nothing bulky," Amos added, "but we thought they might wish to bring some mementoes of their life on Earth."

This is really happening, thought Ben. *We are actually going to leave the Earth*. It was staggering. Beam came into his thoughts. She reassured him, stroked him; comfort flowed to him.

"It is clear to us that this is a difficult decision. We know that in time you will come to understand it was a proper step to take,' Amos told Ben. "We feel your concerns and, yes, fear of the unknown. I told you that we could help you better understand when the time came. Perhaps for you, Ben Green, the time has come to see more of what we know, and share more of what we are."

They led Ben to the center table and lifted him onto it. Above the cone glowed, and for the first time a beam of soft yellow light extended from the core of the cone. It enveloped Ben. This was not the hot ash-producing light that the center table had previously emitted onto the men.

"We have begun to change the programs to what is actually required for your commander processing," Beam said. "Relax and allow your mind to be free."

Ben closed his eyes and relaxed. He felt warm. He felt a palpable warmth that flowed and filled him as though he were absorbing a substance. It expanded within, like air into a balloon. Opening his eyes, he expected to see himself bloated, but he had not changed shape.

Amos' thoughts reached him. *You are growing inside. Your nerves are being tuned. Your mind is expanding. You are sensing parts of your body and mind that you have never felt before. We believe that this internal growth reaches to the part of you that you call the soul.*

Ben relaxed again, comforted by Amos' thoughts. His mind filled again. It rambled at first; bits and pieces of insight … feelings … sensations of anger and love … frailty and strength … random explosions that coursed through his mind and body … touching emotions … then it seemed they gathered in one place, deep inside. He felt his skin and bones were a shell, an outer covering for a delicate, living, existing, strong being that was himself. The thing was without gender or form. Its power was enormous. Its love almost brought him to tears. What he sensed was huge and consuming, clear. Infinite!

He knew. *It is not important what that primitive part of me thinks or fears for itself. We have, inside of us, human and Antarean alike, a life force larger than our existence. We are a part of each other, of the Universe. If it is a plan, then we are part of the plan. If it is existence alone, it does not matter, for we are part of the existence, too. We must always reach and grow. It is a thing we can do together. Now, filled with knowledge of myself, I can be a part of all the others who will join. I can meld with them and we are together a part of one another. We are great together. We are wonderful. To leave the Earth is not to leave the Universe, for we are irrevocably a part of the total wonderful occurrence. We are life. We carry the seeds of tomorrow onward to the stars. We are life. We are together, all life; together we are what we call God, the Master.*

Ben rose from the table. His eyes glowed; so did Beam's and Amos' under their skin suits. The light was the same color and intensity. "Thank you," Ben told them.

He was aware of other things. His thoughts were too full and new to be expressed. Oh, the futility of humanity's effort to express the knowledge he now possessed. But he was compassionate, because he knew, as he had never known, that the struggle to express would eventually bring the race to understanding. Ben knew it would be a slow process, spread over millennia. Yet, as slow as it might be, inexorably, he knew humanity would someday, on its own, unaided by outside influence, find the meaning to existence that, thanks to the Antareans, he now possessed—the beautiful knowledge of self. "Will we all feel this way; know these things I see?"

"Yes," Amos Bright answered. "Those who make the journey will have to be this way; otherwise, they would not be able to comprehend the Parmans, or Antareans or the endless beings we encounter in our travels. Only in this state is the Universe understood."

"Wonderful," Ben whispered. He reached his hands to Beam and Amos and they permitted him to touch them. They remained that way for several minutes gathering and sharing their life force.

CHAPTER FORTY-SIX
INTRUDERS ON THE DOCK

Before Ben left the processing room, he helped to prepare the equipment for processing.

"There are some things that have happened that you should know." Amos said, taking him aside. Beam went to the cabinets to make programming adjustments.

"Three events. The first is that our Mr. Shields and Mr. Parker will be away from the grounds for some time … at least until after we depart."

"You fired them?"

"No, let's just say they have taken some much deserved time off. The second event is that the boats were followed today by some of Jack Fischer's friends. They came in a helicopter looking for him. He has spoken to them and assures us that their curiosity has been satisfied. However, it may be necessary for you to pay them a visit if they become curious again."

"Whatever you say, Chief Commander." It was the first time Ben had addressed Amos Bright by his official title, which up to now he had had suspected but not confirmed.

"The final matter is a bit more distressing. When the boats returned here last night, they were followed by another boat. The person on board was not known to us. Hal and Harry wanted to capture it, but the commanders needed to be brought here quickly. They have been using too much energy and were in need of rest and nutrition. Their old skins were almost destroyed. So we had to let the boat escape. The man aboard could not have seen anything extraordinary. I am not too concerned. The boat is called *Banshee*. It is owned by one Mr. Robert

Miner of Coral Gables. Perhaps tomorrow you can call on Mr. Miner and find out why he was following our boats?"

"Certainly. Mr. Robert Miner will get a visit the first chance we have."

"Good. Then we will see you later."

Ben left as Amos and Beam continued preparations to process the first recruits of their new army.

Arnie honked the horn again. Sandy told him to be patient. "Judy will be down in a minute. She said she had a long casting session last night. She's excited about the job. It pays a lot of money."

Arnie, still mulling over the strange sights he had seen the night before, didn't pay attention. "For someone who wanted to find out about her boyfriend, she sure is taking her time."

"What's eating you, honey?" Sandy asked, concerned. "Everything okay at the office?"

"Yes. It's just that Judy got me so worked up about Jack that I'm curious … and worried."

"Well, I still think that Jack will have a perfectly reasonable explanation."

"I hope so." Arnie clammed up and began figuring how long it would take them to get to the marina, get the *Banshee* under way and then run over to the Antares complex. He estimated an hour and a half. That would make it after 1:00 P.M. He blew the horn again just as Judy appeared at her front door. She waved, checked her mailbox, and hurried to the car.

Ben Green noticed Shields as he was walking back to Building A from the processing room. He wondered what Shields was doing there since Amos told him that the manager would not be around. But he was.

Amos didn't know about bail. He assumed the police would detain Shields indefinitely, or at the very least for several days because he had badly struck another human being. Ben walked out of his way. "Good morning, Mr. Shields. How are you?" His tone was sarcastic.

"Good morning, Mr. Green. I'm fine." Shields was apprehensive about Ben Green after spying on him the other evening and getting hit. "Have you seen Mr. Bright around?"

"Mr. Bright?"

Ben picked up his thoughts. "Oh Amos. Sure. We just had coffee together. Nice guy. We were old friends back in New York."

"Funny, he never mentioned that to me, Mr. Green, especially when I told him about that pool business."

"Pool business? What pool business?"

"Surely you remember when you wanted me to get the pool filled?" Now he was sarcastic. "It was only a short while ago."

"Oh, *that* pool business. Well, there are a lot of old folks named Green in the world. We met a few weeks ago by accident. Sort of a reunion. Small world, isn't it?"

"Yeah, small world." Shields wasn't buying it.

Ben decided to hold him for a moment and contact Amos. "How's the construction coming in Building B?"

"You should know. You're in there often enough."

Okay, Mr. Shields, he thought. *Time to get you off the premises permanently.* Ben quickly relayed his plan to Amos, and they agreed upon it. Then he made Shields swing at him and knock him down. Shields didn't know why he had done it, but here he was again, using his fists and this time against an old man. Ben kept his feeble return blows as soft as possible. Amos had the Dade County sheriff on the phone quickly and they dispatched a car. Ben refused medical attention, but he assured the police he would press charges. There would be no bail for Shields now—two assault and battery offenses in so many day. It was medical observation time, and that was good for at least a week. As the police took him away, Shields was almost incoherent, yelling about a man from the D.A.'s office, a swimming pool, and a conspiracy. *Explain that one to the shrinks,* Ben thought as he lay under the cot lamp for a minute to heal the bruises from the fight. Then he went back to Building A. It was time to turn some neighbors into members of the Geriatric Brigade.

The dock was crowded with the *Manta III* and *Terra Time,* so Arnie nosed the *Banshee* in very carefully. The last thing he needed was to damage his boss' boat. By the time Arnie tied the *Banshee* up to the

Antares complex dock, twenty people had already begun processing.

The activity in the busy processing room was interrupted for a moment. "Visitors," Hal announced. "It's the young lady who was here looking for Jack. She is with two others. One male and one female."

"Why are they here?" All Light asked Jack.

"Looking for me, I suppose. Sorry. I'll go down and talk to them."

"We will monitor through you," All Light told Jack.

"Here he comes," Judy said as she watched her boyfriend make his way down the path to the dock.

"He looks fine," Sandy remarked.

Jack stepped onto the dock and waved a big hello. He immediately went to Judy with his arms open for a hug.

"Not so fast, Mr. Slippery. You have some explaining to do."

Jack backed off and turned to greet his brother and sister-in-law.

Sandy reached and gave Jack a kiss on the cheek. Arnie nodded, but remained distant. "We were worried about you, little brother."

"Worried about what?"

"No more deceptions, okay? We know that when you called us you were not where you said you were. Phil Doyle called and told me you were avoiding him and the rest of the charter boats. Like that … so we're worried."

"I appreciate that, but you people are listening to me. I told you that I had a special charter." Jack looked around, adding a conspiratorial atmosphere to the conversation. He lowered his voiced. "These people are on to something big. And, they're very sensitive about outsiders. I gave them my word that there would be no leaks through me. I have to tell you guys, this is embarrassing. I could lose my charter."

Jack felt All Light send him a message: *Well done, Jack.*

Sandy turned to the others, "See? I told you it was that way."

Arnie still looked skeptical. Judy pushed back.

"What can be so secret that you have to lie to your girlfriend and your family?"

"Treasure, baby. Treasure," Jack whispered.

"Treasure with shiny eyes and copper skin?" Arnie asked.

"What?" Judy asked.

"That's what I said—shiny eyes and copper skin. How about it, Jack?"

"What are you talking about, Arnie?"

Jack tried to buy time to think. How did he know? What did he see? The questions raced through Jack's mind up into All Light. All Light telepathed back: *I will send help.* Hal and Harry were already out the door of the processing room making tracks to their quarters to put on their beach boy coverings.

"I'm talking about the people, or whatever they were, on your boat last night," Arnie said. "I followed you into the canal. I saw them."

"You were here last night?" Sandy asked her husband.

"You bet I was here. I took the boat from my boss, but when Judy had to go for the interview I decided to have a look over here anyway. Captain Jack here had some very interesting passengers on his little yacht. It looked like a Halloween party. Who were they, Jack?"

"I don't know what you think you saw, Arnie. The divers have some special equipment and pressurized suits. That's all I can say. I promised them secrecy."

An awkward moment of silence passed on the dock. Judy noticed two young blond men coming down the path. "We've got company."

"Oh, damn," said Jack. "Thanks a lot, *family*. Now I'm in for it!"

Hal and Harry joined the group. "Anything wrong, Mr. Fischer?"

"No. These people are friends. This is my brother and sister-in-law, and this is my girl friend."

"You know the conditions of the charter, Mr. Fischer." Hal was acting annoyed. "This could be construed as a violation of our agreement."

"Yeah. I understand. I'm really sorry about this. It won't happen again."

As Hal spoke, Harry read the minds of the three humans on the dock. The two women were convinced. He felt reluctance on the part of Jack's brother. He also knew that this was the same man who had spied on them last night in the canal. These thoughts were beamed back to the commanders. They were ordered to detain the group.

At that time, Ben Green and Joe Finley were sitting in Robert Miner's Florida room.

"It's not a serious problem, Mr. Miner. We just like to know who is on our property, and why. I'm sure you understand." Ben Green tried to be friendly, but firm.

"We've promised our clients complete privacy," Joe added.

"I'm sorry, gentlemen, but I don't know what you're talking about."

"We are talking about last night, Mr. Miner." Ben sharpened his tone. "Last night, your boat, the *Banshee,* followed some of our clients to our private dock on Red Lake Canal."

"Is there a law against that?" Robert Miner was a tough man. He had built his advertising agency from scratch to one of the biggest in Miami. At this point in his life, he felt he didn't have to answer to anyone, and if Arnie Fischer was in some kind of trouble, then he would protect him.

Joe and Ben read the man. Now they knew who had been in the canal, and that they were talking to the wrong man. "No, Mr. Miner, there is no law against that … per se. We have some rather special guests at the facility and they value their privacy. No harm done. No harm intended."

Miner was surprised at the fast back-off these two old men were making. It aroused his curiosity. "Who are these special guests?"

"That must remain confidential."

Joe Finley stood to leave. "Thank you for your time."

"No problem. Glad to help, gentlemen." Driving back to the complex, Ben and Joe thought they might have acted too hastily. That was not the last they would hear from Mr. Robert Miner.

CHAPTER FORTY-SEVEN
ALL THAT GLITTERS

Ben and Joe received the message from Beam as they parked in the Antares lot. *Go to Jack's room to help with captives.*

"Your own brother, Jack—I'm your brother. Convince your charter I'm telling the truth."

"I'm sorry, Arnie, but I can't. Like I told you, these people mean business. They're afraid that you'll spill the beans about their discovery and people will be all over it."

"What discovery? I don't know anything about a damned discovery."

"Sorry, Arnie. You brought this on yourself."

"So what happens now?" Judy sat on the bed. Sandy sat next to her.

"I don't know, honey. They're talking it over now."

"Don't 'honey' me, Jack Fischer. I've had it with you."

"I'm sorry you feel that way. I only asked you to trust me."

"With lies?"

"With whatever. That's what trust is."

"Bullshit!" Judy yelled.

Sandy felt this was not the place or time. "I think we'd better figure out how to get out of here and save your lover's quarrels for another time."

Ben and Joe knocked and entered the room. Judy recognized them right away. "I know you. Are you part of this?" Judy asked.

"Hi, Miss Simmons.

Judy introduced Arnie and Sandy to the men. The men seemed to know Jack.

Arnie spoke up first. "Mr. Green, do you why are we being held against our will?"

"I'm sorry for the inconvenience. There are some things here that must remain confidential. My partners and I feel you may have compromised our security."

Judy pointed at the two elderly men. "I was right ... damn it, I was right! Treasure, my ass! These guys are CIA."

"CIA?" Jack said, smiling. "What CIA?"

"He gave it away. Didn't you hear him? Compromise and security. That's the way they talk."

"Who talks, Miss Simmons?" Joe asked.

"The goddamned CIA talks, Mr. Finley!" She was a child of the sixties and a member of the SDS at Columbia. They had been infiltrated by FBI and CIA agents, and the whole thing had blown up. Members were exposed and asked to resign from the college. It had been kept out of the papers, but Judy harbored an intense resentment toward government police and intelligence agencies.

"You are mistaken, Miss Simmons."

"I don't think she is, Mr. Finley." Arnie said. "This detainment smacks of CIA tactics."

Ben and Joe excused themselves. This was out of hand. They had to talk it over with the Antareans. Jack went with them. As they left, they locked the door from the outside.

"Jail. We're in goddamned jail," Arnie said loudly.

Sandy began to feel very nervous.

Amos, All Light, Beam, Jack, Ben, and Joe met in the hallway outside the processing room. The hum of activity from the room filled the hallway.

"It is a problem. What do you suggest?" Beam asked Ben.

Ben was concerned. "We can't hold them too long. The question is, what can we tell them that they will believe?"

"How about the truth?" Jack suggested.

"No. I don't think so," Joe said quickly.. "Too many people are nosing around as it is, and when the others, our recruits, begin disappearing around here it's going to get tougher and tougher. I think we have to hold them."

"We can't hold them for three or four weeks." Jack was adamant.

"Judy has a bunch of TV commercials to do. Arnie has a job. Don't forget they have his boss' boat. If it's not back later, we are going to have the Coast Guard looking for it."

"Good point," Ben agreed.

"Perhaps we can try to create images like we did with Shields and Parker and Mr. Stranger?" Beam suggested.

"Like what?" Amos was interested..

"Well, we told them it is a treasure discovery. Why not show them some treasure? That will be proof and they will have to believe us. Tell them Jack gets a large share. That will keep them quiet."

"I like that," Ben said.

"Yes!" All Light agreed. "Beam will prepare a room to show them."

"I can use the storage area in the basement," she'd suggested. "Bring them down in ten minutes." She turned to Ben.

"What kind of treasure should it be?"

"Gold," he told her. "Old gold coins and gold bars. Spanish. Do you know what I mean?"

"Yes. I have studied your history." She left.

"My God! Will you look at that!" Arnie Fischer gasped when he saw the pile of gold bars and chests of coins that Beam projected in the small storage room.

"Can I touch them?" Judy asked.

"We'd rather you didn't," Beam told her. "The authorities might check for fingerprints if they ever got wind of this."

Arnie was impressed. "Good thinking. I understand. Hey, I'm really sorry about being such a pain in the ass. I don't blame you for being so careful," Arnie was contrite. "Jack warned us, but…you know families worry sometimes.

Beam read the thoughts of the humans. She was satisfied that they were convinced.

"Good," Ben said. "Now, let's take a walk back to the dock and talk about this a bit more. We agreed to show you this in order to convince you. Now I'd like to hear you convince me that what you saw will remain a secret. If you can't, then we'll move and Jack will be out of a job and a most generous share of the profits."

Down at the dock, Arnie, Sandy, and Judy swore that silence was the order of the day. Ben and Joe were satisfied they told the truth as they watched the *Banshee* turn and head slowly up Red Lake Canal.

"I think the little viewing of the treasure room will hold them for a while," Joe said.

"I'll visit with them tomorrow night to be sure," Ben told him. "Now let's get to work. We have an army to prepare!"

CHAPTER FORTY-EIGHT
STORMY WEATHER AHEAD

Far to the south, in an area of the Atlantic known as the breeding ground of tropical storms, the *Tyros* satellite observed a depression growing. Within eighteen hours the weather service attached to the National Oceanic and Atmospheric Administration would name it Ellen. It would become the fifth hurricane of the season, and it would leave its mark on south Florida before dissipating out over a nation that could be missing nine hundred forty-one of its elder citizens.

Maz listened as the phone rang at Phil Doyle's home. "Phil? Hi. Its Mazuski."

"Hi-ya, Madman. Sober up yet?"

"I haven't touched a drop since yesterday afternoon. I've been trying to figure out what happened. Still drawing blanks."

"Me, too. I remember we saw the *Manta Three.*" That's it.

"I'm worried about Jack. He knew it was me up there. It sure looked like he was trying to hide something."

"Want to have another go?"

"What do you mean?"

"I know where he's docking now. Let's go over and have a little talk with him."

"Okay, but I can't do it today. I have a party to take up to Lauderdale. How about tomorrow morning?"

"I'll meet you over at the pad. Hey, Mazuski?"

"Yeah?"

"You have a walkie-talkie we can hook up in my car?"

"Sure. I got you. A land-and-air attack. Good idea."

"Right. See you tomorrow around ten."

"Roger. Bye."

"Bye."

Tony Stranger was not surprised to get a call from Shields. He was, however, surprised that it came from the psychiatric clinic at the county hospital. Shields explained his problem. It had a familiar ring to it, especially the part about Wally Parker and the girl.

"I'm going to be here for at least a week, Tony. Wally is in the hospital here, too. He doesn't know I'm here. I don't know what happened. It's all too confusing."

Tony knew Shields as a volatile man, but not a violent man. He decided not to tell Shields about his adventure with Mr. Bright's secretary. "Look, pal," he told Shields, "you hang in there. I'm going to have a look around that place. I get the feeling that our Mr. Bright is something more than he appears to be. It's bugging me."

He hung up and then called the hospital. "I'd like to inquire about Mr. Wally Parker. I believe he was admitted two days ago."

"Just a moment, please." The operator put him on hold.

A few seconds later a female voice came on the phone. "Fifth floor. Miss Burns speaking."

"Hello. I'd like to check on the status of a patient … a Mr. Wally Parker."

"Yes sir. Are you family?"

"Yes, his brother."

"Yes, Mr. Parker. Your brother can't speak on the phone. He can have visitors tomorrow. His condition is satisfactory and he's resting, but under sedation. We had to wire his jaw. It was broken."

Tony was surprised. "Thank you. Please tell him I called … tell him Tony called. I'll be up tomorrow to see him. Good-bye."

CHAPTER FORTY-NINE
THE ULTIMATE TOOL

Robert Jastrow, a NASA scientist, once wrote that scientists actually have the ability to match the human brain in memory capacity. But the memory bank would be so large it would take up most of the Empire State Building. It would consume electricity at the rate of one billion watts—half the output of the Grand Coulee Dam. It would cost about ten billion dollars. According to Jastrow:

"No other organ in the history of life has been known to grow as fast as the human brain. The growth was explosive—and it was early man's tool-making industry that triggered it off. The possession of a good brain enabled *Homo* to make tools in the first place. But the use of tools became, in turn, a driving force toward the evolution of a better and better brain …"

Mr. Jastrow was right. He was, unknown to himself, writing about the basic theory behind the Antarean processing room. It was not the external use of tools that brought the human brain to maximum; it was the use of the ultimate tool—the brain itself—that allowed the breakthrough. Once activated, the entire brain became a tool of infinite capacity and depth. It was as infinite as the Universe it reflected. It was a mini-Universe, containing all that any life form required to comprehend existence itself.

But in a relatively obscure structure, in a corner of Coral Gables, Florida, nine hundred forty-one human beings made a quantum leap into the full realization of their capacity that would take their own race several thousand years to accomplish.

The Geriatric Brigade was almost complete.

CHAPTER FIFTY
TAKING CARE OF LOOSE ENDS

think it's going to be very close." A concerned Ben Green sat quietly with the Antarean commanders. Three weeks had passed since the processing had begun. Several events, some lucky and some disturbing had occurred. The last action remaining, and perhaps the most unpredictable, was to move the occupants of the nursing home to the Antares complex and process them. Those thirty-six residents would complete the army.

"Ben," Beam said sincerely, "you have all done a wonderful job." Beam, who sat next to Ben, touched him as she spoke. Kindness flowed between them. The warm sensation, although not new to Ben, still surprised him.

"When will you bring them?" Amos asked.

"Tonight. We think they won't be missed by anyone outside the home for at least two days. That should be enough time."

"Yes, that is enough now that we have so much help. We will have to alter the commanders soon, also." Beam said.

"We are ready. Joe and I will be the last. We have to finish the business of the wills. Also there's the matter of Mr. Stranger."

"Have you seen him today?" All Light asked.

"Joe spent some time with him this morning. He is still being unreasonable. That will be Jack's problem after we leave, but I'm sure he can handle it."

"Jack has been so very helpful to us all," Amos said. "I want to reward him in a way that will make his life easier after we have gone."

"Do you have any ideas?" Ben asked.

"I have arranged to meet with Mr. DePalmer at the bank tomorrow. I am going to sign the complex over to Jack, with the suggestion that Jack involve Mr. Stranger in some way to repay him for his detention here these past weeks."

"Good thinking. Stranger responds well to money. What about the other loose ends?"

"They concern me," said Amos. "I only hope that we can hold them off for the few days we need. After that it really won't matter."

Poor Jack, thought Ben. *He's going to have a lot of explaining to do.*

They all heard him and agreed.

Tropical Storm Ellen had flirted with the Florida coast for almost a week before striking the peninsula near Boca Raton. It then swung north, went back out to sea, and in a most unusual maneuver, did a turnabout and went south again, hitting the Florida Keys with hurricane level three force.

But Ellen served the Antareans well. It was the perfect cover for them to bring their mother ship down from the moon's dark side and park it underwater, near The Stones.

Madman Mazuski and Phil Doyle had scouted the Antares complex once, but saw little. The storm kept them away for a week and a half after that.

The control tower at Miami International Airport, and the new radar-tracking station attached to the Strategic Forces Base in southern Florida, both picked up the large Antarean ship on their radar. Because of the size and speed of the image on their screens they both concluded it was an electrical anomaly caused by the depression recharging itself over the warm Atlantic water as it turned and headed south. Besides, since it was stabile moving through the most violent part of the storm, they concluded that it could not have been an aircraft and survive the turbulence.

Had the airlines carefully checked their passenger manifests, they would have observed a slight growth in passengers from St. Louis, Boston, and New York. Had they checked further, they might have found the age of those passengers were older than usual for this time of year. But there was nothing strange about older people coming to Florida.

The missing person calls were up a bit for the Miami police. There had been a few disappearances of older people from the lower Collins Avenue district reported by neighbors. Had the cops checked deeper, they would have found more than one hundred people were actually missing. But most people down there lived alone and had no family. The detectives assigned to the area had little to go on. There were no signs of violence, robbery, or murder. There were no ransom demands. The people were from a variety of backgrounds, races, religions and politics. The only common denominator was their age. None of them was under seventy. They couldn't even stake out any specific part of the neighborhood. It was too large and everyone down there was old. Who would the police watch? What would they watch for? So they wrote the calls off to cranks and people who went to visit someone and didn't tell anyone.

Judy got the Florida Power and Light spokeswomen part in their commercials. The shooting had been delayed because of the storm, but there were costume fittings and rehearsals to keep her busy. Jack spent some time with her on and off for two weeks, until it was time to begin shuttling the processed seniors out to the mother ship on the *Manta III.* Judy was so excited about her job, and about the treasure that Jack would share, that she didn't bother him about his absence. On the last day the Antareans planned to reveal themselves, Judy, Arnie and Sandy, and the truth. Until then, Jack kept the secret.

Arnie and Sandy kept their word to remain silent about the treasure. Mr. Miner, Arnie's boss, did press him about where he had taken the *Banshee,* and why. Arnie satisfied his curiosity by telling Miner he brought some clothing to his brother who was docked there.

Wally Parker was out of the hospital with a wired jaw, a lawyer, and the burning revenge that came from a bad beating.

Ralph Shields was out on bail, desperately trying to talk with Wally, who would have no part of it. He was also disturbed that Tony Stranger had mysteriously disappeared.

Tony Stranger had visited Wally in the hospital, and the caretaker wrote down the events that led to his hospitalization. It struck Tony that what had happened to Wally was too similar to what had happened to him to be coincidence. He knew somehow Amos Bright was behind it. The banker DePalmer wasn't talking. So Tony had gone directly to Building B and when Harry and Hal caught him sneaking through the basement, Stranger raised the roof, screaming and yelling and demanding that the police come. Now he was a guest of the Antareans, in a locked room, a prisoner of his own curiosity. He was frightened, even though one of the old men came to see him each day to reassure him that he would not be harmed.

With the weather clear, Jack, on the *Manta III*, and Harry on the *Terra Time*, began shuttling the processed humans out to the mother ship. Their initial schedule fell short and they were only able to make four trips a day. Each boat could safely carry some fifteen passengers and their few possessions. At that rate they would fall short some two hundred fifty passengers, including the Antareans, by the scheduled liftoff time. So night deliveries for the last three days were to be initiated to make up the difference. Jack sensed that the people at the gas dock were suspicious of his activities, and Phil Doyle had been asking around about the *Manta III*.

"Do you think Mr. Doyle would like a charter himself?" Amos asked.

Jack was hesitant. "Well, he's been nosing around. I guess he's a little pissed off at me for ignoring him when he came over on the chopper. How would I approach him?"

"Why not tell him the truth?" Art Perlman suggested. "You won't be able to lie because he will see our fellow soldiers go over the side and not come up."

"It sure would make it easier," Jack agreed. With three boats we could even get a tank truck over here and save the time it takes to get over to the gas barge every morning. But I don't know how he would take the truth—I mean the actual truth."

"Frankly, I don't want to lock anyone else up like Mr. Stranger." Bernie Lewis chimed in.

Beam suggested that Jack call Mr. Doyle and ask him to come over to the dock. They would prepare a demonstration for him so that there would be no doubt about the job and what Jack had been doing. What Jack never brought up was Madman Mazuski. Jack sat on the bridge of the *Manta III* when Doyle and Mazuski walked onto the Antares dock.

"So there really is a Jack Fischer!" Phil shouted up to him.

Jack slid down the ladder onto the deck. He looked around wondering why the Antareans had let the Madman through. "Hi, guys. Mazuski, how've you been?"

They shook Jack's hand as they boarded the boat. Phil looked around to see if anyone else was on the *Manta III.* "You alone?"

"Yeah. I didn't know you were bringing company."

"He's one of us. I was with him in the chopper a few weeks ago when we saw you over at The Stones. What the hell were you doing there?" A voice came from the dock. "He was working for us."

Hal, Harry, Amos, and No Light were on the dock, standing near the *Manta III.*

"Where did you guys come from?" asked Mazuski. "There was no one here a second ago."

"We came from far, far away, Mr. Mazuski," Amos said as he boarded the boat.

"Very far away," said No Light as he too came aboard. Hal and Harry remained on the dock.

"And gentlemen," Amos Bright continued, "we would like to talk some business with you both. Shall we go below?"

An hour later there were two more helpers, and the Antareans had an unexpected bonus—one serviceable helicopter flown by a pilot who thought he had seen it all until, as the clincher, Jack brought an eighty-five-year-old woman onto the boat. She was Ruth Charnofsky, Rose Lewis' aunt from Collins Avenue. The woman greeted the visitors and proceeded to jump over the side of the boat into the canal. She settled to the bottom, some ten feet below, and remained visible, waving from time to time at the astonished pilot. After ten minutes he gave up. "I believe. I believe. Get her up here. I'm losing my breath."

Mazuski arranged for a gasoline tank truck to park at the dock the next morning and shuttle operation began.

CHAPTER FIFTY- ONE
WHERE DID THE SENIORS GO?

Mr. DePalmer had handled the arrangements for Arthur Perlman to buy the nursing home. The owners were given, as Arthur, given his tawdry past, liked to joke, "an offer they couldn't refuse." The entire staff of the home was given two weeks' notice and replaced by members of the Geriatric Brigade who had not yet been completely processed. Betty Franklin, Bess Perlman's sister, was removed the day the processing had begun. After the original staff departed, she returned to speak to the remaining tenants of the home. These were people who had been left by their families to end their days under the care of strangers. Their families, and in some cases government overseers who were also on the owner's payroll, had ignored their complaints about harsh treatment and cruelty. Had Bess not seen it for herself, it would have been hard to believe that human beings could treat other human beings with so little dignity or care.

Yet Bess and Art were concerned that the resident understood, as best they could, what was being proposed because their task was to arrange to move the people from the home to Building B. Could they pluck these ailing seniors up and send them on such a fantastic journey? Could they take those unable to comprehend them without consent of some kind?

Difficult as it was, the answer was yes. The files were examined and thirty-six of the fifty tenants of the home were found to be alone in the world. They had not had visitors for years. They had no family on record. Some were wards of the state. Some had turned their life's savings over to the home and in return received awful care. Art and

Bess felt that after the processing, these people would be grateful. But it was a responsibility that they took on seriously, after much thought and soul-searching. The families of those left behind would be notified of the change in management and introduced to a new staff by Mr. DePalmer after the mother ship had departed.

Art chose a Sunday night to move the nursing home residents, after visitors, few as they might be, were gone. At two in the morning a charter bus pulled up in front thirty-six octogenarians, confused and frightened, took the first step toward an adventure none could ever imagine. The bus driver was told that there was a gas leak in the building and the people had to be moved to safety. Art hoped the story would hold for as long as they needed. He miscalculated.

Detective Sergeant Matthew Cummings of the Dade County Sheriff's Office had been assigned to the Collins Avenue disappearances for two weeks. He was as baffled as the rest of the force. However, the matron who had been fired by Art Perlman, returned to the home on Tuesday afternoon to pick up a few personal possessions she had left behind. The home was now staffed with members of the Brigade who were in the process of hiring new people to take care of the remaining tenants. The matron, Mrs. Blackwell, was a vindictive woman. She poked around and soon realized that several residents were missing. She also thought that the woman now in charge was somehow familiar, but she couldn't place the face or what right away.

"If you have your things I would appreciate your leaving the premises." Bess Perlman was firm.

"I asked you what happened to the rest of the patients here."

"They are out on an outing."

"Baloney. I know those people. Some of them couldn't walk more than ten steps. You can't take them out like that."

"But we did, Mrs. Blackwell. Perhaps you and the former owners didn't try hard enough to make life pleasant for them."

"Something is fishy here and I intend to find out what. This isn't the last you'll hear from me." Blackwell turned and left in a huff. Bess called Art to tell him about the problem.

Within an hour, Sergeant Cummings had the complaint about the nursing home on his desk. He called Mrs. Blackwell and sent a car to pick her up for questioning. Within another hour the sergeant and Mrs. Blackwell were at the home. Bess had gone back to the Antares complex for a few hours, but the other members of the Brigade held to the story of an outing. The police were told that the group had gone to the Miami Seaquarium and would return in a few hours. Cummings felt uneasy and decided to check out the Seaquarium himself. One of the seniors working at the home called Art Perlman, who, upon hearing the news, instructed his people to leave the home in the care of the few regular people whom they had hired.

"No such group was here today, Detective." The words kept ringing in Sergeant Cummings' ears. Back at the home, when he questioned the residents left behind, one of them said that she thought she saw a bus had take several people for an outing a few nights ago. He put the home under police guard and radioed for his office to begin checking bus charters for the night before last. This was the break he had been looking for in the Collins Avenue missing seniors case. He was sure it tied in somehow.

By the following morning the last of the people from the nursing home had been processed at the condo. All that remained was for the human commanders to be transformed, the equipment packed up, and the final trip out to the mother ship could take place.

Amos Bright met with Mr. DePalmer at the bank. Jack Fischer sat with them, signing the papers that made the Antares condominium complex his property, free and clear.

"Of course, Mr. Fischer, our bank will be delighted to assist you in any matters that you deem necessary. We are at your service." DePalmer was trying to make sure that he kept the business.

"I'm sure we can work things out, Mr. DePalmer, and I'll rely on your help."

"Good. Let us know whenever you need anything." He gathered all the papers and checked them again to be sure things were in order.

Ralph Shields, who had been released after Mr. Bright refused to file charges, had been watching the bank, hoping to have a word with Mr. DePalmer about what had happened. He hoped Mr. Bright might hire him back. He approached the meeting. "Mr. Bright, could I speak to you for a moment?"

DePalmer stood up. "This is a private meeting, Mr. Shields."

Amos stood, offering Shields his hand. "It's okay, Mr. DePalmer. Mr. Shields has something to say and I think we should listen. Yes, Mr. Shields?"

"Well, I wanted to say that I'm not the crazy man you all think I am. Something is going on that I don't understand. I thought maybe you could tell me." He spoke softly and was contrite.

"Perhaps we can, Mr. Shields. Perhaps we can. Why don't you come back to the office with us and we can talk this out?"

Shields was relieved. "Great. I'd hoped you would say that. I'll follow you in my car."

"Good," Amos said. "If you will excuse us for a moment, we have some business to complete. We will meet you outside in the parking lot."

Relieved, Shields left.

"Mr. DePalmer, I want to thank you for all that you have done for me, and for the Antares project. I know you will help Mr. Fischer, and I know the relationship will be of benefit to all."

"Are you leaving town?" the banker asked.

"I'm going away for a while. Mr. Fischer will know where I am."

"Well, have a good trip. It's been a pleasure serving you. And please feel free to call on me if I can be of any help in the future."

"Yes, Mr. DePalmer. The future. I believe you will. Good-bye."

CHAPTER FIFTY-TWO
WHY WE GO

We are aliens!" Ben Green spoke to his nine group commanders. His wife, Mary, the Perlmans, the Finleys, Bernie Lewis, Betty Franklin, Aunt Rose Charnofsky, and Frank Hankinson had all been programmed as the Antareans promised.

"Alien is a strange word to use." Mary told her husband.

"Alien is an alien word," Alma Finley responded. "I understand so much now. What was strange before is no longer strange, but truth. I cannot conceive of any life form as alien."

"Yes. It is only life," Joe Finley added. "But, we're not of this planet anymore."

Frank Hankinson stood and walked to the center of the processing room. "I feel as though…" He searched for words.

"As though you don't belong here?" Betty asked.

"No. As though I never belonged to one place. I feel a part of something much larger."

Aunt Rose spoke. "We did belong here once, and I for one, will not forget how it was. But now we are grown."

Bess touched Art on the neck, close to the place where Beam had made the final incision. "And we will grow even more! Isn't it wonderful?"

Ben stood and surveyed the empty room. "How long ago all this began, or so it seems."

The new commanders understood.

"It's time," Ben said. "Amos is ready. The boats are approaching."

Without another word, the commanders of the Geriatric Brigade left the now empty room that had changed their lives forever.

Only the last words of nine hundred forty-one lives, meticulously transcribed and recorded for their families and loved ones remained with instructions that what had happened remain a secret. In those messages were the new perspectives about life and future. Messages from a new race to one that must develop or perish. Individuals speaking a one—asking that which any human could ask of another—love, peace, respect, freedom, caring, equality. They had come from many parts of the country, each with a personal, final reason; that special desire that gave them the courage to journey into the unknown.

Many wrote to those they loved about love. Extra words and thought were for the grandchildren and great-grandchildren. With their new awareness they knew the potential of a child's mind. They encouraged to reach, to touch a place that would grow that mind beyond the narrowing influence of adults.

Is it curious that they came so readily? As we grow old, they wrote, you understand a great deal more about potential ... human potential. You know the value of life and the wonderful gift that it carries. You have patience, even as you are discarded by the younger who wish to be among the more "beautiful" people. We are a race which finds aging too painful a reminder of what we will become.

If one voice could speak for all of them, it would say, simply: "We have done this to help our fellow beings elsewhere because we were set aside from doing that here. And, because they asked, and because we are needed."

CHAPTER FIFTY-THREE
UNWELCOME PURSUIT

Jack kept the stern of the *Manta III* tight to the right side of the dock. *Terra Time,* now captained by Arnie Fischer, berthed on the left. The *Razzmatazz,* with Phil Doyle on the flying bridge, snuggled close in behind him.

"My God!" Judy Simmons exclaimed. "Is that Mr. Green? What happened to his head?"

"He's a commander now," Jack told her with a hushed respect in his voice. "They are all commanders."

Amos and Beam met the group of ten commanders at the top of the path. They all touched and gathered for a moment. *This is good,* Amos Bright thought to all of them. *What we have done here will always be remembered. Now let us go home.*

They walked slowly toward the dock.

Tony Stranger stood next to Ralph Shields on the deck of the *Razzmatazz* watching the procession approach. They had both been hired by Jack to run the Antares complex under the firm supervision of Mr. DePalmer. "This was worth being locked up for weeks. What a story! Look at them."

Shields was concentrating on trying to recognize the previous tenants of the Antares condominiums. He felt as though he was walking a delicate line between reality and a dream world.

Sandy touched Arnie's arm. "Oh, look at them. Aren't they glorious?"

"Special. I feel very special to be here. To see this." He told his wife. He put his arm around her and held her close.

The tranquil moment was suddenly broken by the crackle of Phil

Doyle's radio and the simultaneous sound of Madman's chopper as it swooped over the pool and hovered over the dock. "Hey, you guys down there. Better haul ass now. This place is crawling with cops. They're coming in from all sides. They're armed and look like they mean business."

All the pieces had finally come into place for Detective Sergeant Cummings. The bus went to the Antares complex. The owner of the nursing home lived at the Antares complex. There had been mysterious assaults at the Antares complex. The owners of the Antares complex had just sold the place, or actually had given the place away to a charter-boat captain. It took two days for all the information to filter through to Cummings, and then three hours to get a judge to issue the court order. Now he was here in force to bust the largest kidnapping ring in the history of the state of Florida...or so he thought!

As he came over the hill running in the direction of the helicopter, he saw the three charter boats, in single file, with engines at full throttle, moving away up Red Lake Canal toward the main channel. He keyed his radio.

"Betters," he called to his partner, "You in the canal yet?" A voice crackled back from the police boat at the mouth of the canal. "Roger, Sarge. We have it covered."

"Okay, watch it. There are three boats coming out at high speed."

"I see them."

The radio crackled and then let out a high-pitched hum so ear shattering that sergeant Cummins had to turn it off.

Farther up the canal, one very expensive police launch inexplicably beached onto a beautifully manicured lawn, crossed it, and stopped in a swimming pool.

"You did that rather well," Amos complimented Ben Green.

"We all did it, Amos," Ben answered. "But I don't think that's the last we will see of the police."

Sergeant Cummings was back at his car on the radio to the Coast Guard. He described the boats and the chopper. He then called for another police launch to meet him at the municipal dock in Coral Gables. He didn't know what happened to Betters and the patrol boat, but he suspected that it was out of action.

As they cleared the seawall and last jetty to the open ocean, Madman Mazuski called in again. "They're on to us, Phil. I can hear the Coast Guard on the radio. They'll be in the air in ten minutes. And two fast cutters will be coming up behind you."

Ben Green took charge. "With your permission, Commander Bright."

"By all means, Commander Green," the Antarean leader answered. "It's your planet." Ben spoke to Mazuski on the radio. "Mr. Mazuski, can you let us know when the helicopters from the Coast Guard are in sight?"

"Roger."

"Once you see them please don't interfere. I suggested you clear the area. At least by a mile."

"You gonna do to them what you did to me and Phil?"

"Something like that. But keep an eye on the cutters for us. "Okay?"

"You got it Mr., uh, I mean Commander Green."

CHAPTER FIFTY-FOUR
DEPARTURE

It was a bizarre sight to behold. Three fishing charter boats offloading what appeared to be elderly people into the water. Two of the newest and most sophisticated Sea-Horse Coast Guard jet helicopters suspended in midair above as a small Sikorsky circled them.

Sergeant Cummings put down the binoculars. "I'll be damned. What in the hell is happening?" His launch rode to the south of the two Coast Guard cutters that were making thirty knots toward the scene. They could not raise their helicopters on the radio.

The last of the old people went over the side and disappeared beneath the tranquil blue-green sea. The Coast Guard helicopters suddenly rose, as though released from a slingshot. It took a minute for the pilots to regain control of their aircraft.

The cutters and the launch approached the three pleasure boats with horns blaring and sirens wailing. The helicopters hovered lower and lower.

Then the ocean began to churn wildly.

All sound disappeared.

The water turned white and began to glow.

A quarter-mile to the north, a huge white needle broke the surface. For three long, fantastic minutes the Antarean mother ship, a craft not of this world, slid from Earth's ocean, pointing upward, and rapidly ascended until it was dot that finally blended into the fair Florida sky and disappeared.

All the humans below heard a single voice in their minds as the travelers sent their final message back to the sleeping Antarean cocoons safely secured and sealed below The Stones:

We will serve the Master for you now.
We are joined with you forever.
Sleep and wait.
We shall find you again and bring you home.
We Love You.